Main

Love and
Happiness

Love and Happiness

by

Ben Burgess Jr.

www.urbanbooks.net

Urban Books, LLC
300 Farmingdale Road, NY-Route 109
Farmingdale, NY 11735

Love and Happiness

ISBN 13: 978-1-60162-911-1
ISBN 10: 1-60162-911-7

First Trade Paperback Printing June 2019
Printed in the United States of America

10 9 8 7 6 5 4 3 2 1

Distributed by Kensington Publishing Corp.
Submit Orders to:
Customer Service
400 Hahn Road
Westminster, MD 21157-4627
Phone: 1-800-733-3000
Fax: 1-800-659-2436

Love and Happiness

by

Ben Burgess Jr.

PART ONE

For Better or Worse

Karen

I was lying on white linen sheets, panting and sweating, in a motel room in Syosset. My breasts rose and fell as I tried to catch my breath. The strong smell of sex filled the room. The air conditioner blew on high, cooling my trembling naked body. I stared at the mirror on the ceiling, wondering how, in a matter of minutes, I'd gone from complete bliss to sadness.

When I had sex with Raheem, it took me away from my chaotic life. He made me feel sexy and unrestricted. I felt like a woman. But when it was over, I fell hard back to reality.

I watched him get dressed and wondered why I kept doing this to myself.

"I gotta go. I'll text you sometime tomorrow," Raheem said. "Okay?"

He kissed me softly, and for that brief moment, it felt real, but I knew our relationship could never be anything more than this. This wasn't *love*. What we had was purely *lust*. Our relationship was merely a quick fix to my problems.

Raheem winked, waved good-bye, walked out of the motel room, and closed the door behind him. I stood up and stared at my reflection in the full-length mirror. I fanned myself and ran my hands down my naked body. My chestnut eyes were the windows to the soul of an emotionally drained woman. For the past three years, I had been living a lie, and every day, I felt like a piece of me died.

My heart was heavy as tears filled my eyes. I started to cry, thinking about what my life had become. I cried because I just wanted to be happy, but I didn't know how to be.

I composed myself, dressed, and headed to the motel office. A maid who had been cleaning one of the rooms shook her head and scowled at me when I put the room key in the return slot. She had seen the wedding ring on my hand. I knew she figured no married woman would come here in the middle of the day with her husband. She was right. Raheem was not my husband.

Raheem had a family too: a wife and three kids. I had my husband, Chris, and my twin girls, Jocelyn and Jaclyn. He cheated on his wife for the thrill of fucking someone else. I cheated to feel validated.

I got into my silver Honda Accord. The judgmental look that the maid had given me would be another thing to torment me as I headed home. I felt even worse than before.

Personally, I didn't think I was asking for too much from my marriage. All I wanted from Chris was for him to pay attention to me. I wanted him to show me romance again, the way he had when we first started dating. Light candles when we made love, and not just try to shove it in me without any type of foreplay. Shower with me, go dancing with me, surprise me with date nights and flowers every now and then. Truly take the time to understand and listen to me. Those things were important to me, and I refused to accept Chris being a good, loyal man as a trade-off for what I needed to have in a loving, stable marriage.

Don't get it twisted. I *loved* Chris. I did. I always had, but I was not *in love* with him. I owed him a lot. I had known he was the one when we met in college, at a campus party.

"Look, I'm not interested," I had said to some random guy who approached me at the party.

"Come on. Enough with the 'playing hard to get' shit. Come here," the random guy had said, pulling on my arm.

"No," I said, scrunching up my face and yanking my arm out of his grip.

"She said no, so leave her alone, before there's a problem," Chris said, coming to my rescue.

"Who the fuck—" random guy began, but then he turned around and saw Chris, Will, and Lou standing behind him. They were all huge, but Chris looked the most intimidating. He was about six feet one and was ripped like a Greek god.

"Trust me, brother, you don't want this type of problem," Chris said as he folded his arms and rested them against his chiseled chest.

"My bad. I didn't know she was with you," random guy said as he walked away.

"Thanks for that," I said, liking how sexy Chris looked.

"It's no problem. I'm Chris, and these are my boys, Will and Lou."

Will and Lou nodded and waved.

"I'm Karen," I said and smiled.

Chris and I got to know each other after that. I loved that he was driven and masculine. He was about *something*, a "real man." It was a huge change from the boys pretending to be men who usually approached me.

Back then, I was reckless and irresponsible. Then Chris came into my life and showed me that I needed to calm down and think about my future, and not only about my past. I toned down my hard partying. I quit smoking weed and cigarettes. I stopped drinking to the point of throwing up and passing out and focused more on school and improving my life. In some ways, Chris saved me. He taught me to want more for myself, and I was truly grateful for that.

When we first started dating, there were several times when my immaturity almost drove him to leave me. Sometimes I'd relapse and go back to my party girl ways. My last big fuckup happened senior year. He was the first person I called that night.

"Chris, please don't be mad at me." I gripped the phone tightly, mentally preparing myself for his reaction.

"What? What's going on?" Chris asked groggily. It was two o'clock in the morning.

"Chris, please wake up, baby. I need you. I got arrested. I'm in jail."

"What did you say? You're where?"

I sighed, knowing that Chris was going to give me some long-ass speech about me fucking up again. Ugh. I hated it when he lectured me.

"Let's speed this up," said the blond douche-bag cop, rolling her eyes and tapping her feet.

I ignored her and continued talking to Chris. "I'm in one of the holding cells at the One Hundred Fourteenth Precinct. They're taking me to central booking. I got arrested for DUI."

Chris sighed. There was a long pause before he spoke again. I thought the call had got disconnected.

"Chris?"

"Yeah. I'm here . . . What happened?"

"I was partying in Queens. I ended up smoking—"

"Smoking weed."

"Yes, Chris. I was smoking weed. Anyway, I guess it was stronger than I thought, because the cops said they saw me swerving and running red lights. Anyway, I got pulled over on my way home, and the cops smelled the weed on me. When they searched my car, they found some bags."

"How much is *some*, Karen?" Chris had that tone in his voice that made me feel like a child.

"I bought a couple bags for days when I'm stressed out."

"How much is a *couple*!" he shouted.

"I don't know exactly. They said it was felony weight, though."

"Jesus, Karen. Who are you? Pablo fucking Escobar? This could've all been avoided if you'd just stop with this bullshit."

"I don't need a lecture right now. I need your help. Can you help me, please?"

Chris bailed me out of jail. Since I had no money, he spent a small fortune on a great lawyer, who found a loophole in the case and somehow got all my charges dropped.

While my legal struggles were over after that, my partying was still putting a strain on our relationship. Chris grew distant. The writing was on the wall. I knew he was close to breaking up with me. I didn't want to lose him for good, so I stopped taking my birth control. I knew he'd never leave me if I got pregnant. It was low down and risky, I knew, but I loved him. I loved him more than anything and anyone. Well, I did get pregnant, and he didn't leave me, but as time passed, our relationship became stagnant.

When I came home nowadays, I didn't feel appreciated or beautiful. Chris and I didn't go out on date nights or do anything exciting anymore. He was always working. When he wasn't working, he was sleeping, watching sports, or tinkering in the garage, restoring his '66 Mustang. I swear, he cared more about that fucking car than he did about me. He didn't pay attention to me anymore. Don't get me wrong. He was a wonderful father. He always took care of our kids and provided for us, but we'd lost something. I felt that *something* when I was with Raheem.

***

I was a couple of blocks away from my house in Levittown when I started breaking down again, so I steered my Accord to the side of the street and parked. I took a deep breath and pulled myself together. I had to look strong when I saw my little girls. I fixed my makeup, put on my shades, and then drove to my house. Chris's black F-150 truck was parked in front. I pulled into the garage and parked next to the piece of shit Mustang he'd been working on for over three years.

I climbed out of the car and walked in the house. At the sight of the toys and the spilled juice all over the kitchen tile floor, which I had mopped that morning, I started fuming. I found the kids in the living room, laughing and chasing each other around our cream-colored couches, with crayons in their hands. Chris was in the computer room, looking at parts for his stupid Mustang, not even paying any attention to the girls.

"Mommy!" the twins yelled when they saw me, and then they ran over to hug me.

"Hey, guys. Did Daddy make you dinner?"

"Yes," they answered in unison.

"What did Daddy make my baby girls?"

"Daddy made us eggs and waffles!" Jaclyn yelled.

I was annoyed that he had fed them breakfast for dinner, and even more annoyed that the sticky plates were still on the kitchen table. The dirty skillet and the spatula were sprawled on top of the greasy stove. I cleared the dishes off the table and dropped them in the sink. Then I stomped to the computer room, picking up the jacket and T-shirt that he had tossed on the floor on my way there, and stood in the doorway, with my arms folded across my chest.

"Hi, Chris."

He sat there in a greasy tank top and blue jeans, his hands filthy from working on his car. He had his feet up, his dirty-ass cement-covered boots resting on the small file cabinet next to the computer.

He didn't even have the decency to look up from the computer screen. He waved nonchalantly and said, "Hi."

There wasn't a bit of enthusiasm in his voice, and he kept searching for car parts, like I wasn't even there. Where was my warm welcome? Where was the show of affection after missing me all day? He didn't even question my whereabouts. It almost bothered me that he made cheating on him so easy.

"Seriously, Chris, why couldn't you clean the table or put the dishes in the dishwasher?"

"Hmm?" he said, not taking his eyes off the screen.

"Can you look at me when I'm talking to you?"

I tossed his clothes at him. That got me his attention. He looked up, glared at me, and shook his head.

"You need to pick up after yourself. I didn't come home from my work to act as your maid."

"As soon as you get in the house, you start with this shit, Karen? Jesus, it'll get done. I had a long day. Can I relax first before you rush in here and start delegating chores for me to do?"

"I had a long day too, and when I come home, I don't want to see the house a wreck. I already know I'll end up cleaning it."

"Nobody told you to clean it. I said I'll do it. Calm down. It'll get done."

"Why can't you clean up before you get involved with your online nonsense?"

"Why can't you just chill out? I'll clean up when I'm ready. Relax."

I left Chris mumbling some shit under his breath and walked back to the kitchen. This was a silly spat that I was making bigger than it needed to be, but I was frustrated about things. I turned on the faucet and rinsed some of the dirty plates.

I thought back to earlier, when Raheem had his way with me. I could almost feel his hands on my body as he sucked on my neck. I got moist remembering how passionately he'd kissed me, how our tongues had intertwined, and his hands had cupped my breasts. I jumped when Chris grabbed a dish out of my hands.

He smiled and said, "Babe, I told you I got this. Hang out with the kids. I'll clean this up."

I smiled, walked into the living room, and cuddled with the kids on the couch. Chris annoyed me at times, but he tried to make me happy. I still loved him. I'd fucked other men, but none of them, past or present, compared to him sexually. He held it down in the bedroom and made sure I was pleased every time we were intimate. I'd had the best orgasms of my life with Chris. I'd dated my fair share of men, and Chris was the first man that made sure I was pleased before he got his rocks off. That alone made him a keeper in my book.

While that was a beautiful thing, what we lacked with our marriage was *passion* and *emotion*. In the past, we'd been intimate maybe two or three times a week, but lately, with everything going on in our lives, it had been reduced to maybe once or twice a month, if that. Our busy schedules kept us apart and gave me perfect excuses to see Raheem and Tyrell, the other man I was cheating on my husband with.

Raheem came in second to Chris when it came to pleasing me sexually. He had a longer penis, but Chris's was thicker, and he had a better stroke. Tyrell had girth but very little length. It was like having sex with a small soda can. He wasn't great sexually, but what he lacked in that department, he made up with by being romantic and sensual. He lit candles, gave me massages, and treated me to dinner at nice restaurants. He made me feel special, something I no longer felt with Chris.

Raheem was a skillful and passionate lover. He was good at creating the illusion that we were making love. When we were together, he seduced me like I was the heroine in a romance novel. I knew he didn't love me. I didn't love him, either, but in those moments when we were intimate, he satisfied my need for affection.

Lately, having sex with Chris felt like fucking, and there was no variation. Don't get me wrong. There were times when I enjoyed the rough stuff, but I needed more than just that. I needed to feel desired and wanted.

My kids' fingers snapped in front of my face.

"Mommy, you're not paying attention to the movie," Jocelyn said, interrupting my thoughts.

My little princesses were nuzzled comfortably under my arms while we watched *Frozen* for the hundredth time.

"I'm sorry, baby. Mommy is a little tired from work."

After the movie, I bathed the girls and put them to bed. Then I went into my bedroom and undressed for a shower. I cleared my throat to get Chris's attention. He was in bed, watching *SportsCenter* on the TV, as usual.

"I'm going to shower," I said, standing naked in front of him, hoping he'd notice and want to join me. I hated that he never complimented me anymore. After having two kids, I knew I was not in my best shape, but I worked out regularly to stay tight.

"All right. I'll be here," Chris said, not even looking at me.

"Do you wanna shower with me?" I asked hopefully.

"Nah. Go ahead. I want to watch the highlights from tonight's games. I'll see you when you get out."

I threw my hands up and let out an annoyed sigh.

"What's your problem?" Chris asked.

I ignored his question and walked into the bathroom. The reality was, our situation was partly my problem. Before we had kids, we did little things like take showers together and cuddle, things couples did to keep their bond strong. Now it felt like we were nothing more than glorified roommates who were raising children together.

I showered alone. Even though his dark, chiseled body looked good lying on top of our red duvet, if he thought I was going to give him some ass tonight, after he turned down my shower invitation, he had another thing coming. I stepped out of the bathroom to the sight of Chris snoring in bed, still holding the TV remote. I gently removed the remote from his grasp, turned off the TV, then placed the remote on his nightstand. More than anything, I wanted Chris to wrap his muscular arms around me, but as usual, I ended up going to bed craving the affection that was missing from our marriage.

Chris

I was exhausted. I jump off the crane I was operating. My hands were dirty and coarse from handling all the debris at the construction site. I closed my eyes and used the cleanest part of the back of my hand to rub the bridge of my nose.

"Chris, you all right? You look out of it," Nadine said as she stood near the crane.

"Yeah, I'm good. I'm a little tired, but I'll live."

"You need to cut back on the hours. You look worn out."

I shook my head. "I got two little girls at home, a mortgage, and all types of bills and expenses. I don't have time to worry about being tired. I gotta suck it up and drink more coffee. I'll be fine. I need the overtime."

We were working on a big water main break at the corner of Murray Street and West Broadway in Lower Manhattan. My kids' school tuition was due a week ago, the mortgage too, and it felt like as soon as I thought I was out of debt and in the clear, an unexpected expense would spring up or something would break down, putting me back in the negative.

"Get some coffee. I'll hold it down here," Nadine said.

She was one of the strongest women I knew. She worked as hard as any man on the site and wouldn't take shit from anyone. Most of the other guys were intimidated by her strength, but I understood her. She was strong, but deep down she was also sensitive and wanted people to like her. She was divorced and had no kids, and while I tried not to check her out, there was no denying she was *gorgeous*. She was born in Barbados. Her green eyes and thick, shapely thighs drove me crazy. She was also my crutch at work and helped to keep me sane. I had mentioned her to Karen a few times, but Karen never listened to me when it came to my job. She thought any woman working construction either was a lesbian or was ugly as hell. I didn't worry about her being uncomfortable about Nadine, because Karen didn't think of her as a threat.

My job was stressful, but right now my mind was on Karen. I viewed my kids as blessings, but when Karen and I had become parents six years ago, our lives had done a complete one-eighty. She'd changed, and I'd changed, and I didn't like it. Every day, as soon as I walked in the door, she was yelling at me about something. I felt like I couldn't do anything right in her eyes. Sometimes I'd rather work late than go home and argue with her.

Things with Karen didn't feel right. We rarely had sex anymore. It was not in my nature to ask, because I'd be damned if I was going to beg her or have her go through the motions out of some sense of duty. I wanted her to *want* me. I was adamant about that, but I didn't know how much longer jerking off was going to pacify me. Karen seemed cool with how our sex life was going, and that bothered and scared me. I had a growing suspicion that she was fucking someone else. Maybe she was not affected by our nonexistent sex life, because she was getting it from someone else.

At the beginning of our marriage, she hadn't had a password on her phone, but now she had one. In the past we'd never been secretive with each other. *Why the change now*? I wondered. She'd been working late a lot recently, sometimes not coming home until after midnight and claiming that she had stayed to put in overtime hours. But her checks didn't have overtime money in them when they were directly deposited into our joint account. Every so often when I used her car, I would find the passenger seat pushed all the way back, and I would have to adjust it. All her friends were short. Who would need to sit so far back?

And lately, she'd been so combative with me. It felt as if we couldn't even talk without getting in an argument. It made me question whether Karen was bored in general or bored with me, our kids, our marriage. And if she was, would she cheat on me to make up for her lack of excitement? I had been trying to give her the benefit of the doubt. I'd been telling myself that I was just being paranoid, but it was all really fucking with me.

I rushed over to the corner store across from the construction site and got coffee for Nadine and me. When I got back to the crane, I handed Nadine her cup and then sat down on a cement block. I took a sip, then rested my coffee cup beside me and massaged my temples.

"Damn. You look stressed," Nadine said.

She put her coffee down on another cement block, walked behind me, and massaged my back and shoulders.

"You have a lot of tension in your neck and shoulders. You need to relax."

Her hands felt heavenly as she massaged me, kneading out all the kinks and knots in my tightly wound shoulders, but I had to stop this. It felt too good. She was hot, but I didn't need this much temptation, especially with the way I'd been feeling in my marriage. I politely stopped her and stood up, my coffee cup in my hand.

"Thanks. I'm good now. I gotta get back to work."

She looked disappointed, but she nodded and smiled. At least I had one woman around who wanted to touch me.

***

It was about one in the morning, and I was just getting home. At least I had had the day off. The house was dark when I walked inside. I headed to my bedroom. The kids were both knocked out on my side of the bed, while Karen was sitting up reading one of her romance novels.

"Hey," I said.

"Hey," she answered softly.

I wished she'd stop having the kids fall asleep in our bed. We had recently broken them of the habit of wanting to sleep with us. It was another factor that had been putting a damper on our sex life.

I carried them to their bedroom, tucked them in, and jumped in the shower. Afterward, I walked into the bedroom and opened my towel slowly. Karen stared at me. I let my towel fall to the floor and stood in front of her, completely naked. Karen looked good in her black and purple bra and panties set. We hadn't had sex in so long that I got hard instantly. I walked up to her, leaned over, lifted her face to mine, and softly kissed her. I rubbed my hands down her body, pulled her thong down, and tossed it on the floor.

While there were millions of women in the world, there'd never been a woman I desired more than Karen. I turned her around, grabbed my erection, and struggled to push into her softness. She was still dry. I spat on my hand and rubbed it on my dick. Then I eased it into her tightness. I pumped away and tried my best to savor the moment. I squeezed her cheeks and slapped her ass. Her juices started to flow. She felt better, moister. I loved hearing her moan. When she moaned, it felt like she was singing to me.

"Ride me, baby," I whispered in her ear.

She nodded and adjusted her body on top of my hardness. Her long reddish-brown hair cascaded down her

face as she worked her magic, grinding and rubbing her clit on my pubic bone the way I liked it. She
placed her hands on my chest and increased her stride.
She was close. I knew my wife's body, and I loved watching her face when she reached that point—her honey-colored complexion glowed. A few moments later she came
and then rested on my chest. She smiled and took me in
her mouth. She deep throated me, and in no time, I was
cumming down her throat. As soon as I finished, Karen
rushed into the bathroom. I heard her gargling with the
mouthwash and brushing her teeth.

It had been so long since we'd had sex that I just
drifted off to sleep, content and satisfied, before Karen
returned to bed. I was so tired from work that I couldn't
keep my eyes open.

Karen

"Chris, make sure the girls finish getting ready, and don't bring them to school late."

"I won't. You know I've done these things a million times before, right?"

"Doing them a million times before doesn't mean you've done them right."

Chris frowned at me.

Bing. A text message.

Our iPhones were on one of the marble kitchen counters. I hated that they looked so identical. I had been constantly dropping my phone and breaking it, and Chris had got tired of buying me replacements, so he'd bought me the same black OtterBox case he had to protect my phone.

"Is that my phone or yours?" I asked him.

Chris handed me my phone without answering. He then poured coffee into my thermos while I rushed to grab my purse so I could head out for work.

"Thanks. I'll see you tonight," I said when he gave me the thermos.

I gave him a peck on the lips and dashed out of the house. After I placed the thermos and my purse on the seat of the car, I checked my phone. It was a text from my sister, Chloe.

What's up, bitch face! I'm in desperate need of a girls' night on Friday.

I texted her back. What did you have in mind?

You can ditch the rug rats with Chris or his dad, and me, you, Lindsey, Vivian, and Judy can all go into Manhattan for a night of shaking our asses and clubbing on Friday night. What do you say, big sis? Are you down for that?

I laughed out loud. Then I sent a final text.

No doubt.

Right now my mind wasn't on my weekend plans, though. My thoughts had gone back to last night's sex session with Chris. It had started off nice. He'd looked so damn sexy standing in our bedroom, naked, with his bald head and muscular body still wet from his shower. I'd definitely been turned on, and I'd wanted him. I enjoyed his few kisses and caresses and was prepared to get the kind of loving from him that I'd been craving for so long, but as it turned out, it was a good thing that my seeing him naked had me somewhat aroused and moist, because he didn't bother to give me much foreplay. Where was the foreplay to get my juices flowing? I knew we couldn't always have marathon sex. Both of us usually had to wake up early to get ready for work, but I needed stimulation. You needed to preheat this oven before you stuffed in the meat. The bastard didn't even offer to go down on me.

Instead, as usual, he climbed on top of me and started poking and pushing himself inside me, going right to straight fucking me. He didn't kiss me at all while we made love, and he didn't hold me after. It was no different than if he was fucking a prostitute. Nevertheless, once I got into it, it was great. But after returning the favor for making me cum, I came back into the bedroom to see his ass asleep. I'd wanted that warm feeling of cuddling together and being held. Instead, I'd gone to sleep, disappointed, while he'd rolled over, satisfied.

***

I was at my desk working on figures for my department. I worked as a derivative accounting manager in the Hicksville, New York branch of National Grid, one of the largest energy suppliers on Long Island. After I had taken a quick look at the reports in front of me, I'd known that something was off with my department figures and that it would take time to get them right.

While I was hard at work, Tyrell knocked on my door and walked into my office, then closed the door behind him.

"Hey, beautiful."

I continued working on the report I was correcting, though I glanced up from my computer screen for a split second and said, "Hey."

"Can you get away tonight?" he asked.

I stopped typing and leaned back in my chair. "I think I can arrange something. What's up?"

"I wanted to surprise you, but I guess I'll tell you. I got us tickets to see *Wicked*."

"What? Hell yeah, I can sneak away for that! I'll call Chris on my lunch break and tell him I'm working late."

Tyrell was nice. He was tall, around six feet four, and had a natural bronze complexion. He wasn't as in shape as Chris or Raheem, but he had a decent build.

He was respectful, romantic, and affectionate. He'd be perfect if he had a longer dick and weren't a minute man. When we had sex, he never got me off during the actual act, only orally or when we used toys. I knew after our outing tonight, I could sex him up quickly and be home before midnight.

I'd met Tyrell a little over a year ago. He was married, but he had no kids. His wife also worked at National Grid, but in our Melville branch. If I hadn't known that she was cheating on him, I probably wouldn't have slept with him. He'd caught her fucking another guy in the company parking lot one night, and rumors of it had spread all throughout National Grid. His work had suffered tremendously because of this, and as his supervisor, I had to let him go. I'd invited him out to lunch to cushion the blow of firing him, but it had backfired bigtime. He had vented to me about his marriage, and I had ended up venting to him about mine. Before I knew it, that night I was bent over in my office, getting fucked from behind. And I convinced HR and the higher-ups to give him another chance. He'd been under me, literally and figuratively, ever since.

At the time, Raheem's lack of availability had been starting to bother me. I couldn't see him whenever I wanted, but I still craved the affection and attention that he provided for me. So I used Tyrell as my substitute maintenance man for the emotional connection I wanted and needed when Raheem was tied up with his wife.

Tyrell walked behind my desk, with a naughty grin. He swung my chair around and showered me with soft, sensual kisses. He hiked up my navy-blue skirt and eased my panties down. He licked his fingers and slowly worked them inside me. I was aroused by his spontaneity, but I had to play it safe.

"We have to be quick. Make sure my door is locked, since you want to be nasty during work hours," I told him.

Tyrell grinned, walked back to the door, turned the latch, and twisted the doorknob to confirm the door was locked. He came back to my chair and, without hesitation, dropped to his knees. He placed his hands under my butt and pulled my pussy closer to his face. He hungrily lapped my clit, switching between firm strokes and gentle nibbles. I held the back of his head in my hands. I felt so in control as I watched him feast on me. My orgasm snuck up on me. I gasped and bit down on my lip to muffle my moans. Tingles swept through me in waves. My body bucked as Tyrell continued to lick me through my climax, despite my reaction. I needed that release. I clamped my shuddering thighs around his head. Then I squealed and panted as I pushed his head away from my sensitive clit.

"Are you trying to kill me, making me cum like that?" I asked. It was more to massage his ego than to tell him the truth, but the boy could eat a good pussy.

Tyrell smiled, got up off his knees, grabbed some tissues off my desk, and wiped his face. "I like to keep you pleased, my dear," he said, smiling.

"You do that well." I paused, a glint in my eye. "Do you want me to return the favor?" I asked, then seductively licked my lips.

"Nah. I want to savor you without any distractions tonight, after our date. Build up your strength, because that was just the appetizer. Meet me at my car when you sign out."

"Okay."

I winked at him. He smiled, walked out of my office, and closed the door behind him. I giggled to myself, straightened out my outfit, combed my disheveled hair, and went back to working on my report.

Wicked was awesome. I loved it! The costumes, the set, and the performances were amazing. When it was over, we ate dinner at Red Lobster on Seventh Avenue in Manhattan.

Afterward, we drove back to our workplace, and I brought him into my office to thank him properly for the wonderful evening.

As soon as we got inside, Tyrell wrapped his arms around my waist and pulled me close to him. His hands traveled down my hips, and he grabbed two big handfuls of my ass.

During the day, I worked in the corporate world, and even though I was a supervisor, I still had to take orders. Right here, right now, I had the control, and I had the power. And Tyrell was about to fall victim to it. I pushed him back on my desk.

"I like when you get aggressive." He laughed.

I hiked up my pencil skirt and yanked my panties down. I stepped out of my panties and then unbuckled his pants and tugged them down, along with his briefs, to the floor. Tyrell lay on his back, with his thick stub of a penis pointing straight up toward the ceiling. I reached down and grabbed his pants from the floor and searched in his pockets for a condom. When I found one, I dropped his pants, ripped open the wrapper with my teeth, and easily put the condom on him by using only my mouth. He thought this was an amazing feat. It took no real skill. His dick didn't have enough length to make it challenging.

I held on to his legs, reached back, and slowly lowered myself down on his dick. I exaggerated the arch in my back as I leaned forward to ride him in reverse cowgirl. He grabbed two handfuls of my ass and started thrusting upward while I rolled my hips on top of him. His squirming and moaning beneath me was definitely a sexy sight, but I clamped my hand over his mouth to muffle his moans.

A vein throbbed in his forehead. He looked like he was on the verge of losing control, and I welcomed it. I liked knowing that I was the cause of this euphoria he was experiencing. I quickened my pace, rolling my hips and bouncing my ass hard on top of him.

"Oh shit! Oh fuck," he moaned, squirming while he came.

Sweat streamed down Tyrell's forehead as he lay on top of my desk, panting and trying to catch his breath from our session. I took pride knowing that I had worn his ass out!

He kissed me. "I enjoy being with you."

"Aw, I enjoy being with you too."

"I'm falling in love with you, Karen."

Ugh. I hated when he got like this. I enjoyed how he made me feel emotionally and physically, but I'd never leave Chris for Tyrell.

I patted his arm. "We agreed we'd just enjoy each other's company. That's it. Don't complicate things."

"I know, I know, but can you honestly tell me you don't feel it too?"

I *honestly* didn't. I liked him. You could even say I somewhat cared about him, but I wasn't in love with him or even close to falling in love with him. As much as Chris irritated me, he was the only man I actually loved.

"Tyrell, I do have feelings for you, but I have a family. I'm married, you're married, and I have kids. As much as I care about you, I'm not breaking up my family. You know this."

"Do you know how hard it is for me wanting you, being intimate like this, and then knowing we're both going home to spouses that don't deserve or appreciate us?"

"An easy alternative to that is to stop this before it goes any deeper, but I don't think either one of us wants that, right?"

"Of course not. I know I'm being soft right now. I just wish things could be different."

I stood up and gave him a kiss on the cheek. "We're good the way we are. We make each other happy and take care of each other's needs. Divorcing your wife would be costly, and it'd be more hurtful than helpful. Enjoy what we have. I'm not going anywhere."

I extend my arms to him. He took my hands, and I pulled him to his feet.

He kissed me and smiled. That little speech should hold him for a while. We dressed and headed home to our separate lives.

I went home to a pitch-black house. The minute I stepped inside, I checked on the girls. They were snuggled under their blankets, sound asleep. I crept to my bedroom. The door creaked as I slowly opened it. The room was dark, but the sparse moonlight from the windows outlined Chris, who was sitting up against the headboard, with his arms folded. I turned on the light.

"Why are you sitting in the dark?" I asked him.

Chris glanced at his watch. "Where were you?"

"I was at work. I told you I was working late."

"Bullshit! I went to your job to surprise you with dinner from Phil's. Your coworkers said you'd gone home hours ago. It's funny, you weren't there, but your car was. I saw it in the parking lot. I waited for you for over an hour."

Damn. I hadn't expected him to come to my job. I was even more upset that the night-shift crew hadn't told me he stopped by when I went back to the office. I needed to think fast. My mind was racing as I tried to come up with an alibi that would calm him down.

"Okay, you caught me . . . I was out with Lindsey," I blurted out.

Lindsey had been my best friend since preschool. I told her everything and trusted her with my life. She knew I fucked around on Chris, and while she didn't agree with it, she always had my back when situations got tight.

"Don't lie to me. You weren't with Lindsey!" Chris shouted.

He was so angry that it scared me, and I started to shake.

"Yes I was. And stop yelling at me! Sometimes I need to have a little girl time. I need to hang out and do things I like to do, besides just going to the gym. I never have time just for me. When I wake up, I have to get the kids ready for school. I bathe them, clothe them, fix their hair, drive them to school, and then I rush to work, where I'm swamped with shit all day. When I come home, I'm making dinner, spending time with the kids, and reading bedtime stories. I'm tired of the usual routine, working all day, then turning on Mommy mode and dealing with the kids all night. I needed to get away for a bit, so I did. We went to see *Wicked*. Then we had dinner at the Red Lobster in Times Square. She drove, which is why my car was in the parking lot."

I had laid my lie down thick. His face softened, and he seemed to calm down a bit.

"I understand . . . It makes sense, but I need you to put my mind at ease. Call Lindsey and let me hear it from her mouth."

"Right now? It's almost two o'clock in the morning."

"I don't care what time it is. Call her now. She lives five minutes away. She should still be up if you guys just finished hanging out, like you claim you did. Call her," he demanded.

He was serious. I was too sloppy, and it was causing Chris not to trust me. I knew I had to be more careful from now on. I couldn't risk losing him.

"Baby, you're being unreasonable," I pleaded. "She's a married woman. She might be up, but that doesn't necessarily mean Jeff is."

"Fine. Before you go to work, call her and let me hear her version of what went down tonight, without you interfering."

"Why are you acting like this?"

"If you lied to me about this, what else could you be lying to me about?"

"I told you what happened."

"Yeah, you did. Now I want to see if it matches up with Lindsey's story."

He slid down in the bed and turned away from me. Something was up, but I was too tired to argue with him tonight. I let him pout. I got undressed, slid into bed, and waited until I heard him snoring. I eased onto my side so my back was facing him. Then I grabbed my phone from the nightstand and texted Lindsey a long message explaining that she should expect a phone call from me early in the morning. I told her what she should say and what I had actually done. She responded right away and said she had my back. I knew she'd cover for me, but I was on edge. I knew I had to tread lightly from now on. Obviously, something had Chris suspecting me. I needed to find out what that was so that I could dispel it. I was not trying to lose what I had. Chris was flawed—you could even say he was damaged—but I wouldn't trade him for Raheem or Tyrell.

My alarm clock buzzed. I rolled onto my back and looked up. Chris was already awake and dressed.

"Good morning," I said groggily.

"Morning, babe. I made you coffee, some eggs, and toast."

"Thanks."

He nodded. "Now that you're up, call Lindsey," he said nonchalantly.

That woke me up. I thought he would've cooled down by now, but he was still fixated on talking to her.

"It's too early for this shit. What's your deal? You think I'm cheating on you or something?"

"I don't know. Are you?"

I couldn't believe it. Even though he was right to wonder, it shocked me that he'd ask me directly. "Are you serious? You're really asking me that? You know what? Fuck you!"

He softened up, sighed, and said, "Wait, I'm sorry. I've been under a lot of stress. I'm not trying to accuse you, but sometimes I get paranoid. I love you. I know I don't say it as much as I should."

When he said that, it reminded me of why I'd never leave him. Under his tough exterior was a caring man who loved me and tried to make me happy. I needed to stop fucking around, but it would take time. I couldn't quit cold turkey. I needed to quell his suspicions while I worked on weaning myself off Tyrell and Raheem.

"If it'll put your mind at ease, I'll call her."

He didn't stop me, which made me realize I needed to do this. I called her, and on the second ring she picked up.

"Hey, bestie," Lindsey said cheerfully.

"Hey, girl. What's up? Last night was fun, right?"

"Am I on speaker?"

"Yeah, we need to go out more often," I said, trying to disguise my answer.

"Let me talk to her for a second," Chris said.

"Hold on. Chris wants to say hi."

Chris snatched the phone from my hand. "What's up, Lindsey? How is everything?"

"Everything is good here. How are you doing?"

"Working. You know how it is. So, you were the one that kept my wife out late, huh?"

"Yup, that was me. Sorry about that."

"Do you guys do that often?" he quizzed.

"Every now and then. Not all the time, though."

I loved her answer. It covered past nights that I'd stayed out late, and it was an excuse I could use in the future.

"What did you guys do yesterday?" Chris asked.

Shit! Why was he still pressing the issue?

"We went into Manhattan to see *Wicked*. After that, we had dinner at Red Lobster."

"Did Vivian or Judy go with you guys?"

"Nah. It was just the two of us. I think they had dates. Karen was my date." She laughed. Chris didn't.

"Did Jeff know about your girls' night?" he asked.

"Nah, it was more of a spur-of-the-moment type thing."

"He doesn't mind you coming home late like that?"

"Nah, Jeff knows I'd never step out on him. I wouldn't jeopardize what we have for anything."

Chris nodded, his shoulders relaxed, and he breathed a sigh of relief. He seemed to believe her. "Okay. Hopefully, we can all hang out soon, so you don't have to kidnap my wife and have fun without me and Jeff."

Lindsey laughed. "Cool."

"All right. Well, I'll give you back to Karen. It was good talking to you. See you soon."

"See ya, Chris."

He handed me the phone.

"All right, girl. I'll text you later," I said.

"Okay. Talk to you later, bestie."

After we ended the call, I turned and faced Chris and said, "If you need me to say it, I'll say it." I took his hands, looked in his beautiful brown eyes, and said, "I could never cheat on you . . . You're the love of my life."

As soon as I said the words, a dark wave of guilt washed over me. I felt dirty. My conscience was eating away at me. When I cheated, I got lost in the excitement. I lived in the moment, and I didn't worry about my actions or his feelings. I knew it sounded selfish, but with everything that was wrong with our relationship, I'd always felt *justified* doing what I'd been doing. Right now, I felt like the scum of the earth.

"Thank you, babe. I needed to hear that. You know I was never the jealous type in the past, because you never gave me a reason to be, but I just felt like something was off, and it worried me a little," he said.

Chris looked deep in my eyes and kissed me, and that warm, loving feeling engulfed me. If only I could have this on a consistent basis.

Karen

"Thanks for watching the girls until Chris gets home, Pops."

"No need to thank me. These are my grandbabies. I love spending time with them."

Just then the doorbell rang. I walked into the foyer and opened the door. My sister, Chloe, and my childhood friends Lindsey, Vivian, and Judy had arrived. They were dressed to kill. I wore a charcoal-colored skirt with a white button-down, short-sleeved blouse.

"Hey, sis. You ready to go? I'm ready to fucking drink," Chloe said.

Pops looked up from his newspaper and shot Chloe a firm look.

"Yeah, I'm almost ready," I said.

"Well, hurry the fuck up, slowpoke."

Pops released a breath, indicating he was annoyed.

I ignored Chloe as I hugged and kissed everyone. Then I led them into the living room and introduced them to Pops.

"These are my friends, Pops, and of course you remember my sister, Chloe," I said.

Always the gentleman, Pops stood up from the couch and gave them each a strong handshake. At that moment, my daughters ran up to Chloe in excitement.

"Aunt Chloe!" they yelled in unison.

Chloe hugged them. "Hey, cuties. Have you girls been good?"

"Yes," they said at the same time.

"Well, me and Mommy have been good all week too, but we're going to be bad tonight," she joked.

Everyone but Pops laughed. Chloe didn't care.

She was spontaneous and carefree by nature. It never mattered to her what anyone thought.

I checked my makeup in the hallway mirror and applied another coat of my chocolate-brown lipstick as Lindsey, Judy, and Vivian talked to Pops. Chloe joked with the kids.

"You see, girls, you got to move your ass like this when you're dancing." Chloe wiggled her ass and gyrated her hips like a stripper as the twins giggled. Pops slammed his palm down on the wooden coffee table.

"That's enough," he said sternly. "Girls, get a game out of your room, and bring it here so we can play."

The girls stopped laughing and did as they were told.

"Do you think that's appropriate behavior to teach six-year-old children? You think it's funny to dance like a skank in front of these little girls?" Pops asked Chloe.

"You need to relax. I was only kidding around. It's not that serious," Chloe shot back.

"It *is* serious. These girls are impressionable. They look up to you and will mirror everything you do. You need to put more thought into what you're teaching them."

"Whatever. Karen, you ready to go?"

"Yeah," I said. Then I walked up to Pops and mouthed, "Sorry."

He nodded, and I gave him a hug and a kiss.

"Thanks again. I'll see you later," I told him.

He nodded again. "It's no problem."

I walked into my kids' bedroom to hug them before I left. They were deep in thought, trying to figure out which game to play.

"Bye, Jocelyn. Bye, Jaclyn. Mommy is going to miss her babies. See you in the morning."

"Bye, Mommy," they said, barely looking up from the shelves with all the games.

Everyone except Chloe said their good-byes to the kids and Pops. After her conversation with Pops, Chloe had gone outside to smoke. I then ushered everyone out the front door, shut it behind me, and rushed everyone over to Lindsey's Mercedes-Benz GL 550. I wanted to get out of Mommy mode as soon as possible.

"What club are we going to tonight?" Lindsey asked once everyone had climbed into the car.

"Oh, let's go to Element," Judy suggested.

"I'm down for that," Vivian agreed.

Everyone else seconded the motion, and so we drove into Manhattan, to club Element on Houston Street.

"Yo, what's the deal with Chris's father being such a douche? I guess I see where Chris gets it from," Chloe said as we drove.

"Not for nothing, Chloe. You were dancing kind of crazy in front of the kids," Lindsey said.

"I wasn't dancing crazy. They're going to learn to dance like that eventually, so what's the big deal?"

"They don't need a crash course called Stripper one-oh-one when they're five, Chloe," Judy responded.

Judy was similar to Lindsey in terms of her personality, but she was the girly girl of the group. Though she was prissy, she had a wild streak. And she was always on the lookout for her Prince Charming. Judy had smooth deep brown skin and big breasts. She made sure to display "the girls" whenever we went out.

"Y'all are fucking up my mood before we even get to the club. I don't need this right now," Chloe said.

Loud and outspoken, Chloe hated arguing with people, especially when she felt she was right. She and I were very close. I was a year older. Although we were sisters, we were the total opposite of each other. Chloe was built like a Kardashian. She had huge hips and a big ass, while I was built more like Vanessa Williams. My complexion was honey colored, but hers was chestnut. I had reddish brown hair, and she had jet-black hair. I enjoyed being wild and spontaneous, but I was also responsible. Chloe lived in the moment and never worried about anything.

She was the only family I had left. Our parents were killed by a drunk driver when I was five, and Chloe and I had to live with our grandparents. When I started college, my grandpa passed. When I finished, Grandma followed him. Now it was just the two of us. We were fiercely protective of each other.

"Hand me a cigarette," I said to Chloe.

"You sure? What if Chris smells the smoke on you?" Chloe asked sarcastically.

I rolled my eyes, then snatched the Marlboro Blacks and lighter from her hand. I lit a cigarette, then took a long, deep, relaxing drag. The nicotine and menthol filled my lungs and calmed my nerves. I blew the smoke out the car window, reached in my purse, and pulled out my cell phone.

"Who are you texting?" Judy asked me when my thumbs got busy.

"Raheem. I'm telling him to meet us at the club," I answered nonchalantly.

"You're still dealing with that guy? Why don't you try to work things out with Chris?" Judy asked.

"I'm trying, but it's going to take time. Being with Raheem is like being on drugs. It's hard to quit cold turkey. I have to ween myself off him."

"Texting Raheem to hang out in a club isn't going to help," Judy said.

"Oh, leave her alone, Judy," Chloe snapped. "I like Raheem better than Chris, anyway. Chris is boring. At least Raheem likes to have a good time."

"Chloe is right. Chris acts like he's Karen's father more than her husband. I want to call my man Daddy in the bedroom, but I don't want him acting like he's actually my father. He is boring," Vivian said.

Vivian was the party girl of the group. She and I had partied hard in my college days. Vivian and Chloe got along because they were both so blunt. Vivian was short, about four feet eleven. She wore designer glasses instead of contacts, and that gave her the sexy librarian look men seemed to love.

"Do you think Chris is boring?" Judy asked me.

"Sometimes," I answered.

"The problem is you guys don't do anything together. Instead of going to this club with Raheem, you should be going with Chris. We could've waited until he got home, and brought him with us," Lindsey said.

"Chris doesn't like clubs," I replied.

"Yeah, and he said he hates seeing her when she gets drunk and stupid," Chloe added.

"You have to explain to him that you want to share things you enjoy with him. You want him to know that you want to have these fun times and experiences together," Lindsey said, not giving up.

I heard the concern and compassion in her voice. Lindsey understood why I did what I did, but I knew she wanted to see my marriage with Chris last.

"If you feel like you need to have other men to fill the void in your marriage, maybe it's time to reevaluate your marriage," Judy suggested.

I shook my head. "No. Chris is the man for me. I'm the one who is fucking up by cheating. I'll stop eventually, but it's going to take some time. Once Chris starts to do his part, I'll speed up my efforts to stop."

"What do you want from Chris?" Judy asked.

"I don't feel appreciated. There's no spontaneity in our relationship. We don't have date nights anymore, and he doesn't surprise me with flowers or things like that. I need romance. I need affection. Chris is dynamite in bed, but what I want goes deeper than sex. I want him to be move vocal and to tell me he loves me. I want him to be more affectionate, to kiss me in public, to hold my hand, but we never do anything I want to do. Like tonight I want to go dancing. If I asked him to go, he wouldn't even consider it."

My phone chimed, letting me know I had received a text. It was from Raheem.

Hey, sexy! I'll be there! I gotta have you tonight. I've been thinking about your sexy ass all week.

I smiled and felt butterflies of excitement. I loved that even through a text, he made me feel desired.

"Look at her. She got a text from Raheem, and she's blushing and shit. I think you should just be with him and cut Chris off," Vivian said.

Vivian and Chloe high-fived. I ignored them and continued to enjoy my cigarette.

We stood outside the club, waiting for Lindsey to park her SUV so we could all go inside together. Five minutes later Lindsey appeared, and we went in. The place was packed. We walked to the bar, got drinks, and headed to the dance floor. Plenty of men begged to dance with me, but I turned them down. I wanted to dance with only one man, Raheem. I wondered when he would arrive.

An hour later, Raheem stepped into the club, looking as fine as ever. He was nowhere near as muscular as Chris, who was built like Michael Jai White, but Raheem was more handsome. He looked similar to Shemar Moore. His rich caramel complexion and his dreamy pair of chocolate-brown puppy-dog eyes were to die for. I turned my back and pretended not to see him. Raheem walked up to me, draped his arms around me, and kissed the back of my neck. I smiled, turned around, and faced him. Raheem slipped his arm around my waist and pulled me close to him. I threw my arms around his neck, and he stared in my eyes and kissed me.

"Hey, baby," he said in his deep, sexy voice.

"Hey."

His big strong hands caressed my arms and sent shivers down my body.

"I love when you touch me," I said.

"I love touching you."

My girls were looking at me. Lindsey and Judy were shaking their heads. Chloe and Vivian were smiling and laughing.

"Get it, girl!" Chloe said, then laughed at me some more.

I giggled and waved her off.

"You look good, baby," Raheem said, rubbing his hands up and down my body.

"Thanks. So do you. Was traffic bad getting here?"

"Nah. I had an argument with my wife before I could sneak out to get here. She was trippin', but I got here as soon as I could. I needed to see you tonight."

Ugh. Whenever he brought up his wife, it woke me up from my fantasy world and brought me back to reality. I quickly pushed those thoughts away and went back to having fun.

We were all gathered around the bar, drinking shots, laughing, and having a good time, when Chris texted me.

I just got home, babe. I wanted you to know that I'm thinking about you. Have fun with your girls. I love you.

His text was sweet, but I was too drunk to care about his message. The alcohol numbed me so much that I experienced none of the guilt I would've felt if I were sober.

"I want you right now. Grab your purse and come with me to my truck," Raheem whispered in my ear.

I nodded. Then I grabbed my purse and turned to follow Raheem.

"Where are you going?" Lindsey asked.

I jumped at the sound of her voice and stopped in my tracks. My words were slurred when I answered, "I'm just going . . . to talk to him . . . in his truck."

"You're going to talk to him, huh?"

"As good as he looks tonight, I might have a long conversation with the microphone in his pants." I laughed.

Lindsey looked concerned. She reluctantly reached in her purse, pulled out a condom, and offered it to me. I smiled and snatched it from her hand.

Raheem and I left the club and walked to his Lexus LX truck. We climbed in the backseat and kissed. His hands hungrily caressed my body. His eyes were full of desire as he unbuttoned my tight white blouse. I excitedly unzipped his khakis and pulled out his dick. I leaned over so that I could reach down a little farther and free his balls from his briefs so all of him was exposed. I lifted his swollen dick away from where it rested against his abs and lowered my head to his lap.

I worked his cock in my mouth. I ran my tongue up the underside of it to tease him. I licked up and down the length before curling my tongue around the head and coating him with my saliva so my hand could easily slide up and down his pole. Then I gripped his cock at the top and plunged down as far and as fast as I could, stopping only to admire how the tip glistened from my saliva. With my free hand, I reached beneath him to lightly massage his balls. Raheem leaned back, with his hands behind his head, and admired the sight of me going to work on his long cock.

"Oh fuck, Karen," he said as his eyes closed and his head dipped back against the headrest.

Next, I deep throated him with even more fervor while I massaged his balls. That drove him crazy. Before long he stopped me, pulled down my skirt, and ripped off my thong. I opened the condom wrapper Lindsey had given me and rolled the condom on him. I maneuvered myself on top of his dick. My eyes rolled back at the feeling of his long, veiny cock slowly entering my pussy. I rode him hard as we kissed.

Raheem unhooked my bra and took my breasts in his mouth. I hooked my hands around the back of his head and increased the speed of my riding. His breathing was thick. I knew he was close to cumming. I felt so powerful and desirable as I made this handsome man lose all composure by being in my pussy. The excitement from fucking him in his car, the intensity of feeling so sexually in tune, and my attraction to him got me close too.

"Oh, shit. Fuck me," I begged.

"Say my name," he demanded.

"Fuck me, Raheem." I screamed his name over and over. The dirty talk was definitely getting both of us off.

When Raheem raised his hips, his penis touched a nerve in me that sent me over the edge. The tingling sensation radiated all over my body, and I moaned in delight. We held each other and panted as we came together. I swiftly grabbed his cock and sucked on the head. I knew he was sensitive, but I liked seeing him squirm. I playfully held him in my mouth for a few more seconds, gently deep throating his softening dick. When he finally pulled away from me, he looked beyond satisfied.

He pulled me back up to him and kissed me. Those butterflies from earlier returned. We dressed each other and held hands as we walked back to the club. I didn't care what my friends thought of me. I was having my cake and eating it too.

Chris

I slept uncomfortably in my truck. No matter which way I moved on the firm leather seats, I couldn't relax. I rested my head on the window and leaned my back against the side of the door, but that was so uncomfortable. I sat up straight behind the steering wheel, with my seat reclined. I was still uncomfortable. I rested my head on the side of the door and lay flat on the seats. Impossible. I just couldn't get comfortable. I felt the same way about my marriage.

Talking to Lindsey had made me feel somewhat better, but I still had a gnawing feeling that something was wrong. That night when Karen allegedly hung out with Lindsey, I had pretended to be asleep after Karen and I agreed I would talk to Lindsey in the morning. But I had heard Karen text someone once my fake snoring convinced her I was asleep. Had she sent a text to Lindsey, asking her friend to cover her? Or had she sent a text to someone else? I didn't think Karen would cheat on me. I prayed to God she wasn't cheating, but there was no doubt we were drifting apart.

I'd been doing overtime at my construction gig and taking some side jobs with my Pops to make extra money to take the family on vacation. Karen and I needed to get away from our regular routines. I knew I hadn't been spending enough time with her or the girls, but I hoped she would understand that I was doing the best I could to balance being a good provider, a husband, and a father. I *needed* this trip. I needed to feel alive again, even if only for two weeks.

Lately, I'd been feeling dead inside. I worked all the time. Even when I was off, I was still working in some capacity. For instance, sometimes Pops needed help with different projects, and I couldn't afford to turn down extra money, not when I had so many bills to pay. Karen worked hard too, but her job was easier than mine. I'm not saying her job didn't have its stress, but my job was physically and mentally draining. Thankfully, Karen was no slouch. She contributed. We split everything sixty-forty. We could split everything fifty-fifty, but I felt a man still had to be a man.

Whenever there was a gift-giving occasion, I went all out with a thought-out gift for Karen, something that I knew she would want and use. She used to match my effort, but now I felt like she didn't even try. Nowadays, for my birthday, Father's Day, or our anniversary, she gave me only a card. It was like it didn't matter when it came to me, but if it were the other way around and I handed her just a card, she would be ready to rip my head off.

Don't get me wrong. Whenever I gave Karen a gift, I did it out of love. I never bought her gifts with the expectation that I would get something better in return. It was not the fact that she wasn't getting me material things that troubled me. It was the fact that she made no effort to do things that would make me happy. Everything was about her and her feelings. Most times, I held my tongue, out of fear that I'd say something that would spark a big argument. Everything I did for Karen was out of love, but when the same love and sincerity weren't given in return, I couldn't help but question whether she loved me and cared for me as much as I loved her and cared for her, or if she was just too selfish and wanted always to take and never to give. These questions still bothered me.

I was not vocal when it came to expressing my feelings. I tried to make my actions speak louder than words. Right now, I was hoping Karen would understand the method to my madness when I took the family on this trip. I still had my suspicions about her. Sometimes she'd stay "late" at work and come home with her breath reeking of alcohol and cigarettes. She knew before we officially started dating that I despised cigarettes. My mother had died of lung cancer. While watching her suffer in her last days, I had promised myself I'd never date a smoker.

Sometimes Karen came home wearing heavy makeup, as if she'd been out clubbing, not working at the office. There were also times when as soon as she came home from "work," she'd quickly jump in the shower.

"Davis! Stop spacing out over there and get back to work," the foreman yelled, snapping me out of my daydream.

I was not concentrating on my job. Lately, I couldn't focus on anything. I had too much going on, and it was affecting my work. Often I was so exhausted from everything that was going on that I slept in my truck at the site to avoid the commute into Manhattan and thus give myself more time to sleep.

While I worked, I called Karen to check on her and the girls, but when we talked, it felt routine and forced. We discussed bills and problems around the house, but our conversations didn't feel like ones a happily married couple would have. They felt mechanical. And she often rushed me off the phone because she was going to some club with Vivian, Chloe, Lindsey, and Judy. She would explain that my father was watching the kids for the night. I knew Karen needed time to relax, but I wanted time too. Ever since the girls were born, my boys Will and Lou had been distant with me. Honestly, I was envious that Karen's friends were still there for her, because I felt abandoned by mine.

A few hours later, my shift finally ended. I was exhausted. As I was heading to the parking lot, Nadine walked up behind me and touched my shoulder to get my attention.

"Do you want to crash on my couch for a little bit before you drive home? You look like you need to sleep."

Normally, I would've said no, but I was too tired to feel guilty. "Sure," I answered.

"I don't live too far from here. Follow me."

Nadine got into her red Nissan Xterra, and I jumped in my truck. We exited the parking lot, and then I followed her to her place. Her house was big and impressive. The exterior was beige stucco, and it had big bay windows.

"This is a nice house," I said as I stepped past the front door.

"Thanks . . . Despite everything, my husband let me keep it."

I felt bad for her. I knew she was still bitter about him leaving her.

"If you don't mind me asking, what happened with that?"

"My husband cheated on me with my best friend, Eva. You know how sporadic and hectic our work schedule is."

I nodded as we stood in the foyer.

"Well, my best friend used to hang out around the house all the time, sometimes when I wasn't home. I didn't suspect anything, because whenever they were around each other in front of me, they acted like they were more like brother and sister than lovers."

I trust my boys Will and Lou with my life, but even I would be skeptical if they hung out with Karen when I wasn't home. I kept my thoughts to myself and listened as she continued.

"One weekend I was cleaning our bedroom, and I found a condom wrapper under our bed. I knew it wasn't from us, because we never used condoms. I confronted him about it."

"What did he say?"

"He admitted everything. He said he loved her. He told me he was glad I had found out, because it gave him the strength he needed to get a divorce. He wanted to be with her."

"Why?"

"I asked myself that question for months. I thought there had to be something wrong with me. Maybe I wasn't pretty enough, or maybe she had more in common with him. Maybe she was better in the sack than I was. I needed closure, so I asked him when we were signing our paperwork to finalize our divorce. He told me I wasn't prissy enough for him. He felt that my job was too masculine, and he felt that I didn't need him for anything. Basically, he felt I was too strong for him." Her gaze left my eyes.

"I'm sorry."

"Don't be. I know I have my quirks, but I want a man who loves me and wants to be with me. It took me a while, but I realized that there were more things wrong with him than there were with me. He helped me by leaving. I wasn't too strong for him. He was too weak for *me*. If he couldn't appreciate me and love me quirks and all, then he saved us both a lot of time, headaches, and aggravation by ending things quickly the way he did. Now I can find a man who will truly love me."

I swallowed. I thought about my fears of Karen cheating. I knew I'd be devastated if I found out she was two-timing me. I loved Nadine's strength. When she got irritated or upset, her West Indian accent came on strong. I could tell that even though she made it sound like she was over the bad marriage, it still ate her up inside, since her accent had been on full display when she told me the story. But she hadn't let this adversity defeat her.

Nadine went over to the hallway closet and took out two pillows and a flannel blanket.

"The couch folds out into a bed. Go ahead and make yourself comfortable. I'll wake you up in a couple of hours."

"Thank you," I said gratefully.

"You're a good guy, Chris. It's no problem."

I stepped into the living room, opened the couch, laid the pillows down, and got comfortable. I needed to relax for a bit.

I woke up to Nadine nudging me. It took me a few seconds to realize where I was. Nadine was holding a cup of coffee, and her hair was down around her shoulders. I had to admit, she looked good. Very feminine.

"Hey, sleepyhead. I made you some coffee."

"Thanks," I said, sitting up. She handed me the cup.

There was a comfortable silence as I sipped my coffee. Nadine sat on the armchair across from me. She had changed into a pair of leggings that hugged her curves and a tight black V-neck shirt that made her tits look amazing. I tried to not think about how attracted I was to her by making conversation.

"So, what are you doing this weekend?" I asked.

"I don't have any plans. I might visit my mom and dad or hang out here with my friends, but that's about it. What about you?"

"Same here. I don't know if my wife made plans to hang out with her girls or if she made plans for the family to go somewhere."

"Well, hopefully, you can go out as a family. It's nice that you like to spend time with your wife and your gorgeous daughters."

When she said that, reality hit me. I shouldn't be here.

"Well, thank you for letting me rest up, and thanks for the coffee. I should be going."

"It's no problem. I wish you could stay longer."

The look on her face told me she meant that. She looked lonely. After working with each other for so long, we were close, and I understood her. I liked all the qualities about her that she considered flaws, but I knew I had to keep my distance. Feelings like these were dangerous for a marriage. I stood up, gave her a quick hug, handed her the empty cup, and headed for the door.

"Drive safe," she said as she followed behind me.

"Thanks again," I answered, then walked out the front door.

About thirty minutes later I walked into my own living room, to the sight of Pops and the girls watching *Wreck-It Ralph*.

"Hey, Pops."

"Hey, son. Karen left a few hours ago. I fed the girls and got them dressed for bed."

"Thanks," I said.

"I'm going to need your help with a basement job in Queens tomorrow."

"No problem. What are we doing?"

"We're going to install a new vinyl floor in the basement and new recessed lighting in the basement ceiling. If we get there early in the morning—figure around six—after cleanup we should be out of there by four in the afternoon."

"No problem . . ." I paused for a moment. "Pops?"

"Yes?"

"Why don't you consider moving in here and selling the old house? I don't like that you're there alone."

"I need my space. I like being alone." My father was stubborn. He always did things his way and on his terms. "Besides, you have a family. You don't need any outside sources controlling how you raise your children. That goes for me and Karen's sister, Chloe. You understand me, son?"

"Yes, sir."

Pops gave me a stern look to make sure I was listening to the wisdom he was giving me. He sat on the couch, with his arms around my daughters. He was wearing his black cargo pants and his polished black combat boots.

I was a carbon copy of my father, with the same features, the same dark skin, and the same stocky build. Even though he'd been retired from the marines for years, he was always clean shaven and neatly dressed. Pops was very direct and commanding, traits he'd learned while in the marines.

I suddenly realized that for him to make that statement, Chloe must've done or said something he didn't like before she left with Karen.

"What happened with Chloe, Pops?"

"That girl Chloe was cursing up a storm in front of your kids, and she was dressed like a damn harlot. Do you want your daughters growing up to be like that?"

"No, sir."

"Good. Fix it." All of a sudden, he coughed violently and clutched his chest.

"You okay, Pops?"

"I'm fine," he said, gritting his teeth.

My father never wanted to be seen as weak and never wanted anyone to think he was. The girls were nodding off on the couch, so I lifted them up one by one and put them to bed. Then I went back into the living room.

"Pops?" I said as I stood near the couch.

"Yeah?"

"I've been saving money to take us to Cancún for a vacation. I want you to come with us."

"I got work to do, boy."

I had to patch up my marriage. I wanted Pops to relax and have fun, but I also needed him there to watch the girls so that I could have alone time with Karen.

"Pops, I need this. Between stress from bills and problems with Karen, if I don't do something, I'm going to fall apart."

"Stop sounding soft. I didn't raise no punk. I raised you to be stronger than that. If you have bills, then you work to pay them. You're a man. If you're having problems with your wife, you fix it. End of story."

I stood up straight and wiped all emotion off my face. My father never wanted to hear about my feelings or my problems. He always treated me like he was disappointed in me.

"I'm not soft. I need time to relax with my family. There's nothing wrong with wanting that."

Pops sat in silence and stared at me long and hard, studying me for what felt like an eternity. He did this often to see if people were lying to him. I didn't break eye contact. I wanted him to see I was being truthful. I think he saw the desperation on my face.

"I'll go. Whatever problems you're having with Karen, fix them on the trip. If you see something stirring, nip it in the bud, before it grows."

"Yes, sir."

We discussed the plans for the job we were handling in the morning some more, but my thoughts were on Karen the whole time. At least one of us was having fun tonight.

Karen

"All right, girl. I'll call you tomorrow," Lindsey said when she was dropping me off in front of my house.

"Ugh. Thank God you were the designated driver tonight. We wouldn't have made it home if it were me. I have a hangover already," I moaned.

"Well, rest up. Good night, bestie."

"Good night," I said and giggled uncontrollably as I climbed out of her Mercedes-Benz.

I was drunk as shit. I walked on wobbly legs to the front door, then stood there and fumbled in my purse for my keys. I finally found my house keys, and after several attempts to put the key into the lock, I opened the door and stumbled inside. I tried my best to creep up the steps without making too much noise and waking up my family. I glanced at my watch; it was four in the morning. I had had a great night partying with Raheem and my girls, but the aftereffects were kicking my ass. I rushed into the bathroom, lifted the toilet seat, and threw up. As I leaned on the toilet, my head draped over the bowl, I thought about Raheem and Tyrell, and about how my cheating had started three years ago.

The cheating had started innocently enough. What led up to it was a simple trip to the mall. Chris and I were driving to Roosevelt Field Mall in Garden City to get outfits for my company's Christmas party. As usual, he criticized everything I did as I drove.

"Jesus, babe. Can you speed the fuck up? You drive too damn slow," he groused.

"I didn't know we were in a rush to get to the mall," I said snidely.

"We're not, but it seems like you're purposely taking your sweet-ass time."

"Next time, you fucking drive, then. Better yet, we can take separate cars, so I don't have to hear you complain."

"Damn. You're extra bitchy today. Is it that time of the month?"

"Chris . . . ooh." I punched the steering wheel. "I can't deal with you right now."

"Trust me, the feeling is mutual."

We continued bickering over petty bullshit. We finally parked, walked inside the mall, and roamed around Express, looking for outfits.

I was feeling a dress I had tried on until Chris looked at me and scrunched up his face.

"What?" I asked, feeling self-conscious.

"You like that one, huh?"

I rolled my eyes and sighed. "What's wrong with it?"

"It's not bad, but it's not the most flattering on you."

"What's that supposed to mean?" I huffed.

"I'm just saying, it's a little clingy, and it makes you look chunky."

Chris's job was physically strenuous. He did a lot of manual labor, which kept him fit and sexy. I mostly sat at a desk all day at my job.

Tears welled up in my eyes. I was coming apart at the seams, but I'd be damned if I'd cry here and embarrass myself in public. I wiped my eyes with the back of my hand, went into the dressing room, took off the dress, came back out, and slammed the dress back on the rack.

"Are you happy now?" I asked him.

"Stop being so sensitive."

"Stop being such an asshole, you insensitive prick. You know I've been dieting. I've lost fifteen pounds."

"I know, and that's good, but you still have a little ways to go, and that outfit wasn't your best, that's all I'm saying. I'm not trying to be a dick about it," he said.

"It's too late for that."

Chris threw up his hands and walked away.

As we went from store to store, Chris thought he was being discreet when he checked out other women, but I noticed. It made me feel insecure when I saw him staring at women who looked like the size I used to be when I first met him.

An hour later we went home and got ready for the party. I put on a dress that I knew he liked, and then fixed my hair in the bathroom mirror. Chris came into the bathroom and sprayed on his Polo Sport cologne and then shook his head as he passed by me.

"What is it now, Chris?"

"If you're going to give me a fucked-up attitude, don't worry about it."

"Say what you want to say."

"Your hair looks better when you wear it up with that dress."

Out of frustration, I styled my hair the way he wanted it. I felt like I was always doing things the way he wanted them done. It seemed like he didn't like me anymore, and nothing I did was ever good enough for him.

I stood in the doorway of our bedroom while he fixed his tie in the mirror above the dresser.

"You never acknowledge any of the positive things I do or the good qualities I have. You're always quick to comment on my flaws. You don't appreciate what I sacrifice to make you happy," I said.

"Look, drop this drama-queen shit. I'm not fighting with you before we go to this party. I didn't mean anything bad by it, all right?"

I put the argument on hold for the time being. I knew that was his way of saying he was sorry, but that wasn't an apology to me.

During the entire thirty-minute ride to the party, neither of us said a word. The radio was off, and we were both lost in our thoughts. Once we got there, we went through the motions and acted like the perfect happy couple, but I was still angry with him and hurting inside.

But when we got home, I decided to put all our bickering aside and make love to my husband. While Chris pleased me sexually, our busy work schedules had reduced our lovemaking to mundane quickies. I knew if I was bored, he had to be too.

To spice things up, I had read magazines, watched porn, and gathered tips from my friends. He loved lacy lingerie, so I wore my black bustier, my black French-cut panties, and fishnet stockings. I lit scented candles and put on soft jazz to set the ambiance in the bedroom. Chris walked in, and his face lit up.

"Damn!" he said.

He tugged on my lingerie to take it off. I couldn't hide my smile. His hands hungrily roamed my body.

"Easy, baby. Enjoy what you're looking at."

I felt self-conscious as he groped me, because his earlier comment about me looking chunky kept replaying in my mind.

We made love. I used a lot of the new ideas I had come across to spice things up, but he didn't seem to notice. Chris always had the decency to make sure I came, but again, we ended up having another quickie, because he had to wake up early the next morning. He rolled over on his side of the bed and went to sleep almost immediately after. I frowned, shook my head, and stared at the ceiling. Was it me? Was this how marriage was supposed to be? Had we both gotten too comfortable?

I decided I would start going to the gym and would get a personal trainer. I hoped working with a trainer would boost my self-esteem and change me enough that even Chris would have to say something positive about the improvements. I didn't imagine then how much it *would* change me.

"All right. Give me two more reps," Ken ordered.

"I hate you! You said that ten reps ago."

"Yeah, yeah, just give me two more."

"No."

"Keep it up and we're going to do another set." His full lips parted into a smile, revealing his beautiful straight white teeth. I fantasized about kissing those soft lips every time he told me to do an exercise.

I was working out at Lifetime Fitness with my trainer Ken Ferguson. His dark skin tone and his mannerisms had drawn me to him because he reminded me so much of Chris. Word around the gym was he did more than just train his clients. I had no intention of doing anything sexual with him. I was a married woman. I thought of him as eye candy, since Chris was always working.

Back then, I thought that if I ever cheated on Chris, the sky would darken, rain would pour down on me, and I'd turn into a horrible *monster*. But I was lonely and vulnerable. I didn't feel sexy anymore. I knew that over the years, I had slipped up a bit and I had let myself go. I didn't intend to cheat on Chris, but I loved the hungry way Ken looked at me. He made me feel desired and wanted. I would often catch him undressing me with his eyes and staring at my ass. Ken always complimented me and made me feel good about myself. Suddenly I started wanting more out of my boring life. I knew about Ken's reputation around the gym, but I didn't care. Curiosity was starting to get the best of me.

"What are you doing after the gym tonight?" Ken asked me after I did two more reps.

"Nothing really. Probably going home to play with the kids and relax with my husband."

"You can do that any night. Hang out with me tonight."

My heart fluttered. It was obvious that he was hitting on me. Hanging out with him would be wrong, but I needed some excitement. I wanted to feel liberated from my stagnant marriage. I knew I shouldn't, but I enjoyed our constant flirting and the chemistry that we had between us. I should have said no, but instead I broke down and agreed to see him.

"I'm sure I can sneak out for the night. Where are we going?" I said.

"I'm taking you to eat the best food you've ever tasted."

"That's a bold statement. What restaurant are you taking me to?"

"You'll see."

I couldn't remember the last time Chris had taken me out on a date night. Lately, his idea of a romantic evening was taking me and the girls to Olive Garden and ordering wine for me and for him.

After my workout session, I showered and changed back into my work clothes. I hesitated about calling Chris. I finally made the call in a stall in the bathroom, because it was less noisy. Was I seriously about to lie to my husband?

"Hey, honey," I said.

"Hey. What time are you getting home?"

"That's why I'm calling you. There are major outages in Seaford. The powers that be said they need a supervisor to stay until we get everything back online. I have to stay late tonight."

"Damn, that sucks. All right. I'll hold it down with the kids. I'll try to wait up for you."

"Okay. See you when I get home."

"Love you, babe."

"I love you too."

I ended the call.

I couldn't believe I had just lied to my husband so I could go on a date, but damn, Ken was so handsome. And he had this swagger and air about him that I was feeling. I figured I'd amuse him and myself by toying with him and flirting a little bit. Maybe I would be more turned on and would fuck Chris's brains out when I got home. I tried not to think about the wrong I was doing and walked back to the personal training office to meet Ken.

We left my car at the gym and drove off in his S-Class Mercedes. I was impressed that he was doing so well financially as a trainer.

My conscience was eating at me the entire ride. This wasn't me. I had second thoughts but figured since I'd already gone this far, I might as well go through with it. We ended up at a condo complex in Garden City.

"This doesn't look like a restaurant to me. Where are we?" I said.

He smiled. "I'm making you dinner at my place."

At first, I thought he had some damn nerve trying to be slick and presumptuous, thinking he was going to get some ass from me by charming me and taking me to his house. He was bold to take me to his place, but there was a part of me that enjoyed being courted.

I shot him a look. "You think you're slick!" I smiled.

"What?" Ken asked, looking off to the side, trying to conceal his laugh.

"Don't play dumb. You know why you're slick. You had this planned the whole time that you were taking me here."

He didn't deny it, but he had a smirk on his face.

"Well, I'm sorry to burst your bubble, but the only thing you're going to be feeding me tonight is food. Now, come on." I laughed.

We got out of the car and walked into his condo, and my eyes scanned everything.

"I can't believe you're so neat," I said.

He chuckled. "I'm not. I'm actually a slob. I pay Molly Maid to clean my place three times a week."

"Damn. I wish I could afford to do that. At home, I'm the maid."

"Well, tonight you're my guest. Relax and make yourself comfortable."

I watched Ken walk into the kitchen. He was young but well versed. Most of the guys I'd met at the gym were complete dummies who could barely put together an intelligible sentence. A part of what attracted me to Ken was his intellect. If I had to describe him in one word, that word would be *charming*.

I heard the clatter of pots and pans as I strolled around his living room and looked over his CD and Blu-ray collections. He had a beautiful black leather sectional couch and a fifty-two-inch flat-screen TV, which was mounted to the wall above his fireplace and came with a home theater system. His apartment was nice but very manly. His rack of movies consisted mostly of action and horror films, and his music collection was primarily hip-hop. A large portion of his living room served as his personal gym. He had an elliptical, a treadmill, and a spin bike in one corner, while his free weights, his kettlebells, and a weight bench were in another. I noticed he had only one framed picture in his living room. I picked it up and looked closely at it.

I figured the woman in the photo had to be his mother.

"Do you like my place?" he whispered in my ear.

I jumped. I had had no idea he was behind me. He scared the shit out of me. I clutched my chest.

"Jesus, I didn't hear you come in here," I said.

"Sorry."

"Very impressive. You've done very well for yourself."

He smiled. "Thank you. You can turn on the TV if you want, or you can keep me company in the kitchen while I cook."

"I'll keep you company."

His kitchen was immaculate. While gazing around in the kitchen, I was struck by his beautiful marble countertops, his rich mahogany wood cabinets, and his state-of-the-art stainless-steel appliances.

I sat on top of his marble counter while Ken made penne alla vodka from scratch. Watching a man cook was very sexy to me. Halfway through his preparations, he fed me a spoonful of the sauce he was making.

"Oh my God! This tastes amazing. Damn. Did you go to culinary school or something?" I said.

"Nah. I used to date a girl who loved to cook. I'm a big believer in self-improvement. Whenever I date someone who has something they can teach me, I'm eager to learn. Now, close your eyes. I want you to taste something else."

I quivered at his request. I closed my eyes, anticipating being fed something delicious, but I gasped when I felt his lips press against mine. I wanted to pull away, but instead I savored the warmth of his soft, full lips. It reminded me of how Chris used to kiss me. I opened my eyes slowly. I couldn't get over how much he resembled my husband. I couldn't lie to myself anymore. I was attracted to him.

After he finished cooking, we ate by candlelight at his oak dining table. We drank chardonnay and talked about all types of topics, with the last one leading to a discussion of sex.

Before I knew it, we were standing in his bedroom. I put my arms around his neck and brought my mouth to his soft, plump lips. We kissed hungrily, hardly coming up for air, while our hands roamed and groped each other's bodies. In my mind, I knew this was wrong and I should stop him, but this was the passion I craved. This was what I was missing with Chris. I'd never done anything like what I felt I was about to do, but I was already past the point of no return. I figured I'd just deal with the guilt later. I closed my eyes to block out these thoughts.

He pulled his shirt over his head, revealing his chiseled chest and abs. Next, Ken tugged my blouse over my head and, with an expert swiftness, unhooked my bra. Our passionate kisses led to the rest of our clothes being thrown around in a frenzy. Once we were naked, his eyes swept over me, taking in my hips, thighs, and my Brazilian wax, where his eyes lingered the longest. Then he stared at my breasts.

"You like what you see?" I asked.

"Hell yeah."

I got on his king-size bed, then lay back on the satin sheets. Ken climbed onto the bed, lowered himself gently beside me, and softly cradled my face in his hands. He snaked his tongue around my left nipple. I grabbed him by the ears and slowly pushed him down to my sopping vagina. I had never thought I'd be in Ken's bed, getting eaten out. At first, it felt foreign. I had been faithful to Chris for so long that I had forgotten what it felt like to be touch by another man. His long tongue lapped at my pussy. The way he did it felt similar to how Chris pleased me, but what made it different was that Ken used his fingers. He curled his ring and middle fingers and massaged the roof of my treasure. He touched so many spots, and the combination of him eating me and touching me drove me wild. I came hard. I felt guilty, but I relished the release. I lay there twitching and shaking.

Ken went over to his nightstand and got a condom. I watched him roll it on his thick, meaty erection. My heart and my conscience were screaming at me to stop, but my body gave in to my desire. A part of me enjoyed just letting go of that repressed part of myself. In that moment, I wasn't a wife or a mother. I was free. I gasped when he entered me. I gripped his back as he worked his hips. His dick was the same width and length as my husband's, but his had an upward curve that touched spots I wasn't used to feeling. His rhythm was perfect. It wasn't too slow. It wasn't too fast. It was exactly what I needed to cum. I moaned. I looked at his face, and my eyes widened. When I looked at Ken, I saw my husband. I cried out, and Ken stopped thrusting.

"Are you okay? Do you want me to stop?" He looked truly concerned.

"I'm fine . . . I'm just emotional right now. I want this . . . I want you. Don't stop. I want you to fuck me."

Once he heard that, he lifted my legs straight up and put them together. He entered me swiftly. Given the angle I was in and the curve in his dick, this felt so good and so deep that I couldn't help but moan and cum over and over again. I wanted to hate myself. I wanted to feel disgusted, but I didn't. I had needed this release.

We marathon fucked that night. I hadn't had sex like that in a long time. When it was over, I was satisfied. I felt beautiful and relaxed. I showered at Ken's house. Afterward, he drove me back to my car, and I headed home. It was late when I got there. I checked on the kids. They were sound asleep in their beds. Chris slept peacefully as I crawled into bed, feeling guilty. I cried myself to sleep, replaying what I had done. I'd broken my promise to Chris, to myself, and to God with my actions.

The next morning the sound of the shower running woke me up. I stretched and rolled over on my side of the bed to check my alarm clock. Chris showered, got dressed, and left for work before I got up. The sunlight beamed through my bedroom window. I looked out, and it was beautiful outside. The sky was blue, and the sun was shining. No storm clouds or dark skies. It wasn't how I had imagined the day would look after I cheated on my husband. I didn't feel like a monster. While I felt horrible, I also felt justified. How many times had I cried to Chris, explaining how I felt? How many clues had I given him?

I took a personal day off from work. I showered, did some laundry, ran some errands, and later made dinner for my family. Nothing bad happened or changed. I realized cheating wasn't as bad as I had thought it would be, and if I could do it once, I could easily do it again.

I continued to see Ken as my trainer and lover. The fact that he was so similar to Chris made it easy for me to cheat with him. It got to the point where my conscience didn't bother me at all.

Eventually, Ken cut me off, though. He explained he wanted to figure things out with the three girls he was juggling on the side. I can't lie. I was hurt. I had known all along that nothing would come out of our affair and that it wasn't destined to last forever, but I had felt comfortable having him around. While the sex had been great, Ken had also provided me with everything that I felt was missing from my marriage. He'd given me spontaneity, romance, and passion. My time with Ken had been like living out a fantasy.

We tried to be cordial and professional when we saw each other at the gym, but eventually, I decided to stop training with Ken. Seeing him and not being able to have him sexually felt torturous. While things were somewhat easier after that decision, I still needed someone to motivate me at the gym. Enter Raheem. He constantly flirted with me whenever he saw me working out. He was handsome and in good shape. It started off with us talking about different routines and eventually evolved into us working out together.

"Damn, Karen. You get sexier by the day," he told me one afternoon.

"Oh, stop flirting. I know you don't mean that."

Raheem looked me up and down and licked his lips. "If I'm lying, I'm dying."

"You're looking pretty sexy yourself." I flirted back, admiring his muscular ass and the rest of his well-built frame as I walked around him and checked him out.

He also had a great smile.

"Sexy people like us shouldn't work out alone. We should work out together," he told me.

"How would your wife feel about that?" I asked, pointing at his ring finger.

"What she doesn't know won't hurt her. If you want, she can hang out with your husband," he said, taking hold of my ring hand.

I smiled. "I'll give you my number. Hopefully, you can keep up with me."

As time passed, our relationship blossomed. We talked about the gym, our passions, careers, and dreams. Raheem worked as a manager for Citibank. He was always dressed to kill and smelled nice and fresh. At home, Chris never noticed the results of my hard work at the gym. He was sexually attracted to me but never complimented me on how slim my legs looked or how toned my arms were getting. That drove me even further away from him. I lost sight of myself by trying to be all things to Chris and to make him happy. It was my turn to take care of things for me and make myself happy.

***

"I can't do this shit," I yelled out during an intense workout at the gym.

"Come on . . . Good. Focus on me. That's it!" Raheem yelled.

I grunted. My legs trembled and sweat dripped down my face as I struggled to do the last rep of heavy squats. Somehow I managed to do it.

"Damn!" I groaned as I rested the weights back on the rack.

"See? When you focus on me, you get eight out!"

"I get ate out?" I asked jokingly.

"You got a dirty mind. I meant you get eight reps out. That was a good set."

It was like sleeping with Ken had unlocked a sexual restriction I had inside of me. My moral compass was lost now, and I didn't know if I would ever find it again. I was bolder now and wasn't afraid to be blunt when it came to what I wanted.

"I hate doing squats," I said.

"Yeah, but they're working for you. Your ass looks fantastic."

I eyed his crotch and saw the huge bulge in his spandex compression shorts. I was impressed with what I had seen so far. Raheem noticed.

"You see what you do to me?" he said.

"No, let me see. Are you a grower or a show-er?" I joked.

I hooked my fingers over the elastic waistband of his shorts. I pulled on it and looked inside. I gasped when I saw the length of his dick.

"Holy shit," I said, blushing and rubbing my ass against his crotch.

Somehow I managed to pull my eyes away from the huge bulge in his spandex shorts. Hundreds of images flooded my mind, each one more perverted than the next.

Raheem wrapped his arms around me. "I'd love to bend you over right here."

The deepness of his voice excited me. His voice alone made me moist.

"So, come through. Let's do this, then." I flashed him a flirty smile and then walked off.

He caught up to me, with a surprised look on his face. "Really? Are you serious?"

"If you don't want to . . ."

"No, no, I want to. Hell yeah, I want to. I didn't think you wanted to."

"What about your wife?" I asked.

"I'm not going to lie. I'm selfish. I love my wife, but she doesn't give it to me as much as I want it. What about your husband?"

"Sometimes I need to feel desired. He pleases me, but he doesn't make me feel beautiful."

"I don't have to try to do that, because I already know you're beautiful." He was trying his hardest to lay game on me, but he already had me.

We left the gym, got in our cars, and I followed Raheem to the Fairfield Inn in Syosset. He got us a room. I *had* changed. I didn't feel guilty anymore. I even had my excuse ready for later.

Raheem opened the door to our room, lifted me up, and carried me to the bed. He laid me down and kicked the door closed. He slowly stripped off my clothes. He kissed me, and it felt so *good*. I wasn't bothered by the fact that I was cheating or that it was wrong. I was living in the moment. Raheem planted a trail of soft, sensuous kisses along my thighs before he feasted on my pussy. He wasn't as talented as Ken or as good as my husband, but I enjoyed it.

Raheem undressed. My eyes grew wide, and my eyebrows went up. I gave him a sultry grin. His penis was very long. Ken's reminded me of my husband's, but Raheem's was different. He had to be at least eleven inches, and he had a huge mushroom head. Chris's shaft was definitely thicker, but I was anxious to feel Raheem. He retrieved a condom from the wallet in his pants pocket, then rolled it on, and slowly inserted himself inside me. I reached around and grabbed his ass while he stroked me and kissed me at the same time. I loved the passion. He sucked on my neck, licked my nipples, and rubbed his hands all over my body.

This was what I wanted from my husband. I wanted him to desire me the way Raheem desired me. Raheem turned me over on my stomach. When he gently stroked his fingertips down my back, tingles traveled down my spine. I shivered. He entered me from behind. In this position, his length felt even greater. His touch, his strokes, and his kisses sent me over the edge. I came intensely, screaming his name.

When we finished pleasing each other, we left the hotel and went back to our separate homes, our separate lives. I went home and acted like nothing had happened. I even slept with Chris that night. Having sex with both of them that day left me sore, but I was satisfied and slept like a baby.

The next day, Raheem and I exchanged frequent dirty messages before I met up with him at the gym.

"Hey, sexy!" he said, circling me and licking his lips.

I smiled and cupped a big handful of his crotch. "Hey, yourself," I said.

Raheem wrapped his arms around me from behind and said, "When can I have you again?"

While I loved the feeling of being desired, if we went further with our friends with benefits, our fuck buddies, or whatever we were going to call our relationship, I wanted it to be more than just sex. I had good dick at home already. Truth be told, Raheem was good, but he couldn't light a candle to how Chris put it down. I didn't need Raheem for sex. I wanted him to be everything that Chris was not. Sex was the icing on the cake, but what was most important and what I truly wanted was the compliments and the flirty text messages every day. I wanted public displays of affection, and I wanted to feel like I was still being courted after we had already been intimate.

"I don't know. I guess that all depends on you," I said solemnly.

"What do you mean?"

"I'm not some desperate housewife looking for a handsome man to fuck her. I want passion. I want to go on dates, to be complimented, to be given flowers and gifts sporadically without it being a special occasion. The whole nine yards."

Raheem nodded as I continued.

"I know that this may seem like a lot to you or that I may sound high maintenance, but that's what I need in order for us to continue fucking. If that feels like it's too much, if you feel like that is something you don't want to do or like I would be too much of a headache, we can keep working out together and accept that we satisfied our curiosity. We can consider it a sort of one-night stand but leave it at that."

"Doing those things with you wouldn't be a chore for me. If anything, the sex is just the icing on the cake."

"That's good to hear . . . I need you to understand that I'm not asking you to break up your marriage. I have kids, and I'm not trying to break up mine, either, but I need a relationship like this for my own happiness."

"Trust me, I get it and I'm up for the challenge."

It felt good to have Raheem cater to me and fill that void that Chris had left unfilled. He made me feel beautiful and told me so, while Chris made me feel like he saw me as nothing more than the mother of his children. Raheem listened to me intently, while whenever I talked to Chris, he acted as if every word out of my mouth was meaningless gossip. Even though we both understood that our relationship would not grow any further than it already had, Raheem gave me what I needed to feel complete.

I jumped up in bed, but I didn't know how I had got there. The last thing I recalled was hanging over the toilet and remembering how my cheating had started. My head was killing me. My eyes struggled to adjust to the darkness of the room.

"Who is Raheem?" Chris asked.

My eyes widened when I heard him say that name.

"Uh . . . he's my trainer at the gym."

"When I picked you up off the floor, you kissed me and said, 'Thanks, Raheem.' Do you kiss him?"

"Baby, I was drunk. I was delirious. I didn't know what I was saying or doing. I worked out before I hung out tonight, so I was probably thinking a million different things while I was on the floor."

"You didn't answer my question. Do you kiss him?" he demanded. He had inherited that commanding tone from his father.

"What are you insinuating, Chris?"

"I'm not *insinuating* anything."

"Yes you are, and I'm getting fucking tired of it. You keep insinuating that I'm cheating on you. If you're so paranoid about me sleeping with someone else, maybe you should take me out sometime and do things with me. Maybe when you're making love to me, you can tell me

I'm beautiful, compliment me, and not just bend me over like I'm a fucking ho."

I sobbed uncontrollably. I didn't know what came over me. I was more emotional than usual, and my response to him indicated what I truly wanted. My unhappiness was pouring out.

Chris's eyes softened once he saw me crying. "I'm sorry. Honestly, I'm scared of losing you. I love you. The reason I haven't taken you out lately is that I've been working more than usual in order to save up enough to take us on vacation."

I searched his expression to see if he was serious. He nodded to confirm his words were genuine.

He went on. "I haven't been home lately for you and the girls, but I needed to make extra money. I booked us a two-week vacation to Cancún. Pops is coming, and I figured he could watch the girls, to give us time to reconnect with each other. You'll always be beautiful to me. That's why I get paranoid that someone would try to take you away from me."

Chris rarely showed his vulnerability, but it was a side of him I loved. If only he were open and honest with me more often, I would stop my cheating.

"I think the trip is a great idea. We need to get away from everything for a while."

I needed this trip. I had to work things out with Chris and reignite the flame that had gone out. If this trip worked out, I'd cut off Tyrell and Raheem for good. Chris hugged me and kissed my forehead.

"You're everything to me. I want to make you happy. I'm sorry for accusing you," he told me.

"I love you."

"I love you too."

I patted his arm and kissed him. On the outside, I was smiling, but on the inside, I was crying. I went to sleep in his arms that night, feeling terrible.

Chris

A few evenings later, we were at Lindsey's house. Pops was watching the kids. Lindsey's husband, Jeff, was in their massive kitchen, checking on the feast he had prepared. Lindsey, Karen, and I were sitting in the living room, on their giant sectional sofa, watching the Knicks game on their enormous flat-screen. They were cool, but I didn't like hanging out with them, because at the end of the night, I always went home feeling like a failure.

"So, we're adding another extension to this house, and we're thinking about buying a summer home upstate somewhere," Lindsey said.

"That's what I'm talking about," Karen said, high-fiving Lindsey.

A moment later Jeff walked out of the kitchen and sat next to Lindsey. He kissed the back of her hand and said, "Yeah, we're going to add a new office for her and a gym for me."

Jeff was about six feet three and was in decent shape. He was fair skinned, his hair was styled in twisties, and he had a goatee. He owned a very successful sports bar in Garden City. With their combined incomes, he and Lindsey were a power couple. They didn't have kids yet, which allowed them to spend most of their free time traveling the world and doing whatever they wanted. I loved my kids, but a part of me missed that feeling of doing what I wanted when I wanted. I missed the freedom that came with not having to worry about bills and family expenses. The truth was, I was envious of them, and so was Karen.

Karen looked at them as if they were the greatest couple ever. She made me feel like we weren't shit compared to them. They'd constantly hold hands, kiss, and look lovingly at each other. Karen would watch them and look at me like she wished I'd be more like Jeff. *I hated that.* Seeing her reaction to them discouraged me from wanting to do those things with her, because I felt inadequate compared to them.

I'd admit I was not the most affectionate man in the world. Being the son of a marine and growing up with my pops hadn't been easy. A big part of my life had been spent moving across the country to different military bases. Pops was a former drill instructor, so he'd expected nothing less than excellence from me. My mother had been the only person who could keep him balanced. Back then, Pops had been a heavy smoker. When I was nine, my mother had been diagnosed with lung cancer due to secondhand smoke. She'd died when I was eleven, and when she passed, a part of my father died too. Pops had never said anything, but I knew he felt responsible for her death. He'd stopped smoking for good once she was diagnosed.

Pops didn't cry when she was on her deathbed or when we were at her funeral. He'd always had a hard demeanor, and he'd raised me to be strong and self-reliant. I was my father's son. I was not very affectionate, and that flaw affected a lot of my relationships in the past. Karen knew how I had grown up, and she'd helped me to change somewhat, but at times I had to stop myself from coming off as cold and unfeeling. I had promised myself I'd never raise my kids the way Pops raised me.

"My baby said she needs her space when she's writing her lesson plans. What my baby wants, my baby gets," Jeff said, bringing me back to the present.

Jeff winked at Lindsey. She bit her bottom lip and playfully slapped his ass. Jeff gave Lindsey a quick peck that made her smile. Their blatant PDA made me sick to my stomach.

"So how is work going for you, Chris?" Jeff asked.

"Good. I can't complain. My construction company stays busy, so work is steady for me."

"Yeah. He's always working. I rarely get to see him," Karen chimed in.

I didn't like how she made it seem like I wasn't there for her, especially when I had told her why I was away from home more than usual lately.

"I'm not the only one who works all the time. You spend a lot of nights working late yourself," I snapped.

We glared at each other. Her look was saying, "Let's not start a fight and embarrass me in front of my friends." Mine was saying, "Don't start no shit, won't be no shit." We let it go. Jeff and Lindsey shared a look but quickly looked away when they saw I had noticed. Lindsey turned and looked at me with a sympathetic expression. I guessed she sensed the tension and felt sorry for me.

A little later, we took our conversation to the dining room, where we ate dinner and listened to Karen and Lindsey reminisce about growing up together. I'd heard the stories a million times, but at least the food was great.

"You're an amazing cook," Karen told Jeff.

He smiled. "Thank you."

"If Chris cooked liked this, I'd be as big as a house," she mused. Again, she was comparing me to someone else and criticizing me.

"I'm sure Chris is a good cook too," Jeff said, then gave me a wink and a nod. He knew she'd been emasculating me all night.

"Nope, unless you consider only being good at making breakfast a good cook. If he had to make us dinner every night, we'd starve."

Lindsey saw the lines of frustration growing on my face and tried to change the subject.

"So, my bestie told me you planned a vacation to Cancún. That sounds nice," Lindsey said.

"Yeah, I owe it to her. She deserves it," I replied.

"I'm sure it won't be as extravagant as the vacations you and Jeff take, but it'll be good for us," Karen said.

At that point, I couldn't hide my irritation. My face was tight as I glared at Karen. I had worked my ass off to give her a dream vacation, and she shit on it, as if the things I did were insignificant compared to what Jeff did for Lindsey. I felt betrayed. I couldn't believe my wife would disregard all my hard work in front of them. I didn't even want to take her on the fucking trip at that point.

Lindsey ignored the comment after seeing how angry it had made me. She said, "Are you guys taking the kids or leaving them with your dad, Chris?"

I stopped scowling at Karen and took a deep breath before answering. "We're taking them, but he's coming too. He knows the deal, so he's going to watch the kids a majority of the time so Karen and I can enjoy each other."

"I think that's awesome!" Lindsey said.

"I'm glad you do . . . Maybe you can convince your friend to feel the same way," I said sharply.

Lindsey laughed; Karen didn't. Karen reached under the dining-room table, picked up her purse, and pulled out her iPhone. I leaned over discreetly, looked out the corner of my eye, and watched her enter the password to unlock her phone. I was a little surprised that she used my birthday as her password, but I was delighted that I had finally learned what it was. She quickly sent a text to Lindsey, which I was able to read.

I need to have a little girl talk with you in the kitchen.

I didn't know if I'd ever use this newfound knowledge about her password, but who knew? Maybe it would come in handy someday. I was more curious about why she wanted to talk to Lindsey alone in the kitchen.

I watched Lindsey casually look at her phone when it vibrated.

"I'm going to grab the dessert. Karen, do you want to help me bring it out?" Lindsey said.

"Sure, bestie."

Karen and Lindsey went into the kitchen, while Jeff and I went back into the living room and sat on the couch. While he channel surfed, I strained to hear what Lindsey and Karen were talking about in the kitchen, but their voices were just above a whisper.

"I don't mean to get in your business, but I see there's some tension between you and Karen tonight," Jeff said.

"Yeah . . . we're both under stress from work, and we lash out at each other sometimes. It's nothing serious."

"I don't want to tell you how to run your marriage, but maybe you should do more than just take her on a vacation. Try to take her out and do things to keep the spice going in your relationship. Compliment her from time to time, and let her know that you could never desire another woman as much as her."

I was livid. Was Jeff really trying to school me on how to treat my wife? Did he think he was better than me? I was insulted. There was no way I was going to sit here and feel like a piece of shit. Karen had told me about their problems conceiving. They'd been having trouble for a few years now because Jeff had a low sperm count, and he was insecure about it. I hated that I was vindictive, but if he was going to say things to make me feel like shit, two could play that game. I'd target his insecurity and hit him where it hurt.

"You're right. I'm going to work on that after the vacation. I see the way you treat Lindsey, and I need to be more like you," I told him.

He smiled. "Well, I was raised by a single mother, so I know how to deal with women," Jeff said confidently.

"True, but things change when you have kids. You'll see. Speaking of which, when are you going to have some little rug rats running around here?"

Jeff's face fell. He squirmed on the couch. I liked seeing him uncomfortable. Now he knew how I felt.

"Um, we're working on that," he mumbled.

"Working on it is the fun part, but none of us are getting any younger. I'm sure Lindsey doesn't want to wait too long, and I'm pretty sure you still want to be in your prime, and not an old man, when you're chasing your kids around."

"We're good right now. We enjoy each other enough for the time being."

"I don't know. Going on dates and trips is nice and all, but life is about legacy. I'm sure there are things you would want to pass down to your kids."

"We will get there soon enough," he said, pouting.

"Well, you know, if you need help, I can donate sperm and help you guys out. Obviously, I can't miss. I got twins on my first try." I laughed.

Jeff went from looking uncomfortable to looking angry. I wanted him to understand that even though my relationship with Karen wasn't perfect, his relationship with Lindsey wasn't, either. My problems could be fixed in time, but he might never be a biological father. His demeanor the rest of the night showed me that what I had said bothered him. Mine softened.

***

"Damn, man. You're watching the kids *again*? You never get to hang out with us," Will said as he sat at my kitchen table.

Will and Lou had stopped by to see if I wanted to go clubbing with them. They had rarely come by to see me since I became a father. In the past, we used to go out all the time. Now I felt left out, because they always hung out without me.

"You need to man up and tell Karen you're going out tonight. It's her job to be home with the kids. You need to be out with your boys," Lou said.

I laughed. "You realize that this way of thinking is why both of your asses are single, right? Relationships don't work like that. She works hard too. She doesn't always get to hang out with her girls, either. I work all the time and hardly get to see my kids. It's not an obligation for me. I like being here with them, and besides, you guys are never around when I do have free time. Y'all can always hang out here with me anytime."

"Nah. I've hung out with you and the kids a couple times, and that shit was like birth control for me. I know I'm not ready to be a father," Will said.

"Yeah, after seeing your marriage, I'm not sure if I ever want to get married or have kids," Lou added.

"It's not that bad," I said.

Will and Lou exchanged looks.

Then Lou said, "I'm not trying to start drama with you and Karen, but I seen her holding hands with some pretty-looking clown at a club in Manhattan."

I didn't need to hear this shit right now. I was already paranoid, and this only made things worse. I couldn't confront Karen about this again, because the last two times had had no proof.

"What club?" I said.

"What club did we go to last week, Will?"

"Element," Will answered. Then he turned to me. "Yeah, man, she was drunk. I'm pretty sure it was her, because Chloe was there, and I'd know that ass anywhere."

We chuckled. Will had a thing for Chloe because of her big ass. Her huge ass, meaty thighs, wide hips, and D-cup breasts were exactly what Will loved on his women.

"Karen was smiling in this dude's face, and he was kissing on her neck and shit. All of them were so fucked up that they didn't even realize we were there. We wanted to let you know so you could handle it," Lou explained.

I sat there, furiously shaking my head. "You guys should've told me this earlier, like that night."

Lou frowned. "Sorry. We got wrapped up in our shit, and it's not something you want to tell someone on the phone, you know. We figured we'd tell you in person."

"You think she's creepin'?" Will asked.

"Nah. She gets flirty when she drinks. She wouldn't cheat on me," I said.

The look on their faces told me that they didn't believe that at all. I was sure they believed there was more to it, but luckily for me, they let it be and did not say anything further on the matter.

"All right . . . Well, we're about to meet up with these girls. We'll stop by next week," Will said.

"We're going to Cancún next week with the kids," I said.

Will and Lou looked at each other.

"I know you love Karen and everything, but keep your eyes open. Don't be blind," Will said as he stood up from the kitchen table.

"She looked really familiar with that dude. It didn't look like she met him that night. It looked like they knew each other, and for a while. We don't want to see you get hurt," Lou said as he, too, stood up.

"I appreciate that. Trust me, I'm keeping my eyes open."

I slid off my kitchen chair, gave them both brotherly hugs, and walked them out. After they drove away, I played with my kids, but I wasn't there mentally. My mind was all over the place. An hour later I put the kids to bed and worked on my car. I spent the rest of the night drowning in my paranoia.

Karen

"Babe, hand me your carry-on bag," Chris said.

We had just boarded the plane, headed to Mexico.

I smiled. "Give me a second, hon."

Raheem had texted me on the way to the airport. He had explained last week that he didn't want to end what we had. I can't lie. It was hard to let him go.

His text said simply, I love you. I just hope you're happy.

I texted him back. I love you too, but this is for the best.

I thought about it for a moment. In many ways, I did have love for him. Then I put down my phone and grabbed my carry-on bag by both handles.

"Here, babe," I said, handing Chris my bag to put up in the overhead compartment.

The kids were excited and were now fighting to look out the window. They were sitting with Pops in the row across from Chris and me. Chris sat down after putting my bag away.

Just then a flight attendant walked up and asked, "Would either of you like some pretzels or something to drink?"

"No thanks!" Chris said.

I nodded and said," No. Thank you."

Chris and I held hands, and I rested my head on his shoulder. I decided this trip would start a new chapter in our lives together. I would try to do everything possible to be the perfect wife, and hopefully, Chris would do what was necessary to remind me why I shouldn't stray.

These past few days had been hard for me. I had spent the entire week lying to Chris so I could spend my last days before this vacation with Tyrell and Raheem. I had taken Wednesday and Thursday off work to end things properly with the two of them. I had ended things with Tyrell first.

In the parking lot at my job on Wednesday, I parked next to Tyrell's Infinity Q50. He was standing there waiting for me.

"Hey, beautiful," he said when I stepped out of my car.

I smiled at him. "Hi, handsome."

We hugged.

"Your chariot awaits, madam." He opened the passenger-side door of his Infiniti for me.

"Change of plans. I'm going to follow you in my car," I said.

"I thought we would at least ride together, since this is going to be our last night together."

I closed my eyes and rubbed the bridge of my nose. "Tyrell, the one rule I want for tonight is we can't mention that this is our last night together. This is hard as it is. Let's just enjoy our night."

Tyrell's face was full of emotion. "It doesn't have to be hard . . . You can at least ride with me," he said.

Even though I understood he was hurt and disappointed, I had to play it smart and safe. I was breaking this off with him, not the other way around. I couldn't risk him getting upset and either leaving me wherever he wanted to take me or refusing to take me back to my car later.

"I promise you, for the most part, I'm all yours tonight, but at some point, I need to get home, and driving all the way back here to get my car would be going out of the way and would be time consuming," I said.

Tyrell didn't respond. He just continued to look sad and irritated.

"Penny for your thoughts," I asked.

"Nothing."

"Your funky attitude is making it look a lot like *something*."

"I can't tell you. According to your rule, I can't talk about it, remember?"

"Look, if you're going to act grumpy the rest of the night, maybe we should just end this right here, right now."

"No, no. I'm sorry. I'm not trying to be an asshole, but I'm mad that after tonight I can't have this relationship with you anymore."

"Tyrell, we will always be friends. You know that."

"Friends . . . Can I at least have a kiss?"

I smiled. "Of course. Sit inside my car, though. I don't want anyone to see us."

He did as I instructed. Once inside my car, he kissed me, and I felt all his passion and feelings in that kiss.

"I have to savor every minute I have with you," he told me.

"Well, let's make this night memorable. Dwelling on our problems isn't going to change or fix anything. Let's make the best of what we can."

He nodded. "Follow me. I have our entire night planned out around Times Square."

"Nice. What are we doing tonight?"

"It's a surprise."

"Can I at least have a hint?"

"Nope."

I followed Tyrell, and we drove into Manhattan. The two of us had a fun-filled evening at the Longacre Theatre, where we saw the Broadway adaptation of *A Bronx Tale*. I loved every minute of the show and actually enjoyed it better than the movie.

"Are you having a good time?" Tyrell asked me after the curtain went down for the intermission.

"Of course. I'm loving this! What made you pick this Broadway show, though?"

"I felt it was fitting in terms of our relationship."

I gave him the side eye. "How so?"

"A guy has to hide his love for a girl out of fear of what everyone will think. We're similar to Calogero and Jane."

"Remember, we said we wouldn't talk about this being our last night together. We're having a good time. Don't ruin it with emotional bullshit."

"You're the boss."

We went to the R Lounge for dinner. I was always impressed with how quickly Tyrell could put together a perfect evening for us. The restaurant was located inside the Renaissance Hotel, on the third floor, and it had a perfect view of the middle of Times Square. In fact, this was the location from which news stations broadcast the festivities on New Year's Eve every year. Once I learned that, I had put the restaurant on my bucket list, and I had been dying to go. The menu featured some great food choices, and everything was cooked well.

When I first started dealing with Tyrell, I had talked to him about how, as a child, I had loved going into the city to see the bright lights and the huge signs in Times Square. I was touched that he had listened to me and had tried to make me happy by bringing me to a place that was steeped in nostalgia.

Tyrell had reserved a gorgeous room for us at the W Hotel on Broadway. While I would have loved for this night not to end, and to spend the entire night in this beautiful room, the clock was ticking, and I knew I would have to get home soon.

"I can't stay here long, so let's squeeze in one last quickie before I go," I told Tyrell once we were inside the room.

"I don't want a quickie. If this is going to be our last time, I want it to be special. I want to savor you. That was the whole reason why I got this room for us."

Tyrell traced kisses along my neck. I unbuttoned his shirt and took it off him. He pulled his pants off, took a condom from his pocket, then pulled off his boxer briefs. He stood in front of me, naked. He unbuttoned my blouse and took it off me, tugged off my skirt, and pulled my thong down over my Louis Vuittons.

"Leave the heels on," he said.

He placed the condom on one of the pillows and eased me down onto the king-size mattress. He rubbed his hands down my thighs and kissed my stomach. Then he worked his way down to my inner thighs, put both hands under my ass, lifted up my hips, and brought his face to my treasure. He swirled his tongue around my wet hole. I wiggled from the feeling of his tongue lapping my labia. He began to tease me, alternating between licking and sticking his fingers inside me.

Tyrell was on a mission. He wanted this session to prove that he was all I needed to be happy. I thoroughly enjoyed it, but this was a temporary happiness, nothing like what I could ultimately have with Chris once I got rid of all the outside factors. Every time my mind drifted to thoughts of Chris, Tyrell seemed to step it up a notch, as if he could read my thoughts. He brought my mind right back to the present when he slipped two fingers into my opening and firmly massaged my G-spot. I felt lost in the pleasure, consumed by how good he was making me feel.

My body was shaking at the sensation and the mounting pressure within me. "Right there . . . right there! Oh shit, Tyrell."

I was so worked up, so on the cusp of getting my rocks off, that it didn't take long until my orgasm crippled me. I clutched the back of his head and held his face to my treasure as I climaxed. He buried his face in my folds and lapped up every drop of juice that came out of me.

Tyrell gave my clit one last suck before moving up the bed and lying beside me. He grabbed the condom off the pillow and rolled it onto himself. He kissed my neck, then dragged his lips down my chest. He licked around my areolae and tugged on one of my nipples with his lips. I opened my legs wide for him. He mounted me and put his face next to mine. I felt him guide the tip of his cock to my treasure and press in softly. I gripped his back as worked his hips and pumped in and out of me.

As Tyrell and I had sex, my mind was on Raheem part of the time. I wanted to cry, because the truth was I would have to go through this all over again the next day with Raheem. I went through the motions, but I was lost in my own thoughts.

As expected, Tyrell didn't last long. I felt him swell inside me. His cock spasmed as he emptied himself, and he moaned into my mouth. He draped himself on top of me. My eyes started to tear. I rolled over on my side. Tyrell threw his arms around me and kissed the nape of my neck, my shoulder, and down my back. I leaned off the bed and reached for my clothes, which were on the floor.

I leaned against the headboard, slipped my clothes back on, and then sat on the edge of the bed.

"So, is that it? Is this how we're going to end off? I spent a lot of money on this room, and you're not going to at least spend the night with me in it?" he asked.

"You already knew that I wasn't, and you already know that I can't, Tyrell. I have to get home."

"To whom? Your husband?" he barked.

I didn't answer him.

He grumbled something under his breath.

"What?"

He propped himself up on his elbows as he spoke. "Leave him," Tyrell said.

"What are you talking about, Tyrell? Leave who?" I knew exactly what he meant, but I was giving him time to get out of his feelings and correct himself.

"I want you to leave Chris and be with me," he asserted.

"That's not going to happen."

"Listen. Hear me out," he said.

I sighed and rolled my eyes.

"I'll divorce Pam, and you and me could be together. I have no problem with having your kids around me, and Chris could visit them whenever he wanted. I need you, Karen. I can't just lose you like this."

"Tyrell, that's really sweet, and you're a great guy, but I'm not divorcing Chris. I like you, but I don't want to be with you, not like that, anyway."

Tyrell looked truly hurt and angered by my response. "You know what? I'm not even going to sweat it. You're going to miss me. You'll try to patch things up with him and pretend that everything is all right, but the problems you have will still be there. In time, you'll come back to me, and you'll see that I'm the man you need."

"Good-bye, Tyrell," I said as I stood up. I started walking toward the door.

"I'm not going to say good-bye. I'll see you again soon."

I walked out of the room with tears streaming down my face. I picked up my car from the parking garage and mentally prepared myself to go through this again with Raheem.

The next day, I made plans with Raheem to meet him at the gym. Raheem was leaning against his truck, holding a dozen long-stemmed roses, when I climbed out of my car.

"Hi!" I said as I approached him.

"Hey there, gorgeous," he said, handing me the roses.

I made a mental note to stop by my office and put the roses on my desk before I went home. I would never be able to explain to Chris why I was coming home with roses when it wasn't a special occasion.

"Thank you! They're beautiful. You look very handsome."

He really did. He had on a dark blue pin-striped suit that fit him like a glove.

I wore my little black dress that left very little to the imagination. Raheem's hand roamed up past my waist and cupped my breasts through my dress. I gently stopped him.

"Not yet. I want to enjoy this moment with you first. Later on tonight we can conclude our night with lovemaking."

As with Tyrell, I told Raheem that there was a change of plans and I'd follow him in my own car.

We drove to Brooklyn, and Raheem took me to the River Café. It was a very upscale restaurant located right under the Brooklyn Bridge. It had a breathtakingly beautiful view of the Manhattan skyline, and there was a cobblestone walkway to the restaurant, which gave it a vintage feel. A pianist played while we ate and drank.

"This restaurant is amazing!" I said as I sat opposite him.

He gave me a small grin and patted my hand. Then he turned my palm down and kissed the back of my hand. "When I did my research on this place, the critics said this is a place where you would bring someone special. I couldn't imagine bringing anyone else here but you."

I couldn't stop smiling. He always knew what to say to get me to smile and make me happy.

Raheem reached across the table and took both of my hands in his. "I don't want our night to end. I don't want us to end."

"Please, this is hard on me as it is. Let's not talk about this and ruin the night."

He nodded. We discussed all types of topics and laughed all the way to the dessert course.

"Are you ready, my dear?" Raheem asked once he had handled the check. "Our next stop is the Brooklyn Escape Room. I figured our last date could be innovative and fun."

"Sounds like a plan."

We made our way over to the Brooklyn Escape Room. I loved this part of the date. It was spontaneous, it was innovative, and it was fun. Unfortunately, it made me think of Chris. The point of the escape room was to work together to accomplish a task. It made me think of the fact that instead of working on my marriage with Chris, here I was on a date with another man. I shook those thoughts away. I reminded myself that this was the last night I would be doing anything like that and focused on enjoying my time. Raheem and I were teamed up with another couple inside the fallout shelter room. It was challenging, but we escaped the room in eighteen minutes.

When it was over, we sat down in the lobby.

Raheem asked, "Did you want to try another room?"

"I'd rather just spend our last night in bed with you."

"That works too." He stood up. "Shall we?"

I reached for his hand, and he helped me up from my chair.

We walked back to our cars, and I followed him back to Long Island. We went to the Marriott Hotel in Farmingdale, on Route 110.

Once we were inside our room, Raheem gently stroked my cheek with his fingertips. "We don't have to stop this. What we have works."

I didn't answer him. I closed my eyes, trying my best to stay strong through this night. Truth be told, I didn't want us to end, either, but I had made up my mind, and I was going to start being loyal to Chris.

It didn't take long before I was down to just my bra and panties. I helped Raheem remove his clothes, and then I stood there admiring his body as he stood in front of me in his briefs. I ran my hand across his sculpted arms and chest. Raheem reached around my back, his strong hands found the hooks to my bra, and he unlatched the clasp. I rolled my shoulders forward and let the straps slide freely down my arms. He slid my panties down my legs until I was able to step out of them, and flung them on the side of the bed.

We held hands. I looked in his teary eyes, and I felt that we shared the same pain. We didn't want what we had to end, but we knew it was going to. I needed it to. I was trying my hardest not to get caught up in his eye contact. I needed to be strong and to stick with my decision.

Raheem started kissing my neck and then dragged his lips down my breasts. He slid one arm around my back, the other around my knees, scooped me up in his arms, and gently laid me on the bed. He slipped a condom over his stiff cock, and his large, muscular body mounted me.

"Are you ready, baby?" he whispered.

I nodded.

He sank deep into me with one motion, and tingles traveled up my spine. I wrapped my legs around his back and pulled him closer. With each stroke, Raheem and I felt as connected as lovers could be. My nails dug into his back, and I held him tightly to me, relishing the feeling.

Raheem worked his magic on me, hammering me with deep, full, forceful strokes. I felt his frustration as he plunged himself inside me all the way to the hilt. The pressure was building inside me. My orgasm was close. I wanted to cum. I wanted my orgasm to whisk me away from all the negativity and problems that plagued my mind, even if it was just temporarily. I wanted my orgasm to take me away from my reality.

Raheem sped up his pace. My hips and legs were wiggling around in the sheets. We came together. Raheem buried his head in my neck, and I wrapped my arms around him. We collapsed next to each other on the bed and lay there, enjoying our post-orgasmic bliss. We held each other tightly, covered in sweat, lost in the intensity of our final time being intimate together. After a few moments of cuddling, I got out of bed and started getting dressed. Raheem lay there, watching me.

"What?" I asked.

"Where are you going?"

"I have to go home, Raheem."

He reached for me without uttering a word, put his hands on my shoulder, and brought me back onto the bed. Finally, he broke his silence.

"Don't do this. Don't end what we have," Raheem said.

"It has to end."

"Why? Both of our marriages have problems. Our relationship makes sense and makes both of us happy. Why do you want to stop that?"

"Because it's not right. Chris isn't perfect, but he doesn't deserve this. We both have families. Every time we see each other, we're risking losing them. We both know we don't want that."

"How many times do we end up doing things to make our significant others happy? How often do we sacrifice our happiness for them? Sometimes, even though the things we do aren't right, we need to do them for our sanity."

Raheem was wearing me down. His words were making sense, but I knew I couldn't listen to them.

"You're right, but I can't be selfish anymore," I insisted. "I'm not perfect, either, and I'm sure I do things that stress Chris out, too, but he isn't cheating on me."

"How do you know that? How can you be so sure? He's oblivious about you seeing me, so who's to say you aren't oblivious about him seeing another woman?"

He was good. He used all the information I had given him as ammunition to fight for us and keep our relationship going. He was preying on my fears.

"Chris is a lot of things, but he's not a cheater. He loves me unconditionally."

"Okay, if you need me to say it, I'll say it. I love you. I love being with you, I love seeing you, and I love what we have. I don't want to lose you."

"You don't love me, Raheem," I said gently.

"I do."

"You don't. Your dick and your pride are causing you to say shit you don't mean."

"I mean it."

I left the bed and finished getting dressed. I was feeling emotional. I needed to leave the room and get away from him. I was scared. I was confused. I didn't know what I wanted anymore. I wanted to believe him, but I knew what we had wasn't real. What I had at home waiting for me was real. My family, my husband. They were not worth losing for a relationship with Raheem that would go nowhere. I sighed deeply and fought back tears. I gave Raheem a long kiss.

"Good-bye, Raheem."

"Don't go like this," he pleaded.

"I have to go. We can't do this anymore. I'm sorry."

I walked out of the room and closed the door softly behind me. I sighed and took a deep breath to try to get a handle on my emotions, but this didn't help. I got in my car and cried the entire ride home. When I pulled into the driveway, I dried my eyes and gathered my composure. When I went inside, Chris was sitting in the living room, watching the news.

"Hey," I said.

"Hey, babe."

"Where are the kids?"

"I put them to bed. It's late . . ."

"Good."

I rushed up to him and kissed him passionately. I pushed him back against the sofa and started to take off his clothes.

"Damn, babe. What's got you hot like this?"

"I need you. Now."

Since the kids were already asleep in their beds, I fucked him right there in the living room. I needed to be penetrated by Chris. Every stroke felt like I was letting go, releasing the hold Tyrell and Raheem had on me and my heart. I kept picturing Tyrell and Raheem instead of Chris. I felt ashamed of myself for thinking of other men when my husband was making love to me.

Before long, Chris was swelling inside me. I knew he was close. As much as I enjoyed having raw sex with him, we couldn't risk having more kids. I pulled him out of me and positioned myself so that his manhood was directly in front of my face. I palmed his ass and pushed his hips forward, then took him in my mouth. I sucked and sucked and sucked, using both hands to firmly stroke him simultaneously. I sucked him like my marriage depended on it, because in my heart it did. He didn't deserve the shit I had been doing behind his back. I felt the muscles in his thighs tighten, and then his hips swayed and his legs started to shake.

His orgasm spewed into my mouth. I milked his dick and swallowed every drop. I felt guilty; my eyes filled with tears. Chris noticed.

"You okay, babe?" Chris looked genuinely concerned.

"Yeah . . . It was just so intense."

"I loved it."

"I'm going to go hop in the shower. I had a long day."

"All right, babe," he said, grinning.

I forced myself to smile and rushed upstairs to shower. I turned the hot water on until the steam fogged up all the mirrors. I didn't want to see myself. I adjusted the water temperature, took off my clothes, and stepped inside the shower stall. The water cascaded down my weary body.

In the shower, I cried until my throat was sore. I felt disgusting. I felt horrible. All the guilt from cheating crashed down on me all at once. I had no one to talk to. I always showed my friends my strength. I never let them see me during troubled times, because I tried to portray myself as a strong woman that had her shit together. But I was falling apart at the seams.

Chris tapped me on the shoulder, snapping me out of my thoughts. "You all right? You looked like you were deep in thought," he said.

"I'm okay," I said, glancing out the airplane window. "I'm just wondering if I did everything I had needed to do before we left."

That wasn't a total lie.

"Don't worry about work or anything else. This is our time to enjoy each other."

Chris kissed my hand, held it, and looked at me lovingly. I smiled, took a deep breath, and prepared myself for my new life without anyone on the side.

I sat on a wicker beach chair, wearing my sunglasses, and enjoyed the gritty feel of the sand between my toes. I loved the fresh ocean air and the way the cool breeze was gently blowing through my hair. The warm sun tanned my honey skin. Chris reached over and fed me a chocolate-covered strawberry. The look in his eyes was so passionate. I could tell he loved taking care of me and treating me like a queen.

Our vacation had been perfect so far. We had an ocean-front room at the Le Blanc Spa Resort, while Pops and the kids were staying at the Club Med Cancun Yucatan. We had done some family activities, but most of the trip was geared toward Chris and me reconnecting as a couple.

We had taken the kids to the Croco Cun Zoo, near Puerto Morelos, where they'd fed the crocodiles and deer. We'd gone to the Ruinas del Rey, and the kids had enjoyed watching the huge iguanas there. We'd soared through the jungle on the Selvatica zip lines. Chris, Pops, and I had tried it alone, while the kids had been strapped to a travel guide. We'd swum in the cenotes. The kids had tried to outdo each other by seeing who could make the biggest splash when jumping off the rocks. At first Pops had been uptight about them jumping, but in time he'd relaxed and seemed to enjoy himself.

While it was good to laugh and have fun as a family, the best part of the trip was being with Chris alone at our villa. Waking up with the man I loved in Cancún was everything I had hoped it would be. Every morning Chris and I worked out together. Usually, our schedules conflicted, so we never had time to do that at home. After we worked up a good sweat, we made love in the shower. Chris covered my body with light kisses as the water cascaded over us. He wanted the trip to show that we were a great team. We had breakfast together every day and went to the golden spa suite for the "Just for Two" spa treatments.

Chris also treated me like a queen every night. He let me choose the activities. We sang together at the karaoke bar, and although Chris wasn't a big fan of clubs, he didn't complain when we went to a few. Certain nights we stayed in our room, had dinner delivered to us, cuddled, and watched movies. Besides engaging in all the pampering and fun activities, we finally talked without fighting. We shared our frustrations, and it was those intimate conversations that brought me closer to him.

While we were cuddling in our room one night and having one of those intimate conversations, we seemed to reach a critical turning point.

"I know you love me, Chris. I'm having a great time here with you, but when this is over, I'll still need all these things," I told him.

Chris held my hand and pulled me closer to him while we spooned. Usually, he'd get defensive, and our conversation would turn into an argument, but now he was really listening to what I had to say.

"I want to make you happy, babe. Sometimes I don't know what you need."

"It doesn't have to be complicated. I need affection. Now and then, surprise me with a sweet text or take me somewhere spontaneously. Compliment me now and then, open doors for me, and send me flowers . . . you know, things like that."

Chris kissed my neck.

"I *need* you to make time for me, and not just when we're with the kids. I mean just for me. Hold me, talk to me, and pay attention to me."

"I'm sorry. I didn't know you felt I wasn't doing those things."

"I told you this lots of times. See, Chris, you heard me, but you weren't listening. There's a difference. They're not the same thing."

"I know, and I promise that from this day forward, I'll be a better husband to you." He turned me around to face him. "I love you, Karen."

Seeing the sincerity in his eyes when he said, "I love you," meant more than words to me. It made me feel warm. I realized Chris was the only man I needed.

An elderly white woman sat down in the lounge chair next to me and interrupted my reminiscing. I watched as she and her husband exchanged a warm smile.

"Do you want another Malibu bay breeze, babe?" Chris asked me from his lounge chair on the other side of mine.

I smiled and nodded.

He winked and stood up to get my drink.

The elderly woman leaned over. "I love seeing young people in love. How long have you two been married?"

"We're going on seven years in May."

"I've been married to my husband, Doug, for fifty-three years. You two make a beautiful couple."

"Wow. That's amazing. Thank you. You and your husband look very happy together."

"I'm sorry. I'm so rude. I'm Grace."

"I'm Karen. That's my husband, Chris."

"You know how I can tell he loves you?"

I shook my head.

"His eyes. It's obvious by the way he looks at you that you're his everything. He adores you the way my Dougie adores me."

Her face was filled with love and admiration when she looked over at her husband. He was now talking and laughing with Chris at the bar.

"I'm so lucky to have him," she added.

"What's your secret to a happy marriage?"

She gazed contentedly at her husband again and said, "Nothing worth something comes easy. You have to work at it. Both of you have to be willing to sacrifice, to constantly communicate, and most importantly, both of you have to appreciate what you have."

I nodded and watched Chris joking with her husband at the bar.

"Dougie and I have never been wealthy. We've struggled and fought more times than I can count, but he loves me. He's given me four beautiful children, a house, and no matter the obstacle, we go through it together and we come out stronger."

Chris and Doug came back with our drinks. Doug kissed his wife and squeezed her breasts. She playfully slapped his hands and pinched his ass when he went to sit down. I envisioned Chris and me being the same way when we reached fifty-three years of marriage.

Soft R & B played as Chris closed the blinds and lit candles around the room. I licked my lips at the sight of his naked, muscular dark-chocolate body. He kissed my hand as I handed him my wineglass. We were alone in our room for our last night in Mexico. I lay naked on my stomach. Chris kissed my neck and rubbed his hands over my hips. He placed soft kisses down my spine. I shivered from the sensation. I felt his tongue lick the small of my back and giggled as he nibbled on my butt. I turned to face him and spread my legs wide, inviting him to my treasure. Chris moved up to kiss me and worked his way back down to my peach. He devoured me, curling his tongue around my clit. It felt heavenly, but I needed more.

"Use your fingers," I moaned.

Chris worked my wet pussy with one finger, then two. The sight of his dark face as he lapped up my honey and worked his magic with his strong, thick fingers sent me through the roof. My breathing was thick. I clutched the back of his head and held his face in my treasure.

"Hum . . . hum on it, baby," I begged.

Chris followed my instruction. He held my ass, pulled me closer, and hummed on my pussy until my eyes rolled back in my head from pleasure. I bucked, squirmed, and arched my back while Chris held my hips down. I twitched and tried to push him away to catch my breath, but he continued to suck on my clit and work his fingers in me. I couldn't take it anymore.

"I want to feel you inside me."

Chris slipped his fingers into my mouth. I sucked on them while he used his other hand to roll on a condom and then hold his cock and enter me. I wrapped my legs around his waist. It felt so good to give myself completely to him. The sensation and pressure of his well-endowed penis plunging into me felt heavenly. Trey Songz was playing in the background, but the sounds of our love-making were their own music. I was close. I gripped his back and my vaginal muscles clamped down on his dick as he continued to thrust through my orgasm. I was lost. I couldn't stop cumming as he stroked me.

"Shit, shit, shit," I moaned.

Then, with one hard thrust, Chris roared and came hard before he collapsed on top of me.

I was completely spent, but I had never felt more satisfied and relaxed in my life. I was convinced that my marriage with Chris could work. My love for him eclipsed any feelings I had ever had for Raheem or Tyrell. People said that no one changed unless they wanted to. Chris had proved he could be the man I'd always needed him to be. We would return to our realities, but I was confident things would be different. He had changed, and so had I. I was ready to have my happily ever after with Chris and only Chris.

PART TWO

What's Done in the Dark Comes to Light

Chris

"Shit! I'm so late," I yelled as I looked at my watch and rushed to get dressed.

The kids were sitting on our bed, fussing with Karen while she combed their hair for school. I searched frantically in the living room for my keys. Karen and I had woken up early for an intense sex session and had lost track of time.

"Babe, they're on the kitchen counter, next to our phones," Karen shouted.

"Thanks. I'll text you later."

"All right. Have a good day, babe."

I grabbed my keys, my wallet, my phone, and ran out the door. I drove like a madman, cutting people off and maneuvering through traffic. This was my first day back to work after vacation; I couldn't show up late. With the grace of God, I arrived exactly on time. My phone vibrated in my pocket as I got out of my F-150 truck, but I ignored it and went straight to my assignment on the construction site. As I settled in, my phone vibrated again, reminding me that I had a text message. I pulled the phone out of my pocket, looked down at it, and saw I had grabbed Karen's by mistake.

The message was from Raheem. I paused and stared at the notification. I was curious to see why this guy was messaging my wife, but I questioned whether I should read the text. A small part of me felt I would violate her privacy and trust by reading it. It was probably nothing, anyway. After all, Raheem was her personal trainer, and he was probably just setting up their next appointment. Our vacation had renewed my faith in Karen. But as I continued to contemplate reading the text, I realized I still had this gnawing, lingering suspicion. I loved my wife to death, but I didn't want to be played for a fool, either. I punched in her password and unlocked the phone. I opened the message.

I couldn't believe my eyes. Staring me right in the fucking face was a picture of a dick with the words *He misses you.*

Anger radiated throughout my body. My hands trembled as I scrolled through and read some of their previous conversations. My breathing was choppy, and sweat dripped from my pores. My heart felt like it was beating out of my chest. I read until I couldn't bear to see any more. I didn't care if I got in trouble at work; I needed to settle this shit with Karen right now.

I told the foreman that I had a family emergency and that I couldn't stay, because my kids were sick. I guessed the look on my face proved to him that something was wrong. He let me go without a complaint.

I needed to know more. So I sat in my truck and scrolled through her entire text history with Raheem. As I read her messages, I squeezed the phone in my hand. I wanted to die. This was more than an affair. They had a relationship. She had met up with him more than a few times; she had seen him on numerous occasions before the trip. He'd even texted that he loved her. What made it worse was seeing that she had texted him back, I love you too. That meant it was more than a physical thing; feelings were involved.

As I scrolled through her text messages, I discovered she had *another* guy on the side, somebody named Tyrell. The more I read, the deeper into a depression I went.

Reading the conversations from Karen—the mother of my children, the woman I had sworn before God always to be faithful to—and seeing that she talked dirty to other men hurt me more than any physical pain could. What was really fucked up about this phone situation was that she used my birthday as her password. That meant whenever she was doing her dirt, she was fully conscience of what she was doing, because I had to come to mind when she entered my birth date to unlock her phone. The signs had been there all along, but I had been too naïve and trusting to pay attention to them.

I copied the numbers for Raheem and Tyrell on an old gas receipt I had lying around on the console. Then I put the receipt in my glove compartment and slammed the compartment shut. I didn't know what I was going to do, but I had to do something. Her text messages with the two men indicated that she knew Raheem from the gym and Tyrell from work. I wasn't totally sure that Karen had my phone at the moment. It was possible that she had realized it was mine right away and had left it at home, but I sent her a text message, anyway.

Karen, come home now!

If she didn't respond, I'd show up at her fucking job. If she did respond, we'd settle this shit at home. I didn't know how I'd react when I saw her or what I'd say or do. I felt so fucking stupid. I gripped the leather steering wheel tightly and banged my head on it.

Before I knew it, I was speeding on the Grand Central Parkway. I was on autopilot. I tried to collect my thoughts, but visions of other men fucking my wife ran rampant through my mind. That was when Karen called me.

"Chris . . . I can explain," she said when I picked up.

"Explain it when I get home," I yelled.

"Please try to understand. We had a lot of problems and—"

"I'll see you when I get home."

I ended the call. I didn't care what excuses she had. No matter how bad she had believed we were, there was no excuse for cheating. If our problems had been so bad, she should've left me. Our marriage wasn't perfect. We had our problems—all marriages did—but no matter how big our problems had been before, she could've talked to me. Sleeping with one guy was bad enough, but sleeping with two was unforgivable.

Karen

After Chris left for work, I rushed to finish Jaclyn's and Jocelyn's hair. Their hair was so thick that it took time and effort to get it done neatly. When I finally finished, I walked into their bedroom and put the combs and the hair grease on their dresser. They followed me into their bedroom, and I quickly dressed them. Then I gathered my phone, my purse, and my coffee and rushed out the door with the girls. After I got them in the car, I drove the girls to school.

"Mommy is going to miss you. Have fun at school and be good," I told them as I ushered them out of the car and up the sidewalk. Their teacher was waiting for them in front of the school.

"Bye, Mom," they yelled and waved after I handed them off.

"Bye, babies," I said, waving at them, as I stood still on the sidewalk.

I continued to wave back until their teacher took them inside the classroom, and then I made a mad dash back to the car. I zoomed down the Long Island Expressway, which locals called the LIE, hoping to get to work on time. Thankfully, I was on time, but I had so much work to catch up on that my nerves were on edge.

I waved to a few people when I got to the office, but I didn't speak to anyone. Some of the employees were whispering and saying things under their breath, but I was used to the usual haters now that I was a supervisor.

Tyrell waved at me, but I acted like I didn't see him, and headed straight to my office. I sat down at my desk, turned on my computer, sipped my coffee, and began to look over reports. Minutes later someone knocked on my door.

"Come in," I shouted.

Tyrell walked in and closed my door behind him.

I sighed and rubbed the bridge of my nose. "What's up, Tyrell?"

"I texted you ten times over the past two weeks, and you never responded back. I'm not happy with us. I don't like that you just cut me off when it was convenient to you. I deserve more than—"

"Look, save it. We're done. You're married, I'm married, and what we were doing was wrong. I'm trying to fix my marriage, and so we're not doing anything sexual anymore. We can be friends. We can grab a coffee now and then, but we aren't doing anything more than that. Now please, I have a lot of work to catch up on, and there's nothing more to discuss."

I pointed to the door. Tyrell slammed it on his way out.

About an hour had passed when there was another knock on my door. I was engrossed in highlighting reports and making corrections on work that was done while I was away, so I found this second interruption really irritating.

"Come in," I shouted again.

This time it was my director, Roger Bedore. He had Helen, our Human Resources representative, with him.

I put down my pen. "Good morning, Roger. Good morning, Helen. How are you two today?"

Helen remained silent.

"I'm well. Karen, we need to talk," Roger said.

He had a grim look on his face as he closed my door. His bald head shone as he bent over slightly and stroked his graying beard.

"Are you aware there are rumors going around the company about you?" Roger asked.

I was confused about why someone from HR was with him, and I was annoyed that shit was being said behind my back at work.

"Rumors? What rumors?" I asked.

Helen cleared her throat and said, "There are rumors that you're having an affair with one of your subordinates, Tyrell Stevens. Employees are saying that because of your affair, he has been shown favoritism, despite his performance being substandard. Is this true?"

"What? No. That's ridiculous. I'm not having an affair with anyone in this office. I treat all the employees here equally. There is no favoritism."

"Tyrell's wife, Pamela Stevens, begs to differ. She has gone on the record and reported that she saw inappropriate text messages between you and Tyrell," Roger said.

My heart was beating fast. "That's not true." I paused for a moment. "Does she still have them?" I asked.

Roger gave me a skeptical look when I asked that question. "No. She and Tyrell fought over the phone, and he erased his text message history," Roger explained.

That was good to know. Without the texts, she had no real proof.

"Some of your subordinates have stated that Tyrell has been seen going into your office for unknown reasons and has been staying for long blocks of time," Roger said.

A wave of heat came over me. Sweat dripped down my neck. Roger's and Helen's eyes pierced through me. I felt like they already knew I was hiding something.

"Some employees have even said they've seen the two of you leaving work together," Helen revealed. "We value you here, but you know the company's strict policy and procedures when it comes to relationships with employees under your supervision. There is a pending investigation regarding this situation. I advise you to talk to your union representative and prepare yourself to answer questions and face the allegations once the higher-ups want to close out the investigation. I'll inform you of anything else that develops." She paused. "Try to enjoy the rest of your day."

Helen quickly exited my office, but Roger stayed behind.

"If you're involved in some type of relationship with him, don't tell me. I don't want to know. I don't want to be put in an uncomfortable position, where I would be obligated to say something on the matter. I think you're a competent supervisor and a hard worker, but even I can't help if they want to make an example out of you and either fire or demote you," Roger said.

I was emotional. I couldn't believe I had just come back to work, and I was already under so much stress. I tried hard to hold back tears. This was business, and I couldn't cry in front of my director.

"Roger, do you have any idea what the higher-ups plan on doing?"

"No. Nothing yet. But seeing that Tyrell's wife works at our Melville office, I highly doubt that if they are going to discipline you, they'll demote you or ship you out to a different office. Instead of firing you and thus hurting your chances of finding another position with a different company, as a courtesy, they'll probably ask you to resign."

Roger looked concerned. I was terrified. Losing my job was not an option; it wasn't even a possibility. Chris and I wouldn't be poor, but we couldn't survive long on his income alone. In this economy, finding another job with a salary even half of mine would be hard, maybe nearly impossible. I couldn't put that burden on Chris. How would I even explain to him the reason for me being fired or forced to resign?

"Hopefully, the investigation will go your way, and this will all blow over," Roger said, trying to console me.

"I can't believe this is happening right now. I just had a much-needed vacation, and I return to work to hear that I may lose my job."

"I'm sorry you're going through this, but you know the policies and procedures. The only advice I can give you is to pray for the best and tread lightly. Don't make any waves or bring attention to yourself."

There was nothing more I could say. I thanked Roger for the heads-up. After he left my office, I just sat there holding my head in my hands. Suddenly, my cell buzzed. I reached into my purse to get it, but when I pulled it out, I realized it wasn't my cell phone. Chris had texted me from *my* phone. Fear washed over me. I read his text.

Karen, come home now!

I'd been sloppy. I had procrastinated and hadn't deleted my old texts. I had too many incriminating messages, so if Chris was demanding I come home, then chances were he had read some of them. I knew it wasn't anything with the kids, because the school would've called me at work since I was usually closest to the school. Chris worked in different parts of the city all the time; plus, he was often at locations with no cell phone signal. So, this had to have something to do with me. I panicked. Between the stress from work and now this, I felt lost and confused. I called Chris.

"Chris . . . I can explain," I said when he picked up.

"Explain it when I get home." He was so loud, I had to pull the phone away from my ear.

"Please try to understand. We had a lot of problems and—"

"I'll see you when I get home." Chris abruptly ended the call.

I stood up from my desk so fast, my chair spun around. I headed to Roger's office. I had to leave work now. I knew this would hurt things with me here at work, but this was my family. This was my life. One of my other subordinates, a guy named Wesley, was leaning over Tyrell's desk and talking to him. He purposely stood up straight and bumped into me when I walked by.

"Oops. I'm sorry, boss. If you need me to help you with something in your office, just let me know," Wesley said. He then put his hands out, moved his hips, and motioned like he was fucking.

I was so upset that I almost started to cry. I looked at Tyrell. He had a huge smirk on his face, but he didn't look up from his computer. If this was any other day and I wasn't under investigation, I would've cursed his ass out. I would've been at HR so fast to have him fired, his head would have spun, but right now I was powerless. I was defenseless at my job and helpless with my marriage. I swallowed my pride and continued on to Roger's office. I knocked on his door.

"Come in," Roger said.

Once I stepped inside his office, he motioned for me to close the door.

"Roger . . . I have a family emergency. I have to leave."

He looked skeptical. "Is everything all right?" he asked.

I wanted to be honest. I wanted to tell him the same shit I was being investigated for at work was biting me in the ass now at home. I wanted to tell him that I was terrified, and that I didn't know what was going to happen next, but I couldn't get into a long, drawn-out conversation about my family life. Rather than getting too personal, I lied.

"No, my kids are sick. Chris is in the city, and their school needs me to pick them up. I really need to leave."

Roger looked unconvinced but said, "Sure, sure. Family comes first. Take care of your children."

"Thank you."

I left Roger's office, with my hands shaking and my eyes puffy. I hadn't even faced Chris yet, and I already felt mentally and emotionally drained. I hurried to my office to get my purse. The workers were gossiping and pointing at me as I went. I guessed the rumor was spreading like wildfire. I was sure that allowing them to see me distraught like this didn't help, but I'd have to deal with that later.

I rushed home and got there first. I sat on our couch and tried to figure out what I'd say to Chris to explain the reasons for my infidelity. I had never wanted to hurt him. I had thought I could bury all this dirt under the rug, but everything had reared its ugly head. I mentally prepared myself for a life-changing argument. Things between Chris and I may never be the same again. I jumped when I heard Chris's key in the lock.

Chris

I pulled into the garage, and Karen's car was already parked inside it. I sat in my truck, mentally preparing myself for what I'd say to her. I pulled the case off her phone and dropped it on the passenger seat. I put her phone in my pocket, took a deep breath, got out of the truck and, with a woeful countenance, walked inside the house.

I entered the living room to see Karen sitting with her feet up on the couch, rocking back and forth. Her arms were wrapped around her legs, and her forehead was pressed against her knees. My cell phone was on the coffee table in front of her. She looked up and continued rocking and holding herself. She looked like she'd been crying. I walked over to the couch, pulled out her phone, and threw it against the wall. The phone shattered. Glass and debris were strewn all over the carpet. Karen was shaking when I walked past her and sat on the couch. Fear was on her face when I faced her, my glare unwavering. She couldn't look me in the eyes.

There were countless questions I wanted to ask, but I summed everything up with one. "Why?"

"Chris, I know I was wrong. I never intended to hurt you. I ended everything with those guys. Our trip showed me that our marriage could be saved. I don't need anyone else—"

"Save the bullshit! I want to know why my wife felt the need to fuck two other men!" I shouted.

There was a long pause. She opened her mouth to speak, but nothing came out. Karen stared at me but offered no explanation or apology for her infidelity.

"Answer me! You owe me that much," I demanded.

Karen looked down as tears slipped from her eyes and soaked her blouse. Her voice was shaky when she finally spoke. "There wasn't one specific reason why I cheated on you. I wasn't happy. I was bored, and I felt that you didn't appreciate me. You were always working, and we never went anywhere or did things together. Sometimes you'd be home, and I'd still feel lonely. I felt like you cared more about restoring your stupid car than you cared for me."

I couldn't believe what I was hearing.

Karen continued. "You weren't giving me the emotional intimacy I needed. I'd come home from work, and you'd barely even look at me. You treated me more like a friend than your wife. The Mexico trip helped us a lot. I felt closer to you and fell in love with you again. It's what I needed to realize that I didn't need the other guys to fill the void I felt with you."

Her words sounded truthful, but I didn't give a shit. It was all excuses to me.

"If you were so unhappy, why didn't you talk to me? It should've never gotten to this. If you were so miserable, why didn't you just leave me?"

"I . . . d-don't . . . please . . ."

Karen's stammering was frustrating me. "Spit it out!" I yelled.

When I saw her eyes darken, I knew the argument was going to get ugly. She crossed her arms over her chest and faced me. "You see that shit right there? That's the problem. Why didn't I talk to you? Because talking to you is like talking to a drill sergeant. You're just like your father. When you're angry, there's no reaching you. You yell at me. You talk down to me like I'm stupid, and you make me feel like I'm beneath you. I'm your wife."

"Don't act like you're the victim here. I have my quirks, but I've always tried to make you happy. You know that. I was only unreachable when I felt you were cheating on me, and clearly, I was right. No matter how angry I was with you, I would never have cheated on you. I loved you too much. How long have you been fucking these other guys?"

"I'm trying to explain everything, and you're not listening to—"

I shook my head. I didn't want to hear all her emotional bullshit. I wanted to know the fucking truth. "How long?"

"I told you about this before. You hear what I'm saying, but you're not listening. I know I hurt you, but I was dying inside. I wanted to feel desired. I wanted to feel alive again. I used to just come home and go to work. Compared to my sister and my friends, my life was stagnant—"

"Did Chloe suggest this? Did she know? Did everyone know about these other guys?"

"Chloe didn't suggest anything. It was my decision. Chloe and my friends had nothing to do with it, but yes, they knew about Tyrell and Raheem. Men cheat on woman all the time, trying to fulfill something that's missing. This wasn't any different."

Karen's betrayal was bad enough, but the fact that her sister and her friends knew about it hurt my *pride*. I stood up and started to pace. I felt humiliated.

Then her last statement sank in, and I said, "Don't give me that bullshit about men cheating on women. I've never cheated on you." I was silent for a moment. "So, *everybody* fucking knew? You made me look like a fool to everyone? If Lindsey knew, then Jeff knew."

Then it hit me. That night at Jeff's house, he hadn't tried to insult me. That had been his indirect way of warning me. I felt stupid for not catching on.

"So, all those times you said you were hanging out with Lindsey or working late, you were really with them?" I asked.

"Most of the time, yes," Karen answered softly.

"You looked me in my eyes and lied to me. You told me that you could never cheat on me, that I was the love of your life, yet now you're telling me you were miserable. Did you ever *really* love me?"

Karen sighed loudly. "You know I love you. You'll never understand or see things from my point of view."

"It's always about you, Karen. It's always about how you feel, about how you're so unhappy. You're so busy pointing fingers that you never acknowledge when you've fucked up. Did you ever think about how I felt? Did you ever think that maybe I was lonely? Or that maybe I needed you here with me? Or that maybe I might've needed you to show some support and uplift me? You're so fucking selfish. I tried my hardest to make you happy."

I sat back down on the couch and slammed my fist down on the coffee table. The ceramic lamp on top of the table fell off and broke into pieces.

I went on. "Did I always tell you I loved you? No, but my actions should've spoken louder than words. I never complained to you when my foreman was giving me shit, or when I was exhausted from working overtime, or when Pops belittled me and made me feel like a failure almost on a daily basis. I'm not completely happy, either. The only thing I felt made me remotely close to being happy was my family, and you ruined that for me. The little happiness I felt I had died today, when I found out my wife wasn't the woman I thought she was."

Karen looked hurt by my words. She uncrossed her arms and looked at me. "I know I hurt you, but think of our kids when you need to be happy."

"You're giving me that advice? Why didn't you use it? Are the girls even mine?"

"How dare you ask me that? Of course they're yours. I can't believe you'd even question that."

"I never thought in a million years I would have to, but after today I don't know what to believe anymore. You lied to me about cheating, so how can I trust you're telling me the truth about them? How long have you been seeing these other guys?"

Karen was seething and was rapidly tapping her foot out of frustration. In reality, I didn't doubt the girls were mine, but I wanted her to feel hurt, embarrassed, and ashamed. I wanted her to suffer, even if it was just a fraction of what I was going through.

"The girls are yours!" Karen screamed.

"You know, when you got pregnant, I thought about leaving you and just giving you the twenty-five percent in child support. I'd always be there for my kids, but I wouldn't have to deal with you too much. I questioned if I was making the right decision being with you. I honestly regret that now. All those times your friends smiled in my face, or when your coworkers saw me when I went to visit you at work, they knew I was being *played*. How long has this been going on?"

She paused for a few moments before answering. "I've been with Raheem for three years and with Tyrell for a little over a year."

I felt a pain in my chest. It hurt so much I could barely breathe. There it was, the truth. We had been married for only seven years, and she had cheated on me for half of them. Karen put her head in her hands and wept. I guessed she felt guilty for hurting me so deeply. I gathered myself and faced her.

"Three fucking years! *Three fucking years!* You mean to tell me, the majority of our marriage has been a lie? If you were so unhappy for so long, you should have just left me."

"Would that really have helped, Chris?"

"Yes. This is a million times worse."

"The signs were there, Chris. You just didn't pay attention to them, or to me, for that matter. My friends saw it. Why couldn't you?"

"Your *friends*? You're taking advice from lonely bitches who can't find men for themselves? The only friend you have with any intelligence is Lindsey. The rest of them are fucking miserable, but you'll take advice from them, right?"

"Don't talk about my friends. My friends have nothing to do with us."

"As much as you hate Will and Lou, they've never suggested that I step out on you. Let's be real. I know Chloe hates me, and your friends don't like me. They've been encouraging you to do this, haven't they?"

Karen stared at the carpet. I knew it. I stood up from the couch, grabbed my cell phone off the coffee table, and headed to the garage.

"Where are you going?"

"To work on my car. I need time to calm down and try to think."

"See? When I need you to talk to me, you always avoid the problem and do something stupid, like work on your fucking car. You've been trying to restore that piece of shit for years now. It's never going to work. It's a fucking lemon. Why can't you get that?" Karen shouted.

Her question stopped me in my tracks. I turned sharply and faced her, staring her directly in the eyes.

"Why does everything I like have to be stupid? The car runs fine. I'm restoring it slowly because I want everything to be perfect. I need to get away from you right now. I can't even look at you."

I walked into the garage, but I didn't work on my car. I got into my truck, started it, and backed down the driveway.

"Chris, wait. I'm sorry . . . Wait . . . Please talk to me," Karen pleaded as she ran out of the house.

I ignored her, and when I reached the street, I sped off. I didn't know where I was going; I just needed to go somewhere. I needed to find someplace to let go of all this anger.

Chris

I drove aimlessly down Jericho Turnpike. I was hurt, I was angry, and in many ways, I was lonely. Eventually, I pulled over. I pick up my cell phone and held it in my calloused hands. This stupid device pulled me out of the dark and showed me that my wife was fucking around. I opened my glove compartment, then pulled out the wrinkled receipt with Tyrell's and Raheem's phone numbers on it. I wanted answers. I needed to know more than the bullshit Karen had told me. I called Raheem first. The phone rang for a few moments, and then, when his voicemail message played, I heard the voice of the man who'd been fucking my wife. I quickly ended the call without leaving a message. I called Tyrell next.

"Hello?" he said.

"Is this Tyrell?"

"Yes, speaking. Who is this?"

"I'm the husband of the woman you're fucking."

"Shit. Look, man, this is between you and her. She was giving it up, so I took it. You would do the same shit if you were in my shoes."

I didn't like how he made it sound like Karen was some whore, and I especially didn't like how he said, "You would do the same shit," as if he knew me. I swallowed hard.

"How many times have you . . . been with my wife?"

"What do you mean by 'been with'? If you mean how many times have I fucked her, then countless times. If you're asking how many times I've been out with her . . . well, I guess that's the same answer. I've seen you around. You'd come to the office and bring dinner for her from time to time. She used to talk shit about you and fuck me all in the same night."

Was he purposely fucking with me? Did he want me to whup his ass?

"You sound real tough for a guy on a phone. If you got so much to say, why don't I come to your job and we can settle this like men?" I said.

"Nah. Like I said before, I've seen you. You're way stronger than me, and besides, I'm a lover, not a fighter. Just ask your wife how good of a lover I am."

"You know what? I'm on my way there right now to fuck you up. Say all this shit when I'm—"

"I wouldn't do that if I were you. First off, everyone here knows I was fucking your wife. It's all over the company, and she's under investigation for it. You wouldn't want to speed up the process and make her lose her job, now would you?"

I wanted to kill him. I hated him for fucking my wife. I hated him because he was so haughty about it, but most of all, I hated him because I couldn't do anything about it. I couldn't kick his ass, because I would risk Karen losing her job. And even if I could, I would have only temporary happiness from hurting him, and it wouldn't negate the fact that he had been with Karen.

I gritted my teeth and said, "Fuck you!"

"No, thanks. I get enough from your wife." He laughed at me and ended the call.

My hands stung as I slapped the steering wheel. I felt humiliated. This all had started with Raheem. He was the source of my problem. He was the one she'd said she loved. I suddenly had an idea. I decided to text him as Karen so I could meet him in person.

Raheem, it's Karen. My husband found out about us and destroyed my phone. I'm texting you from my new number. Meet me at the gym. I need to see you right now. I need you.

I sat in my car and waited for a response. It came a few minutes later.

Okay. See you at five.

He had responded pretty quickly, but it had felt like an eternity to me. I texted him back.

Meet me in front of the gym.

I drove to the gym, found a parking spot close to the entrance, and waited. Fifteen minutes after five, I saw a real pretty-looking guy—about six feet four and in decent shape—standing in front of the gym. He was wearing a gray tank top and black running tights. I watched him reach for his phone, and soon after I got a text.

I'm here.

There was my confirmation. This was the main source of my problems and my pain. I got out of my truck and walked toward him. He had no idea who I was when I stood next to him. He was taller than me, but I eclipsed him in term of my width. Muscle wise, he had nothing on me.

"Excuse me. Are you Raheem?"

He looked confused. "Yes. Do I know you?"

"I think you do. You're fucking my wife."

His expression changed from one of confusion to fear. Before he could do anything, I kicked him in the dick as hard as I could with my steel-toed work boots. When he doubled over, I grabbed him by the back of his head and kneed him in the face. Blood and snot squirted out of his nose. He landed on his back. I kicked him and stomped on him.

Gym members and pedestrians passing by saw the mayhem and ran inside to get help. I didn't care who came. I didn't care who saw me. I wanted Raheem to feel my pain. I needed him to take this and more because I couldn't get to Tyrell to give him the same punishment. While many passersby saw what was going on, none of them helped him. Finally, two personal trainers from the gym ran out and grabbed me. One guy was about my size and weight. He looked like a younger version of me, like he could have been my son or something. *Ken* was written on his name tag. *Joe* was written on the other guy's name tag.

"Get the fuck off of me!" I yelled.

Ken tried to restrain me when Joe let go of me so he could check on Raheem. Raheem was bloody and bruised. He was conscious, but I'd inflicted a lot of damage. I wiggled and squirmed, trying my hardest to break free from Ken's grip.

"Sir, please . . . Stop. You gotta calm down," Ken said.

"This guy fucked my wife! He ruined my life."

Ken's grip loosened a bit, which allowed me to break free and kick Raheem in the face again. Ken grabbed me, turned me around quickly, and looked at me as if he had realized something. Maybe he had seen Raheem and Karen together around the gym. He leaned in close to me.

"Look, I know you're pissed about Karen, but no woman is worth going to jail for. You have kids, man. Do you want to do time for this shit? I'm going to let you go, but you need to get out of here. You understand? Get out of here," Ken whispered.

I was taken aback by what he said. As one man to another man, I respected what he was doing for me. He was right. I was acting out of anger and other emotions and not thinking of the consequences. He loosened his grip on me, and I freed myself. I ran to my truck, started it up, and sped off.

As I drove, I thought about what Ken had said. He knew my wife's name. He knew Raheem wasn't her husband. I felt like the entire world knew she'd been cheating on me, and I'd been the dumb ass in the dark, oblivious to it all.

Karen

I swept up the pieces of my cell phone and the broken lamp. I poured the debris in the dustpan into the kitchen garbage can. Chris didn't have to tell me he was disappointed in me. The hurt and pain on his face said more than any words could.

About ten minutes later I heard voices at the front door. My kids were home from school with Pops. The door opened, and the girls ran in. I looked in the hallway mirror and attempted to fix myself up the best I could, but to no avail. My eyes and nose were swollen and puffy from crying all day. My hair was a mess, and my clothes were wrinkled and disheveled. I tried to muster up a smile and look happy when my daughters saw me.

"Mommy!" they yelled excitedly.

"Hey. How was school?" I asked.

"We made this for you and Daddy," Jocelyn said, waving a sheet of construction paper in the air.

"Isn't it pretty?" Jaclyn asked.

At the top of the paper were the words *My Happy Family*. Underneath the girls had drawn a picture of the whole family, including Pops and Chloe. I thought about what I'd done and about how Chris had stormed out, and I started to cry.

"What's wrong, Mommy?" Jocelyn asked.

"You don't like it?" Jaclyn looked disappointed.

"No, no, I love it. It's beautiful. Mommy is crying because she's happy," I lied.

Pops stared at me. I assumed from his glare that he suspected something was wrong. "Girls, why don't you play in your room for a while? I have to talk to your mother about grown-up stuff."

"Okay!" they yelled in unison and then skipped off to their bedroom.

As soon as they were out of earshot, Pops faced me. "What's wrong?" he asked.

"Pops . . . I did something horrible. I don't think I can tell you."

"You cheated on Chris, didn't you?" he asked calmly.

It stunned me that, that was his first guess. I nodded.

He sighed and looked at me. Pops had this stare that made you feel like he could read your soul. I hoped he could read mine.

"We were having problems. I never meant to hurt him—"

"Stop. I understand. I'm going to tell you something I haven't even told Chris. Years back, I got orders that I was returning home from deployment. I wanted to surprise Chris and his mother, Eleanor, so I didn't tell them I was coming. Chris was in school and Eleanor didn't work, so I figured I would come home and surprise her first. When I walked in the house, I heard her moaning up a storm in our bedroom. I opened the bedroom door and caught her in the act with one of the military policemen from the base."

My mouth dropped open.

Pops turned and stared out the window as he continued. "I was naïve. I believed that since she came from a military family, she knew what the role of a soldier's wife was. I had neglected her. I hadn't written letters or called her, because I had needed to keep my mental edge when I was in combat. I couldn't think about being home or about my family, because I believed the moment I did,

I'd get killed in battle. I had thought she understood that, but she had needed affection while I was away, and she'd felt that since I didn't care to contact her when I was deployed, she wouldn't care if she cheated on me with another man."

For once, he looked like he was going to show some emotion, but he quickly composed himself and went on. "I got over it. Chris will get over it. I'll talk to my son, and then you two can figure out how to make your marriage work. Your marriage isn't about you two anymore. You have children. Everything should revolve around them. Where is he?"

"I don't know. We argued, and he drove off. He said he needed to get away from me."

"Call him."

"He was so angry, he broke my cell phone during the argument."

"I'll call him." Pops pulled out his cell phone and called Chris. The call went straight to voice mail.

"I'm worried about him," I said.

"He'll be back. I raised him right. He knows better than to desert his family."

"Pops, can you watch the girls for me while I get a new phone and search for Chris? I know you said he'll be back, but for some peace of mind, I just need to look for him."

"I'll watch the girls. Take care of your business."

I hugged him. He acted so robotic at times, but for that one instant when he talked about his wife's infidelity, he seemed human, emotional even. I saw how deeply it had hurt him.

"Thank you for understanding," I said.

He nodded. I didn't know if I was thanking him for understanding why I cheated, for watching the girls, or for giving me time to get a new phone and search for Chris.

I grabbed my bag and headed to the Verizon store.

"Mrs. Davis, your new iPhone is activated and ready for you," said the cashier at the Verizon store.

"Thank you."

I left the store, got into my car, and was bombarded with missed text messages. First, I got one from Tyrell that read, Your husband called me today. We had a nice little chat.

At first, I didn't believe it. Chris didn't have his number, but then I received several text messages from Raheem. The first text said, Your fucking husband pretended to be you and set me up.

My heart beat wildly inside my chest. I quickly read the rest of the text messages from Raheem.

He told me to meet him at the front of the gym at five.

The motherfucker came out of nowhere and called my name and attacked me.

The trainers at the gym broke it up, and your punk-ass man left before the cops got here.

I swear on my life, I'm going to get that motherfucker back!

I called Raheem after reading all the texts. He picked up on the first ring.

"Hello, Raheem? Oh my God. I'm so sorry. I didn't know he had your number."

"How the fuck did this happen?"

"He found out about us today, destroyed my cell phone, and left. I didn't know where he was going or that he would contact you. I'm so sorry."

"He caught me off guard, but if I see him again, I'll be ready for his ass."

Raheem was handsome, but he wasn't a fighter. Chris had been an all-American wrestler in college. He and

Pops sparred a few times a week to stay sharp. There was no way Raheem could beat Chris in a fistfight, but I let him talk tough.

"I'll talk to him. I'm sorry he attacked you," I said.

"Nah, I don't want you to talk to him. I want to beat his ass. Karen, out of respect for you, I'm not going to have his punk ass arrested, but you tell him if he ever tries some shit like that again, not only am I going to fuck him up, but he's also going to jail."

"Thank you for not getting the cops involved. I'm going to go and try to find him now."

"Yeah, you do that. Don't forget to tell him what I said."

I rolled my eyes. "I won't."

We hung up. I thought about searching for Chris, but I needed to know more about what had happened today. I called Tyrell. I needed to know exactly what he'd said to Chris. Chris didn't usually do anything this reckless. Maybe Tyrell had said something to set him off.

"Hello, Tyrell," I said when Tyrell picked up.

"Hello, yourself, Karen. To what do I owe the honor of this call?"

"What did you say to my husband to set him off?"

"I only told him the truth. The truth sets us all free."

"Stop playing with me and talking in fucking riddles, Tyrell. This isn't a game. This is my life! What did you say to him?" I yelled.

"First of all, calm down. He asked me how many times we'd fucked. I told him, 'Countless times.'"

When I heard him say that, I felt a knot form in my stomach. I was filled with guilt and regret. I could only imagine how Chris felt.

Tyrell continued. "He asked me how many times you had broken plans with him to be with me, and I told him it happened all the time. He tried to threaten me. He wanted to stop by the office and teach me a lesson, but I let him know that wouldn't be wise, with the investigation about you pending."

I hated that Tyrell had this type of leverage against me. Information was spread too easily at my job. This situation brought out a nastiness in Tyrell that I hadn't seen before. He'd never shown me his arrogance before, only his compassion.

"I let him know that while he might be able to beat me up physically, you needed me sexually," he added.

"Don't flatter yourself. You weren't that good. I didn't sleep with you for anything you did sexually. I needed you emotionally. That was it."

"Oh please. I had you hollering and screaming for Jesus every time I touched you."

"Truth be told, you're small. Orally, you're fairly decent, but other than that, you're whack. Unless you were going down on me or we were using toys, you did nothing for me sexually."

Tyrell made an irritated grunt that told me what I'd said hit a sore spot and touched home. I didn't care. The situation had escalated because of what he'd told Chris.

"Well, I might be small, but there's a *big* chance you won't have a job soon, bitch," Tyrell spat out.

"Don't take your anger out on me because your wife is still cheating on your ass and I cut you off."

"Let's see how you feel when you lose your job *and* your family. You'll be begging me to come back."

"You think after all this, I would ever touch you again? You realize you're at risk too, right? I guess you never read the code of conduct at work. If corporate discovers that anything happened between us, you're going to get fired too. Then we'll both be unemployed, and I'll still have cut you off, and your wife will still be fucking around on you."

There was silence on his end. I guessed it hadn't occurred to him that he could get fired too.

"Did you purposely tell her about us?" I asked, breaking the silence.

Tyrell cleared his throat. When he spoke, his voice trembled, like he was nervous. "Yeah. I kept hearing around the office that she was still seeing other people, so I wanted her to know two can play that game. I didn't know she was going to get corporate involved. I knew she was mad, but I didn't think it would go this far."

"Well, this is why I told you to keep your fucking mouth shut. Now we're both in danger of losing our fucking jobs. Pray that your pride didn't fuck us up and that we won't be fired. Lose my number, asshole."

I ended the call. I massaged my temples, gathered my composure, and drove past Will and Lou's place. Chris's truck wasn't there. Next, I drove past Pops's house to see if maybe he'd gone there, but his truck wasn't in the driveway. After driving around for about an hour, I decided to head home.

When I walked through the door, Pops and the kids were sitting at the kitchen table. Pops was watching the girls as they colored in their coloring books.

"Did you get in touch with Chris?" Pops asked.

"No. I couldn't find him anywhere. I'm starting to get worried."

I didn't want to tell him that Chris had fought with Raheem or that he had had an argument with Tyrell. Pops was always hard on Chris, and I'd done enough to hurt him already. He didn't need added aggravation from his father.

"This is unacceptable. I'm going to call him again, and he better answer me. He should be handling his problems like a man, not like some pansy." Pops pulled out his phone, dialed Chris's number, and put the phone on speaker.

"Yes, Pops?" Chris answered. He sounded apathetic.

"Boy, where are you?"

"Pops, I don't need this right now. Karen has been cheating on me and—"

"I know what happened. She told me everything. Handle your situation like a damn man and get over it!"

"I'm not you. I can't act like nothing happened. She hurt me and—"

"She hurt me," Pops said, mimicking Chris. "Boo-hoo. Man up. Come home right now and talk to your wife. You should be here for your family, not running away like a brat. When you have children, your marriage is no longer about you or your wife. It's about raising your children to be respectable and responsible adults. You should be leading by example."

"I don't need this lecture right now, and I'm not coming home. I'm not ready to see Karen yet."

"Boy, if you don't come home—"

"I'm not a child anymore, Pops. I'm a grown man, and I make my own decisions. I'm not coming home." Chris ended the call.

"God damn it!" Pops slammed his fist hard on the kitchen table and stood up. The sound scared the girls; they looked at me to see if everything was all right.

Pops called Chris back several times, but the calls went straight to voice mail. After hanging up, Pops clutched his chest, and his breathing was heavy. He had a weird look on his face.

"Are you okay, Pops?" I asked, concerned.

"I'm fine," Pops barked. He walked slowly to the kitchen cabinet with the glasses. His hands shook as he reached for a glass and then filled it with water from the faucet. He sat down at the table and drank the water. "I'm okay. I'm just a little upset," he said.

I wasn't sure if that statement was for the girls or for me, but I wasn't angry at him for his outburst, because I knew he was frustrated.

A few hours passed, and Chris still hadn't come home. I put the girls to bed and talked to Pops some more. I tried to explain what had led me to cheat. I didn't tell him because I was trying to justify my infidelity or because I wanted him to understand. I just felt like I needed to hear myself say it out loud to gain a better understanding of why I had done it. Pops listened without interrupting me, but his face was emotionless when I finished. I couldn't read his expression to get an idea of what he was thinking. I was not sure if I wanted to know. He didn't say if he agreed or disagreed, if he understood, or if he was still confused. He just apologized for Chris not being there and headed home.

I sat in my living room, staring at the ceiling, wishing I could restart this long, shitty day.

Chris

"I knew that bitch was cheating!" Lou yelled.

After I sped away from the gym, I stopped by Will and Lou's place. They owned a two-family house in Dix Hills. I parked my truck six blocks away from the house because I didn't want Karen to find me there.

"I'm not a fan of Karen right now, but she's still the mother of my kids. You need to chill with the name-calling," I said.

Lou nodded. "My bad, brother. I apologize, but I knew something was shady by the way she was smiling in that dude's face that night in the club."

"There was more than one guy . . . There were two of them," I revealed.

"Damn!" they said at the same time.

Will's and Lou's jaws dropped, and their eyes widened to the point where I thought they were going to pop out of their faces. They shook their heads in disbelief.

We were sitting on the couch in Will's living room, watching the Yankees game and drinking Coronas. I had met Will and Lou during my freshman year at Adelphi. At the time, we had all been studying business and had convinced each other that we were going to be the next great African American billionaires. We'd made a pact that we would move in together one day and be successful bachelors. They'd kept up their end of the deal. They were successful investment bankers on Wall Street now. My life had gone in a different direction.

"That's fucked up, man. What happened? Start from the beginning," Will said.

I told them about mixing up cell phones this morning, seeing Karen's text message history with Tyrell and Raheem, calling Tyrell, and fighting with Raheem.

"Be honest, Chris. With all the bullshit she's been putting you through over the years, you never thought about stepping out on her?" Lou asked.

"Nope."

Lou tilted his head. "Why?"

"My parents were the perfect examples for me. I always wanted the type of relationship that they had. Love like theirs took work, and my dad would never cheat on my mom and vice versa. I figured that in order to have that same type of love, I had to be the same way. After this, though, I don't think I'd ever be able to have that type of love with Karen."

"I get what you're saying, brother, but we don't live in that era anymore. Nowadays everyone is out for themselves. Karen is a prime example of the modern-day woman. I'm always going to do my thing. I would rather have one up on a bitch than find out later that she was fucking around on me," Lou said.

I didn't respond to his statement.

"Anyway, I need to be away from Karen and my Pops for a while. Do y'all mind if I spend a few nights here?" I asked.

"Hell nah, we don't mind, brother. Now things can be like how we planned them in college," Lou said excitedly.

During college Will, Lou, and I had saved money to buy a spacious three-family house. At the time, Karen had hated the idea, because she'd felt like she wasn't in my long-term plans. She had questioned what future we had if I wanted to buy a house where I would be living with my single friends.

"So, will you finally divorce this bit . . . this woman now that you know what you know?" Lou asked.

"Right now, yeah, but I don't know. It could all change. I have kids to think about."

Both of them ignored the last part of my statement and celebrated, high-fiving each other.

Neither Will nor Lou had made it a secret that they didn't like Karen. They thought she was too needy. And Karen wasn't fond of them, either. She thought they were womanizers. So, seeing them high-fiving and laughing when I told them that I intended to divorce her did not surprise me.

This was not the first time I had contemplated leaving Karen. Back in the early days, Karen and I had fought constantly. I'd been on the verge of breaking up with her when she told me she was pregnant. Even though I'd felt she wasn't totally right for me, I'd thought that would all change once we had a family together. And for the most part, things had changed. Starting our family had made me love Karen even more. Motherhood had made her more mature and more responsible. She had built a great career, had been a good role model for our daughters, and had become a good, nurturing mother.

We had had our fair share of arguments and quirks. All marriages did. At the end of the day, I was still a man. But while I'd looked at the occasional ass and breasts whenever a hot woman would walk by on the street, I'd never acted on it. I hadn't even entertained the thought of straying. When it all came down to it, I took my wedding vows seriously, and no woman was worth losing my marriage and my kids over. I had thought Karen felt the same way, but I guessed I was wrong.

"You can crash in one of the guest rooms," Will offered.

"Cool," I said.

"I hope you don't mind hearing me sexing my loud-ass women at all times of the night," Will joked.

"I remember the routine from college. I'll be okay," I assured him.

"We got to make up for lost time, Chris. If Karen wants to do her thing, you need to do yours too," Lou said.

I nodded, not in approval but in acknowledgment of his statement. I had no idea what the future held for me. I wasn't sure if I could work things out with Karen, but I couldn't ignore the possibility that we might get divorced. It looked like that could soon be a reality.

The odor of cigar smoke was strong in the black and pink private room. My naked ass was stuck to the cushion of the warm black leather chair, while my pants were down around my ankles. My hand was on top of the stripper's reddish-brown hair. Her head was bobbing in perfect rhythm as she went down on me. Her thick lips and honey-colored complexion reminded me of Karen, which was why I had picked her. It felt good. I felt good. And although it wasn't right, I tried not to care. I was at J's Gentlemen's Quarters in the Bronx with Will and Lou. Will was sitting in a similar chair across from me with a Hispanic stripper with sienna-colored hair. She was riding him, reverse cowgirl, while he held on to her massive ass. Lou was with a white bleached-blond stripper. He was standing up, hammering her doggy style, while she knelt in his chair.

We'd hung out every night for the past week, meeting and fucking all types of nameless women. In all honesty, at first, a part of me felt validated by what I had done. By going through with it and sleeping with other women, I felt like I was getting payback for Karen ripping my heart out and hurting me all these years.

To Will and Lou, this was living. At this stage in my life, it was exciting, but I didn't want this anymore. We used to do this type of stuff in college. They hadn't changed. This lifestyle wasn't for me anymore. I missed my family. I hadn't seen Karen or my kids the whole week.

The nameless stripper quickened her rhythm to break my drifting thoughts. Her deep light brown eyes were focused on me, and she looked determined to please me. Beads of sweat dripped down my forehead, my mouth was dry, and my body tensed up. I tried to will myself not to cum too quickly, tightly squeezing my shaft to cut off the sensation, but she quickly moved my hand away and used hers to jerk my dick up and down while she simultaneously sucked me off. I couldn't hold back any longer. I shouted, "Karen," and came in her mouth. She swallowed every drop and continued sucking on the head of my manhood to make me squirm.

"Really, dude? You got this badass stripper slobbering your knob, and you're calling out your wife's name?" Lou said, shaking his head. He hadn't missed a beat while screwing his stripper.

The stripper I was with got off her knees, straddled my lap, and said, "Don't worry. When I'm finished with him, he won't remember her name."

"Oh shit. That's what I'm talking about," Will said excitedly as he bit his bottom lip and slapped his stripper's ass.

"What's your name?" I asked her.

"You can call me Cinnamon, baby."

Cinnamon kissed my neck and stroked my dick to keep me hard. I was still sensitive from cumming, but she kept me turned on. Cinnamon's skin had the same cucumber-melon scent as Karen's, and she wore chocolate-brown lipstick, just like Karen. Her hair had a similar texture and smelled of coconut, like Karen's did. I dug into my shirt pocket and handed her a condom. She opened the wrapper with her teeth and slowly rolled the condom onto my dick. Cinnamon spread her thighs. Her eyes were closed as she took my manhood inside her. She gripped my shoulders and bounced rapidly on my hardness. I grabbed her ass and moved my hips upward. She leaned forward, drowning me with her huge breasts.

"Damn, baby," she moaned.

"Yeah, get that shit, Chris!" Lou yelled.

I was getting into it, but as I watched her face and saw she was enjoying it, I thought about Karen riding Raheem. I pictured her enjoying getting fucked like this stripper. I lifted her off me. Her eyes lit up. She gave me a sultry look as she licked her lips and caressed my arms. I guessed she was turned on by my strength.

I turned her around and took her from behind so I wouldn't see her face. I pounded her. Her ass vibrated heavily from the impact. Her skin took on a reddish glow. I felt the heat coming from her skin. The harder I fucked her, the more she enjoyed it. She held the top of the chair with one hand and massaged her clit with the other. Her hand worked energetically. Her knees shook, and her body writhed in pleasure. Her vagina tightened around me. Her moans of pleasure echoed off the high ceilings in the room as she came loudly. Her body went limp for a moment, but she gathered her composure and backed up onto my hardness. My palms were moist from our sweat. I grabbed her hair and came hard. I panted as I pulled up my pants. Cinnamon moved so I could sit down, and then she sat on my lap.

Will and Lou had finished banging their strippers sometime while I was fucking Cinnamon. They had enjoyed watching me have a good time.

"We're just getting started. You wasted years with Karen. While you were out being faithful, she was fucking other dudes," Lou said.

Cinnamon and the other strippers looked at each other. I knew what he was doing. He wanted me to stay angry. He wanted me to keep those thoughts alive so my conscience wouldn't eat me about all the women I'd slept with this week. Will and Lou were my boys. In their own twisted ways, I knew they thought they were helping me, but was this the solution to my problems? Would sleeping with other women in return negate the fact that Karen had been sleeping around for years? I felt lost.

I completed a long-ass day doing construction on a residential building on West Fifty-Seventh Street in Manhattan. My late-night partying with Will and Lou, along with my work schedule these past two weeks, had me exhausted.

Will and Lou didn't know how long I'd be staying with them, so they had put money together to get me some clothes and things they thought I might need so I could avoid stopping by my house and getting into another heated argument with Karen. But I had made it an absolute requirement that I talked to my kids every day. The first night I called them had been the hardest.

"Chris, can we please talk?" Karen had asked.

"I don't have anything to say to you right now. Just put the kids on the phone."

"When will you have something to say? You see, even after everything I said to you, you're still not listening to me—"

"This is why I'm not coming home. I don't want to fight. I just want some fucking peace until I can calm down and figure shit out."

Karen sucked her teeth. "Pops thinks you need to come home, and I agree," she said.

I sighed.

For a while, Pops had called me every day, but I had sent him straight to voice mail each time. I didn't feel like being chewed out over my decision to stay away. When he'd realized I wouldn't answer his calls, he'd resorted to texting me at least three times a day. He'd write things like "I raised you better than this, son. Be a man." And "A man handles his problems like a mature adult. He doesn't hide and cower from his issues like a child." One I always thought about was, "Your responsibilities are to those kids. Be the father I raised you to be."

"I'll come home when I'm ready. Put the girls on the phone," I told Karen.

"What if I say no? What if the only way you'll talk to our girls is if you come home?"

"Haven't you done enough damage? You being spiteful like that would only hurt me and the girls more. Just give them the phone."

There was a long pause. Finally, Karen called the girls to the phone.

"Girls, your dad is on the phone. He wants to talk to you two."

In the background, I heard the girls running excitedly to the phone.

"Daddy, when are you coming home?" Jocelyn asked.

"Soon, baby. Daddy has just been working a lot."

"We miss you, Daddy," Jaclyn said.

"I miss both of you too. I promise I'll be home soon. I want you both to know how much I love you."

"Love you too, Daddy," they said in unison.

"All right. I'll talk to you girls soon. Love you."

I ended the call.

Most nights went like that. Others ended with me hanging up after I talked to the girls, though Pops wanted to give me his two cents. I missed my kids like crazy. I missed my family in general. I had never wanted to be away from them like this. Karen and I had our problems, but I hadn't known that they were this bad and that it would come to this. I hated being away from them, but I was still embarrassed and upset and wasn't sure when I would go home.

While I still wasn't ready to go home, I knew I couldn't stay with Will and Lou anymore. That lifestyle wasn't for me. I didn't know if I'd go home, sleep in my car, or stay in a motel, but I knew I needed to get away from partying and having meaningless sex every night. So before I left for my construction job in Manhattan this morning, I thanked them for letting me stay, then packed the few belongings I had there and put them in my truck.

So, like I said, I was exhausted after putting in a full day's work on that residential building on West Fifty-Seventh Street. While I was stowing away the last of my tools, Nadine walked up to me.

"Hey, Chris," she said.

"What's up? Are you doing anything tonight?"

Nadine looked taken aback for a moment. "Nah. I'm free. What's up?"

"Do you want to get dinner with me?"

She nodded. "Sure. Where do you want to go?"

"How about Lucky's Famous Burgers on Twenty-Third Street?" I said.

"Sounds good."

Nadine followed me in her car to the restaurant. After searching for what felt like an eternity, I finally found parking and met her inside the restaurant. We ordered, and I treated her to dinner. While we were eating, we talked a little bit about work, but the conversation eventually got to the topic of what was going on in my life.

"Chris, you know I enjoy hanging out with you, but what's going on? Before today you never wanted to have dinner with me after work. What's the deal?"

I didn't know how to answer that question. She was right. In the past, we'd shared a quick snack at work, but I wouldn't have dinner with her. I'd thought it wasn't right, but I didn't know what to think anymore. Maybe I needed a friend, a female friend, who'd give me a woman's point of view. Will and Lou were great, but I needed a friend who wouldn't tell me to fuck my pain away. So I told her everything. When I finished, she held my hand and looked deeply in my eyes.

"Chris, despite everything, do you still love her?"

If she had asked me that question two weeks ago, there would have been no hesitation on my part, but after everything that had happened, I honestly wasn't sure anymore. Karen had hurt me deeper than anyone ever had. I didn't think I could ever again love and trust someone as blindly as I did her, but despite everything, I didn't hate her. Karen was the mother of my children. We had a history together. I knew it would be hard to forgive her. In my heart, I knew I loved her, but I wasn't sure if I could love her the way I had before she cheated on me.

After a few moments I said, "Yeah, I still love her."

"Then go back to her. Try to salvage what's left of your relationship."

"Do you think she was justified in cheating on me?"

"I don't think it's right for anyone to cheat, male or female. I was cheated on, and it devastated me. I wouldn't wish that pain on anyone."

"Thanks for listening, Nadine. I really appreciate it."

"Chris, you can talk to me anytime. I'm always here for you. You give me faith that there are still some great men out there."

Listening to Nadine gave me the strength to talk to Karen. She made it seem possible that we could work things out with our marriage. Nadine and I finished our meal, hugged, and said our good-byes.

I got a room for the night at the Americana Inn in Farmingdale. I didn't sleep well. I kept thinking of my conversation with Nadine. Talking to my children a few minutes a day wasn't cutting it anymore. I missed my kids, and even though I didn't want to admit it, I missed Karen. By five in the morning, I was up, showered, dressed, and headed back home to face my demons.

Karen

"I want my Daddy!" Jaclyn cried.

"Where's Daddy?" Jocelyn screamed.

Pops knelt down on the floor and picked them up. "Girls, I know you're upset. Daddy is a little busy at work. He should be home soon. He told me to tell you girls that he loves you," he said, trying to console them.

I was emotionally sapped. It had been two weeks since I'd seen Chris or heard from him. Pops had been a godsend. He'd been taking care of the kids while I worked.

Tonight I needed to relax. Pops had agreed to watch the kids while I hung out with my girls. Chloe was picking me up at the house, and at the appointed time, I got a text from her.

Hey, bitch face. I'm outside. Hurry up, so I don't have to fight with Chris's punk-ass daddy.

I looked out the living-room window and saw her red Acura TL parked in the driveway. She was using her vanity mirror to put on her eye shadow. I kissed Pops on the cheek, thanked him again for all his help, hugged the kids, and told them I'd see them in the morning. I then headed out for a night of hard drinking to calm my nerves.

"What's up, K?" Chloe asked when I got in the car and fastened my seat belt.

"Nothing. I'm still stressing over this Chris situation."

"Cheer the fuck up. What was he doing looking through your phone, anyway? You look for shit, you find shit."

"Whenever you're with a guy, you always snoop through their phones," I reminded Chloe.

"Yeah, but women are inquisitive by nature. Unless he's a bitch, he shouldn't have looked in your phone. Besides, most of the time, I'm bored with the guys, and I'm looking for a way to kick them to the curb, anyway."

We laughed.

"You should be happy Chris found out. Now you don't have to worry about hiding things," Chloe said gleefully.

"Does Chris piss you off that much? You always sound like you hate him," I replied.

"I don't hate him. I just don't feel he's the right man for you. Plus, when y'all first started dating, he told me that I didn't have the self-discipline to finish college, and that I should aspire to be more than a cashier at a grocery store."

"But you hated school and didn't finish. And you despise your job at the grocery store."

"Yeah, but it's bad enough I kind of feel like a failure. I didn't appreciate his bougie ass judging me. Besides, I'm head cashier at the store now." She chuckled.

"Well, excuse me, Miss Thang," I laughed.

"Seriously, K, have you considered that you cheated on him because he's not right for you? You want someone who's affectionate. You want someone who's going to compliment you and make you feel special. What if he's doing the best he can, but his best just isn't enough for you? Should you settle? Should you sacrifice your happiness because that's all he can give? Should he sacrifice his happiness by trying to be something he's not to make you happy? Love shouldn't be hard. If you feel it's too much work with someone, then you shouldn't be with them."

I didn't agree with everything she'd said, but there was some truth to her statement.

"All relationships take work. You'll never find everything you want in one person," I said.

"You can believe that shit if you want, but I'm looking for Mr. Right, and I'm not settling for Mr. Right Now."

I put my elbow on the armrest and my fist against my cheek and looked out the window. I thought about what Chloe had said as we made our way to Lindsey's place. What if Chris was doing the best he could do, but his best just wasn't enough for me? Should I settle? Should I sacrifice my happiness because that was all he could give? In my heart, I still believed Chris was the man for me, but I couldn't lie to myself. Those questions were still heavy on my mind.

When we got to Lindsey's, Lindsey, Judy, and Vivian met us at the door. Jeff was entertaining some of his coworkers and friends in the living room. He waved at us and then went back to laughing with his guests.

"Y'all ready to go?" Lindsey asked.

When everybody nodded, she said, "All right. Who's driving?"

"Not me," Chloe said.

"I came with Chloe," I said.

"I drive a two-seater," Judy laughed.

"My car is a wreck, and I'm low on gas," Vivian chimed in.

"You guys suck. I always drive," Lindsey pouted.

"You got a big truck, bitch," Chloe joked.

Lindsey smiled and rolled her eyes.

We walked out of Lindsey's house and piled in her Mercedes-Benz. As we headed to Webster Hall in the city, I told everybody about the horror that was my life.

"I know he's upset about finding everything out, but he's a douche for leaving you to deal with the kids by yourself," Judy said when I was done.

"He's just a douche, period," Vivian said.

Chloe and Vivian laughed together. Lindsey didn't say a word.

"Are you going to divorce him and get that alimony and child support money?" Vivian asked.

"I don't know if we're going that far yet," I said, feeling uncomfortable even thinking about us getting divorced.

"It's something you need to think about. If he wasn't giving you what you wanted *then*, what makes you think that after finding this out, he'd give you what you want *now*?" Judy asked.

"I don't know. I don't know what I want to do or what I want in life anymore. I wish I could just start over. I wish that Monday had never happened, and that this was all a bad dream," I said as tears welled up in my eyes.

"Wasn't Raheem better than Chris in bed, anyway? Forget Chris and stick with what was making you happy," Chloe said.

"He was good, but Raheem wasn't better than Chris. I enjoyed sex with Raheem, but Chris has always been the best. It was never about sex, though. I wanted passion. I wanted to feel appreciated and desired. Now I just feel stupid. All this shit is crashing down on me. I might lose my job. Chris hates me. I just can't right now . . ."

I broke down and wept. Chloe and Lindsey already knew everything, but while Judy and Vivian consoled me, I told them more about the drama at work, Tyrell's talk with Chris, Chris attacking Raheem, and my talk with Tyrell. My girls all tried in their own way to cheer me up.

"Your drinks are on me tonight," Judy offered.

"I'm going to find you a man tonight," Vivian said.

Chloe reached in my purse and pulled out my cell phone.

"What are you doing?" I asked.

"I'm texting Raheem to tell him to come out tonight. You need some dick bad."

I tried to snatch my phone away from Chloe, but she maneuvered her hand so I couldn't grab the phone, then finished her text and sent it to him.

"I don't need any dick right now. My stupidity and *dick* are what got me into this mess," I sighed.

"What's done is done." Chloe shrugged.

My phone chimed, letting me know I had a text message. Chloe read it.

"See, he said he's going to come out tonight. You have so much fun when he's around. Take this time to enjoy yourself and stop worrying about Chris," Chloe said, handing me my phone.

"No. I'm not dealing with this shit tonight. I just want to have a drama-free time," I insisted.

I texted Raheem back.

That was my sister that texted you with my phone. With everything that's going on, I think it's best if we don't meet up at the club.

I got a reply from Raheem right away.

You seem to be having a problem with people getting hold of your phone and messaging me.

I didn't know how I should respond to that, but I needed to drive the point home that I didn't want to see him.

It won't happen anymore. I promise you that. Stay home.

He wrote me back right away.

I want to see you tonight. We can put all the other shit behind us. I just want to have a good time with you.

I knew that was out of the question.

No. I need to fix my life right now, and seeing you won't help either of us.

He texted me right back, refusing to give up.

You're saying that now. Once you see me in person, you'll feel differently. I'll see you there.

I kept my next text short and to the point, hoping that would dissuade him.

No, seriously, don't come.

He didn't respond this time. I sighed and hoped he wouldn't show.

Moments later we pulled up to Webster Hall.

"I'll drop y'all off here. Karen, can you stay with me while I look for parking?" Lindsey said.

Usually, Lindsey had no problem finding parking on her own. This had to mean she wanted to talk to me alone.

"Sure," I said.

Judy, Vivian, and Chloe hopped out and immediately started flirting with some guys standing in front of the club. Lindsey drove around the block and double-parked. After shutting off the engine, she turned to me.

"Karen, you need to work things out with Chris."

"I don't know what to do. I just want to be happy. I wish I had what you and Jeff have," I told her.

"You can't have what Jeff and I have, because you're not me, and Chris is not Jeff. I wish I could have what you have. I want to be a mother and have children more than anything in the world. I might never get the opportunity, and it's not a major concern to Jeff. He loves me, but he likes the freedom of not having to be responsible for kids. I want kids more than I want jewelry, trips, or a big house."

I saw the sincerity in her eyes. Maybe I had been so busy dwelling on what I didn't have that I'd stopped appreciating what I did.

She went on. "The truth is, we're never satisfied. We always want what we don't have. I want your life, and you want mine. You need to put a lot of thought into what's really important to you and what makes you happy. What might be good for me might not be good for you. We all gave you advice tonight, but you have to decide what's best for you."

"As always, thanks for being the voice of reason, Lindsey."

"I'll always have your back, bestie. You now that."

We hugged while tears streamed down our faces.

We circled around for a while, found parking, and then met the girls inside the club. Chloe was sitting on a guy's lap, while Vivian was laughing with another guy. Judy was standing by the bar, waiting for drinks. Lindsey and I walked to the bar and commenced our night of heavy drinking and dancing.

Raheem arrived around eleven. I'd spent the past few hours trying to drink my troubles away and praying he wouldn't show, so I was smashed when he got there. Lindsey had stopped drinking a while ago, because she was the designated driver, and so she watched Raheem like a hawk. She had always been protective of me, and I loved her for that.

"Hey, Raheem," Chloe slurred from her perch on that guy's lap.

"What's up, Chloe?" Raheem said.

"My sister here needs some dick! You think you can help her out?"

"Chloe!" I shouted, feeling embarrassed.

"Don't be ashamed of it." Chloe turned and addressed the guy whose lap she was sitting on. "I'm going to get some dick tonight too. Right, buddy?"

He grinned and nodded.

"She doesn't speak for me. Dick is the last thing I want tonight," I said.

"Is that right?" Raheem asked, looking at me hungrily.

"She's fine, Chloe. Karen's right. That's not what she needs right now," Lindsey said. She was sitting right next to me at the bar.

Raheem frowned at Lindsey. Chloe shrugged her shoulders and went back to flirting with her new guy. I downed three more tequila shots, and then Raheem playfully pulled me to the dance floor. Surprisingly, he hadn't had a single drink.

In my absence, Judy asked Lindsey to keep her company after she found out the guy who'd been hitting on her all night was married.

I had drunk way too much. I was at the point where I could barely stand, so dancing was out of the question.

"Let me take you home," Raheem offered as we stood on the edge of the dance floor.

I was so drunk I would've agreed to anything at that point. I laughed and nodded yes. On wobbly legs, I stumbled my way to the entrance. Lindsey must have seen me heading out with Raheem, because she met me at the coat check and grabbed my arm.

"Where are you going?" she asked.

"Oh, leave her alone, Lindsey. Let these two adults enjoy their night," Chloe said. She had followed Lindsey to the coat check.

Raheem winked at Chloe and took my arm. Lindsey reached for me, but at that very moment, Vivian grabbed her hand and pulled her to the dance floor. Lindsey looked concerned as she gazed back at me. I was so drunk that I felt like I was watching a movie. Before I could even comprehend what was going on, Raheem and I were picking up his truck from the valet.

Raheem put me in his truck and drove us somewhere. When we got there, he came around to the passenger side of the car, opened the door, took me by the hand, and pulled my wobbly body from the seat. I was way too drunk to take in my surroundings, but the next thing I knew, I was being placed on a bed. Then my clothes were being taken off. I heard the clank of his belt as his pants fell around his ankles. I heard him rip open the wrapper of a condom.

I felt Raheem grab my ass and maneuver me until I was positioned the way he wanted me, with my ass in the air and my face mashed into the bedsheets. I struggled to angle my head to the side so I could breathe. Suddenly, I felt the fullness of his dick push inside me. I didn't complain. I didn't want sex right now, but I didn't fight it. I was too emotionally exhausted to fight. Even in my inebriated state, I knew this would be a life-altering mistake.

"Can . . . we . . . just . . . talk? I need to . . . talk right now," I said, slurring my words.

"Go ahead. Talk," Raheem said as he continued to pump inside me.

Raheem turned me over and laid me on my back. He grabbed my knees and forced my legs apart. I thought about Chris and how my life was so chaotic right now. I kept hearing Chris's words in my head.

You're taking advice from lonely bitches who can't find men for themselves? The only friend you have with any intelligence is Lindsey. The rest of them are fucking miserable, but you'll take advice from them, right?

Was Chloe really happy? Were Judy and Vivian really happy? They had all slept with their fair share of men, but their relationships didn't last. While I was envious of Lindsey, she had confessed that she was envious of me.

My buzz was wearing off now. And Raheem panting and sweating on top of me was making me feel filthy.

"Can we talk, Raheem?"

Raheem just grunted, then roughly turned me around, pressed my face into the pillow, and fucked me from behind again.

"We are talking," he said as he sped up his rhythm.

He wrapped my hair around his hand, shoved my face deeper into the pillow, and pounded me relentlessly. His grip on my hair tightened so much that my scalp started to burn. I screamed from the pain, but the louder I screamed, the harder he fucked me. I grabbed the bed-sheets, gripped them tightly, and my fingers clawed the mattress. The headboard slammed repeatedly against the wall.

I felt disgusting, useless, and ashamed. I felt like a whore. Tears streamed down my face. Raheem didn't care; he continued pounding me. Reality finally hit me. I loved the illusion that Raheem cared about me, but the truth was, I was just a piece of ass to him.

In one swift motion, Raheem pulled out of me and turned me over.

"Open your fucking mouth," he yelled.

I shook my head no.

Raheem forced my mouth open, ripped the condom off, and shoved his dick in my mouth. I struggled to pull my face back and push him away, but he batted my hands away with his right hand and squeezed my jaw with his left, forcing my mouth to stay open. Raheem let out a low groan through his clenched teeth, fisted his cock, and forcefully jerked himself until his cock erupted and a stream of hot, sticky cum shot onto my face. I twisted my head to avoid getting any more of it in my mouth. Not wanting to swallow, I closed my eyes and mouth while he continued to pump his dick and finish cumming all over my face. Most of the cum was around my mouth, but some got in my hair and on my chest. I almost threw up, but I managed to grab tissues from the box on the nightstand to spit the warm cum into. I wiped off my face and hair and then threw the tissues in the garbage bin next to the bed. I had never felt so disrespected.

"Turn that ass around and give me some more of that sweet pussy," Raheem yelled, shoving me back down on the bed.

He fucked me raw without a condom throughout the night. I let him have his way with me. When he finally collapsed, exhausted, on the bed, I turned away and pulled the covers over myself, feeling ashamed, used, and humiliated. I curled up in the fetal position and cried myself to sleep.

The next morning, I woke up to find Raheem in my bedroom, closing one of Chris's dresser drawers.

"What are you doing?" I asked, squinting in the early morning light. My head was pounding, and my throat was dry.

"I can't find my socks. I was going to take a pair of your punk-ass husband's."

I looked around the room as it dawned on me that we had fucked in my house . . . in my bed.

"What's wrong?" Raheem smirked.

"What do you mean, what's wrong? I can tell by the smug-ass expression on your face that you know exactly what's wrong. Why the fuck did you bring me here?"

"I asked you if you wanted me to take you home, and you said yes. I looked at the address on your driver's license, plugged it into my GPS, and took you home. You handed me the keys to your door, so I thought everything was cool and you were inviting me in."

"You know damn well I was drunk. Why the fuck would you do that? You know I don't do shit in my house. I would never sleep with you in the same bed that Chris and I share."

Raheem shrugged. "Oops. My bad," he said, chuckling.

I covered my face with my hands and shook my head. I wanted to hide under the covers and pretend none of this shit was real. "Oh my God! This can't be happening right now," I moaned.

"Who was that old guy watching TV on your couch last night?" Raheem asked.

My heart felt like it was going to explode. Pops had babysat the girls last night. I prayed he hadn't seen Raheem taking me to my bedroom.

"What happened when you saw him?" I asked nervously. I stood up. My hands trembled as I grabbed my robe off the floor and put it on.

"I saw him. I said hello and told him not to worry, that I'd make sure I put you to bed."

I looked at him as tears streamed down my face. Last night we'd been *loud*. I was so ashamed of myself. I didn't know how I would ever face Pops again. I was married to his son, and he had heard me have sex with another man in our bed, in our house, while our kids slept a few doors down. I wanted to die. The air reeked of the stench of our late-night sex. I dug in my closet and found some strong vanilla-scented candles to try to mask the aroma. I lit them, but who was I fooling? I was sure Pops already knew what had gone down last night.

"Oh yeah, that candle will definitely cover the sex in the air in here." He laughed.

"Get out! Get the fuck out. How could you do this to me? Why would you bring me here? Why would you fuck me in my house? Why would you talk to Chris's father?"

I slid down onto my knees and buried my face in my hands.

Raheem had used me, but I was furious with myself for letting it happen.

"Next time, maybe your husband will think twice before attacking someone when their back is turned. I hope his father tells him what it sounds like when a real man fucks you."

I jumped up and rushed him. Swinging wildly, I punched him in the chest and face. Raheem grabbed my arms and tossed me onto the bed. I fell back onto the sheets, then slid down to the floor, taking the comforter and two pillows with me.

"Get the fuck out! You're ruining my life," I cried.

"Calm it down, drama queen. I didn't do shit to you. You did this shit to yourself," Raheem said coldly.

"I don't interrupt your family life. You don't see me calling your wife or going to your house," I retorted.

"Truth be told, I don't have a wife for you to call."

"What?"

"I've been divorced for over five years. I didn't want you to get all clingy on me and think we'd be more than what we were. All I really wanted from you was a steady piece of ass." Raheem sneered.

That hurt. He had played me like I was some silly teenage girl. He had had me believing he loved me, but everything he'd said was lies and bullshit. He had hurt me, but I was not going to cry. He didn't deserve my tears.

He opened my bedroom door and made his way downstairs. I slowly followed behind him. Pops was sitting at the kitchen table, eating a bowl of cereal, watching Raheem and me. I couldn't bring myself to look at him. I was ashamed of myself. Raheem smiled and gave Pops a nod. Pops's eyes narrowed. He slapped the table and stood up. He stomped toward Raheem, ready to kick his ass. I quickly ran in front of Pops to slow him down.

Raheem bolted out the door, got into his truck, and sped off.

"Who was that?" Pops yelled.

"Pops, please let me explain—"

"You disrespected me, my son, yourself, this house, and your family. I love my grandchildren more than anything in this world, but I will not allow you to blatantly disrespect my son. From now on, you're on your own. I will no longer be your babysitter when you want to cheat on my son."

I held on to his arm, but he pulled away from me.

"Pops, please . . . It's not like that. I was drunk. Raheem tricked me—"

"I heard you two last night. It sounded like you enjoyed being tricked. When you two came in the house, you were laughing and kissing on him. It didn't look like there was a lot of resistance on your part." Pops looked at me with such disdain.

"Pops, I was drunk—"

"That's no excuse. You're an adult. You're responsible for your actions. You know your limits. If you're drinking so much that you can't control yourself whenever you go out, then you have a problem and should get professional help."

I hated being chastised. I hated it when Chris did it, and I didn't appreciate Pops doing it now. I had to take a deep breath before I said something I'd regret. Everything was falling apart. With Chris being MIA and with my troubles at work, I needed Pops more than ever to be around for the kids.

"Pops, please. The kids need you right now. I don't know when Chris is coming back."

At first, he looked like he was softening, but he went right back to being rigid. "No. I'll visit them as much as I can. I'll even pick them up from school from time to time, but as of now, make other arrangements, because you and Chris are on your own. I have my own problems to deal with."

I knew there was no reaching him. The only thing I could do was beg Pops not to tell Chris about last night.

"I'll make other arrangements, Pops, but please, can you not tell Chris what happened last night?" I begged. "I'll talk to him and work on our marriage, but if he finds out about this, it will ruin any chances of us getting back together."

"I don't know. After what I witnessed last night, I don't know if it's best to work things out. It's one thing if you actively work on improving your relationship. It's another to just want to stay married to my son because it's comfortable for you."

Something in my face must have changed his mind, because Pops sighed and shook his head.

"I'm not going to tell Chris. I'm going to put the responsibility on your conscience and decency as a human being to tell him yourself."

He picked up his leather veteran's jacket and put it on. I could barely look him in his eyes. I couldn't imagine what he thought of me.

"Pops, wait." I hugged him, but he didn't say anything. "Thanks for everything. My whole world is going up in flames—"

"Spare me your bullshit! I don't have time for your crocodile tears."

He pulled away from me and walked to the door. When he opened it, Chris was standing there with his keys in his hand.

"Hey, Pops," Chris said.

"Son," he replied, then walked past him and out the door.

I stood there, shocked to see that Chris was home. Of all the days for him to return, it had to be today. I prepared myself for another drama-filled morning.

Chris

"What's his problem? Is he still pissed because I haven't been here?" I dropped my duffel bag and backpack on the floor.

Karen hesitated to answer. She nodded, ran to me, and hugged me. "He's a little disappointed in you, but I don't care. I'm just happy you're home."

I was tentative at first, but I warmed up and accepted her embrace.

"I missed you so much, Chris. I'm so sorry. I was stupid. I don't want to lose you."

As angry as I was with Karen, there was a part of me that didn't want to pull away, so I let her hold me.

"The kids are still sleeping. I want to talk to you upstairs while we have some alone time," she said.

"Okay."

We went upstairs to our bedroom. The comforters and pillows were on the floor. Karen quickly picked them up.

"I had a hard time sleeping last night," she said.

It showed. She looked worn out. Her puffy eyes and her hoarse voice were telltale signs. Karen started talking as soon as I sat down on the bed. I could tell she was nervous.

"These two weeks you've been gone have been hell for me. I'm so sorry for hurting you, Chris. I was stupid. I was selfish. And I didn't know what I had until you were gone. I'll do whatever it takes to make us work. I never want to lose you again," she pleaded.

She had so much guilt and remorse in her eyes, I couldn't help but kiss her. Her tongue tasted like she'd been drinking. I wondered if she'd been drinking alone in our bedroom because she was depressed that I wasn't here.

Karen wrapped her arms around my neck, and we kissed passionately. I'd slept with a lot of women while I was away from home, but I had longed for Karen. I loved her, even after everything she'd done. She was the only woman I wanted. I opened her robe as she held my face and kissed me frantically. I kicked off my boots, took off my belt, unbuttoned my blue jeans, and pulled them off. When Karen took off her robe, I stared at her naked body. So many thoughts flooded my mind. Her thick, shapely legs had me turned on, but I kept thinking about her with Raheem. I kept imagining them fucking. I pushed the thoughts away, lifted her up, and placed her gently on the bed. I spread her thighs wide and put my mouth on her love. I wanted to savor her.

I licked her from the bottom of her vagina to the top of her clit. I sucked on it, basking in the sounds of her moans and groans. Hearing her pant and seeing her shudder as she came made me feel like a man. It felt good knowing I could still please my wife. My hands roamed her body. I sucked on her neck and rubbed her thigh. Karen moaned again and reached for my hardness. She locked her legs behind me and pushed me inside her. We made love unprotected and uninhibited. I thrust hard inside her as she coated me with her juices. Our grunts only added to our frantic, emotionally driven sex. I searched her eyes for happiness, but what I found was distance. She looked as if she was just going through the motions. She stopped me.

"Let me get on top, baby. I miss riding you," she said.

Karen maneuvered on top of me and rode me wildly. Her head hung back as she held on to my chest. Karen bit her bottom lip and rocked her hips steadily on top of me. I could tell she was relishing the moment.

"Mmm. That's it, baby. Ahhh. Mmm-hmm. Oh yeah," she moaned.

I watched her enjoying herself. The sunlight coming through the window glinted off Karen's wedding ring and hit my face. Knowing that she had probably worn that ring every time those other men fucked her infuriated me. All I could think about was her moaning the same things to Raheem that she did to me. I imagined him fucking her and pictured her enjoying it the same way. I wondered if they had worn protection or if she'd been free spirited about it, like she was with me right now. Before, when all I'd had were suspicions, I hadn't had a real face to picture in my mind. But that had all changed. Raheem was *real*. I'd seen his face. I knew he'd fucked her countless times right under my nose. I didn't know if she was *in love* with him, but I did know that she *loved him*, and that hurt. What made things even worse was I knew that there was another guy besides Raheem. I gradually lost my erection. I went limp inside her. Karen noticed and looked surprised.

"Are you okay, baby?" she asked.

I wasn't okay. I felt like a fucking loser. My wife had me, my marriage had failed me, and now my body was failing me. Karen shifted off me, then stroked my manhood and went down on me. She revived that manly part. I wished she could revive my pride. When I was hard again, Karen slid under me. This time I was more attentive; I tried to focus on the act at hand. Karen's legs were wrapped firmly around my back, and her eyes were closed tight. I opened her legs wide and pushed her knees back until they were by her ears and almost touched the headboard. I dove deeper inside her with each stroke.

"Mmm. Damn, baby! Yes! Give it to me," she moaned.

When I thrust harder, she winced and closed her eyes.

"Look at me," I ordered.

"Ooh, baby, I love it. Don't stop."

"Karen, open your eyes and look at me," I demanded.

"Damn, baby."

"Look at me!" I shouted.

Karen opened her eyes. She looked scared. I didn't want her thinking of Raheem or Tyrell while we were making love; I needed to know she was here with me. I increased my pace. Every time Karen tried to close her eyes, I rammed my dick in her harder. She panted; her pussy pulsated on my manhood. Sexy moans and groans escaped her. Karen reached for a pillow, clutched it tightly to her face, and moaned into it to muffle herself, trying not to wake the kids.

Her body stiffened and then shook violently as she came.

"Oh my God! Cum inside me, baby. I want you to cum inside me!"

I didn't want to cum. As I tried to fight the inevitable, I trembled. I didn't want to enjoy it, but then my floodgates opened. I didn't care that we were fucking raw. I didn't pull out. I needed to feel like *a man*. I needed to feel like she was *my* woman. I held on to her shoulders, pushed myself deep inside her, and let my cum spew into her. When I was spent, I fell down onto the bed, exhausted. Karen rolled over onto her side. There were no words spoken or loving embraces. Silence engulfed the room. Now that our passion was sated, reality hit us, and our problems came back to the surface.

Karen reached out to touch me, but I pulled away. I didn't want to be touched. She looked hurt. She shook her head and stood up, with her head down. Her voice was choked with emotion when she announced, "I'm going to take a shower."

I nodded.

Karen picked out black boy shorts and a black bra from her dresser drawer. "I love you, Chris."

I didn't respond. I just stared at her.

"I understand if you can't say it back to me yet . . . Can you?"

"I'm trying, Karen, but we can't just slap a Band-Aid on our bullet wound of a relationship and think things are going to be patched up and fixed. Fucking me doesn't negate that you were fucking other men."

She looked hurt. We stared at each other for a while. Then, with her head down, Karen slowly walked into our bathroom. When I heard the water start to run in the shower, I sat up against the headboard. I was torn. I had enjoyed making love to my wife, but I didn't like envisioning other men fucking her. I decided to surprise Karen in the shower. I got up and went to get some fresh underwear. I opened my dresser drawer and saw a folded piece of paper. I picked it up and opened it. Inside was a used condom. I couldn't believe my eyes as I read the note.

Your wife loved this dick! Ask your old man how it sounds when she gets fucked properly. Call me when you see this so I can give you some pointers.
Yours truly, Raheem

I started to hyperventilate. The room spun. My hands shook. The condom had been in my dresser, which meant that Raheem had been here.

Ask your old man how it sounds when she gets fucked properly. Did Pops know? Did he fuck my wife in my house, in my bed, while my father was here? Where were my kids when this was happening? I needed answers now. I grabbed my phone out of my jeans, scrolled through my recent calls, and found Raheem's number. I called him.

"What's up, bitch?" Raheem answered.

"You sound real tough on the phone. Why don't we meet up so I can fuck you up again?"

"I got something for you. I figured I'd fuck you up with this instead. Hold on. I'm gonna send you something."

What can he possibly send me? I thought.

A few seconds later I received a text with a video. I swallowed; sweat dripped from my forehead.

"Go ahead. I'll hold. Watch the video," Raheem said confidently.

My heart beat wildly as I pressed PLAY. Hatred and rage coursed through my body as I watched Raheem fuck my wife in the same bed I'd made love to her countless times. I heard the same moans and groans that she'd made with me. I watched him peel off the condom and cum all over her face and mouth. My stomach turned. He was right. He'd inflicted more pain with this video than any punch or kick could ever deliver.

"Did you finish it? It was good, right? I left the condom in the drawer for your bitch ass," he said.

"Fuck you!" I yelled.

"Oh, and just so you know, the rest of the night, I fucked her raw. Don't worry. I'm done with her. I hope you didn't kiss that bitch today. You wouldn't want to taste the remnants of my dick in your mouth, would you?" Raheem laughed.

"Fuck you! Fuck you! Fuck you!" I yelled until I was hoarse.

"Checkmate, bitch!" He laughed and ended the call.

I hurriedly put on my clothes. My first thoughts were to just get the fuck out of there, but I needed answers.

I put my phone in my pocket, then trod heavily to the closed bathroom door. The humidity from her shower seeped under the door. I kicked the door so hard, it flew off the hinges. Karen screamed, backed away from me, and slipped in the shower. She cowered in fear as I stood over her.

"I can't fucking believe you! Did you fuck him in our house? In our bed?"

Karen was terrified. She sat in a corner of the shower, shaking. "Chris, please! Wait! I can explain—"

"Explain?" I yanked her up off the shower floor, my grip tight on her arms. "Explain?"

"Chris, please listen to me. I was drunk. He took advantage of me. I never would've done that on purpose. I love you."

"He took advantage of you?" I yelled.

I let her go, then pulled out my phone and showed her the video. Karen covered her mouth.

"It doesn't look like he was taking advantage of you. It looks like . . . it looks like . . . you fucking enjoyed it. How could you do this to me? How could you disrespect me like this in our home?"

I put my phone back in my pants pocket and grabbed her again. I shook her vigorously.

"Answer me. Haven't you humiliated me enough? Why do you want to hurt me? What more can you take from me?"

"Chris, please . . . You're hurting me."

Karen tried to free herself, but my grip was unyielding. Suddenly, I heard a knock on our bedroom door.

"Mommy, Daddy, what's going on?" Jocelyn yelled.

"Daddy, why are you yelling?" Jaclyn asked, concerned.

"Let me go, Chris," Karen shouted.

I released her. She put on her robe, ran to the bedroom door, and opened it.

"Girls, Daddy and Mommy are just talking loud. It's nothing to worry about. Go downstairs and watch TV. We'll come down soon," Karen explained. Her voice was shaky, but she tried her best to sound calm.

"Okay," Jaclyn said, then led her sister down the hallway.

I walked out of the bathroom and sat on the edge of the bed. Karen sat next to me. I got up. I didn't want her near me.

"Tell me exactly what happened. I want to know how you could fuck another man in my bed while my father and our kids were home."

Karen took a deep breath. She crossed her arms over her chest and looked at the floor. "I was drunk . . . Raheem asked if he could take me home—"

"Whoa, whoa, whoa. Hold up. Where were you, and why were you with him in the first place?"

"I was at a club in Manhattan. Um . . . Webster Hall. Chloe saw I was upset with all the drama that's been going on with you and me, and—"

"And she thought it was best to bring the root of the fucking problem out with you guys? Real fucking smart."

"Chris, please. Chloe sent him a text asking him to meet us at the club. I had way too much to drink. He got our address from my driver's license and took me here. I honestly didn't know what was going on. This morning I woke up and realized we were here. Your father helped me out last night and watched the girls, because he knew I was depressed with everything that was going on with you. Don't be mad at your father. It wasn't like Pops wasn't angry too. When he saw Raheem, he was ready to kick his ass this morning."

I had a knot in my stomach. I couldn't believe Pops had heard Karen having sex with another man. I tried to think.

"If Chloe and all your friends knew you were that drunk, why did they let you go home with him?" I asked.

Karen was wringing her hands. She stopped, stared at her wedding band, and didn't answer. Her face was filled with shame. At that moment, I hated her. How could she have cheated on me again? How could she have let this happen?

"I can't do this shit anymore . . . I'm done. I want a divorce." I shocked myself when the words left my lips.

Karen stood up and got right in front of me, with tears streaming down her face. When she hugged me, I gently removed her arms from my waist.

"No, Chris, you don't mean that. We can make this work."

"No we can't."

"Chris, we can. Please don't do this right now. Give me a chance."

"I came back here today to give you a fucking chance, and I found out you're guzzling fucking cum from other men in our bed when our kids are home."

I walked to the bedroom door with my head down.

"Where are you going?" Karen asked.

"Away from you."

I opened our bedroom door and ran down the steps. Karen followed after me, crying hysterically.

"Please don't leave me again, Chris!"

I ignored her and grabbed my duffel bag and backpack. I stomped out of the house and slammed the door behind me. Everything happened for a reason, and this proved what Will and Lou had been telling me all along: Karen and I just weren't right for each other.

I sat in my truck, not knowing where to go. After a few minutes, I pulled out my cell phone and dialed a number.

"Pops, I need to talk to you," I said when he picked up.

"I'm working, boy. If you want to talk to me, you can help me at this job site and talk to me while we work."

Pops gave me the address where he was working in Queens. When I got there, he looked at my expression, then gave me a sledgehammer to use to break down a wall while he took measurements for the Jacuzzi he was installing.

"Pops, Karen slept—"

He held up a hand to stop me. "We'll talk about your problems after our job is done. Right now, we work. Focus your energy on that."

I faced the wall; my head swirled with so many thoughts. How could Karen do this to me again? How could she fuck Raheem in our bed? If Pops knew what was going on, why didn't he say something or stop them? How could she embarrass me in front of my dad like that? I couldn't take it anymore. I lashed out, taking all my frustrations and anger out as I swung the sledgehammer as hard as I could against the wall. Plaster and other debris flew across the room.

Bam! Bam! Bam!

The video of Raheem and Karen replayed in my head. I heard her moaning and saw his hands wrapped around her waist.

Bam! Bam! Bam!

I hit the wall harder and harder, until I was covered in sweat. I saw him shove his dick in her mouth. I saw him fucking her raw. I heard him laughing on the phone. It was all too much for me. My chest tightened. I couldn't breathe. My knees buckled and I sank down.

"Boy, get up," my father yelled.

"I need to talk to you, Pops. I don't know what to do. I can't eat, I can't sleep, and I can't—"

"Get up off your damn knees! I raised a son, not a daughter. Stop talking soft."

I couldn't take it anymore. I needed him, and all he cared about was me talking soft. I turned away from him and punched the wall.

"God damn it. Can you turn it off for one fucking day, Pops? One fucking day? I don't need a soldier right now. I need my father."

"Boy, have you lost your damn mind? Don't you cuss at me! Calm down. I raised you to be tougher than this."

"I can't be like you. I can't be withdrawn and just *deal* with things. Why can't you just listen and try to understand what I'm going through? Sometimes you act more like a robot than a person. When Mom passed, you didn't even shed a tear. You stood up straight and consoled everyone else when it was you who should have mourned the most."

The expression on his face showed me that my words had hit him.

"When your mother died, I cried more than anyone. I just didn't do it in front of you. I tried the best I could not to have any outward display of emotions in front of you. You didn't need to see me when I was weak. I needed to have a level head and be strong for both of us. I needed to show you how a man handles his problems."

"I needed sympathy and compassion too, Dad."

"Your mother gave you that."

"My mother wasn't alive anymore. When she passed, I needed those things from you too." I shook my head. My emotions brought me back to my present problems with Karen. "I did everything I was supposed to with Karen, Pops. I was faithful. I was loyal. I was responsible. I gave her everything, and it still wasn't enough."

His expression softened. He put down his tape measure and helped me up from the floor. He walked over to his lunch cooler, pulled out a cold soda, and handed it to me.

"Son, I'm going to tell you a story that I hope will help you. There were times when I was deployed and engaged in combat—"

"Pops, please *talk* to me. No talks of the marines or combat. Just talk to me. Father and son."

"Chris, this is who I am. I can't turn it off. This story has a point, so hear me out. When I was in combat, things were chaotic. I didn't know if that day would be

my last. I saw some of my best friends die in front of me.
There was nothing I could do. In those moments, I was
scared, alone, and angry. I didn't have time to mourn
or get consumed by all the horrors that were around me.
The war was still going on. I had to keep fighting, or I
wouldn't make it. My point to you, son, is that right now
your life is chaotic. You feel alone and scared about what
the future holds. You're hurting, you're in pain, but you
can't let it consume you. You have to keep fighting. The
war is still going on."

He hugged me. I could probably count on one hand
how many times he'd done that in my lifetime. It felt
awkward, but I welcomed the warm embrace.

"I know I'm hard on you, Chris. I'm tough on you and
expect so much only because I want you to be a better
man than me."

I sat down on a stepladder. I closed my eyes and
rubbed my temples.

"Why didn't you tell me what happened, Pops? Why
didn't you tell me she brought a guy to the house?"

I reached in my pocket for my phone, scrolled through
my messages, and showed him the video Raheem had
sent me. Pops grunted and turned his head away. The
look of disgust on his face showed me he was upset and
understood my pain.

"Son, I try not to get involved in your marriage. This
hurts me too."

"What happened, Pops? I want to hear it from you. I
heard her side of the story, but I don't know if I can
believe anything she says anymore."

Pops sighed like it hurt him to tell me. He picked up
his tape measure and worked while he talked. "Karen
told me what happened between you two. While you
were gone, she was stressed over taking care of the kids
by herself and dealing with work."

"Work," I scoffed. "Did she tell you she might lose her job? She was sleeping with another guy there too."

"No. I didn't ask, and she didn't tell. I gave her a break from the kids last night and told her I'd watch them while she spent time with her friends. If I had known she was going to use her free time like this, I wouldn't have told her to go out with them. When Karen and that man came stumbling into your house last night, drunk, I wanted to kill both of them. I was sitting on the couch, with your daughters asleep next to me, when the man said hello. My first thoughts were to stomp his guts out.

"I stood up, and I looked at your children sleeping peacefully on the sofa. I didn't want your children to see their mother in that state. I didn't want them to see me fighting a man in your house. I didn't know where you were or when you were coming back. I couldn't risk being arrested and being away from my grandchildren. I took a deep breath and had faith that Karen wouldn't be crazy enough to disrespect either of us in your house. When she did, it took everything in my being not to go in that bedroom and hurt both of them, but I had to keep myself together for the sake of your kids."

"Well, this is the straw that broke the camel's back," I said. "I'm done with her. We're getting a divorce."

"Son, do you want to be a man who has children, or do you want to be a father? They're not the same."

I sighed. "Pops, you know I love my kids. I'll always be a good father to them."

"Getting a divorce will affect that. Do you want to see your kids whenever you want or when it's convenient for Karen? Going through a divorce will turn you into a glorified babysitter."

"Karen is a lot of things, but she wouldn't use the kids like that."

"Divorces are never civil. They get ugly. I have seen many of my marine buddies think the same way you do right now, and they got a rude awakening once they went through their divorce. When you're 'seeing your children,' she'll be out dating other men. Would you be okay with that? Would you like having another man, possibly the same man she brought to the house last night, around your kids more than you are? Do you want to miss out on special occasions and milestones because it's not your time to see the kids? You need to work things out for the sake of your children and yourself. You don't want them to grow up in a broken home."

I thought about what he'd said. While I wouldn't want any of the things he'd mentioned, I couldn't see myself forgiving Karen after everything that had happened.

"I love my kids, but I can't keep them happy if I can't make myself happy. Karen cheated on me countless times, and I can't be in a loveless marriage. I'm getting a divorce."

"You know I'm not a believer in that option, but I'll support you, son. And after these latest events, that might be for the best."

"Do you mind if I stay with you for a while?"

"I know you're in pain, son, but no. You can't keep leaving your children behind."

"If I take them with me, can I stay with you?"

Pops looked uncomfortable. "Fine. If you bring them, you can stay for a week, tops. After that, you can work on getting your house in order."

"No problem. Thanks, Pops."

We continued to work and talk. After I had finished working with him, I headed home to get my children.

PART THREE

Things Fall Apart

Karen

My daughters were playing with a small blue ball in the living room. Jocelyn kept throwing it against the hallway wall. As I sat on the couch, I held a glass of Hennessy in one hand while I pressed the palm of my other hand against my forehead. My migraine was killing me. I still had a hangover and shouldn't be drinking, but fuck it. I needed it. Listening to the constant bouncing of the ball only made my headache worse.

"Jocelyn, stop bouncing that damn ball in here before you break something."

"No!" she said defiantly.

I set my glass down on the coffee table, stood up, and walked over to her. "What did you say, little girl? I know you're not telling me no."

Jocelyn kept bouncing the ball, ignoring me. My nostrils flared. I grabbed her by her shirt and pulled her close to me.

"When I tell you to stop doing something once, you stop doing it. I'm not going to repeat myself again. Do you understand me?"

Jocelyn looked away from me and asked, "Where did Daddy go? Why did you make him leave again?"

I didn't need this right now. Between everything that was going on with Chris and her acting up, I felt like ripping my hair out.

"I want Daddy," Jaclyn chimed in.

I put my head down and massaged the back of my neck. I had no idea where Chris was.

"Why did Daddy leave again? Why were you yelling at each other this morning?" Jocelyn asked.

They were too young to understand what was going on. I was distraught, ashamed, and I couldn't hold myself together. I sat back down on the couch and put my head in my hands. "What's wrong, Mommy?" Jocelyn asked.

"I'm not feeling well, babies. Daddy went to get Mommy some medicine."

Seeing the tears in my eyes, Jocelyn apologized and hugged me. "I'm sorry, Mommy. I miss Daddy a lot."

"When will he be back?" Jaclyn asked as she sat next to me on the couch and patted my arm.

Tears filled my eyes. I could only shrug my shoulders. My daughters were young, but they weren't stupid. I knew they sensed something was wrong. I needed to talk to someone. I had to get things off my chest before I lost it. I sent the girls to their room to play. Then I called Lindsey.

"What's up, girl?" Lindsey said when she answered the phone.

"I need you right now," I sobbed.

"Oh my God. What's wrong?"

I told Lindsey most of what had happened with Chris. Lindsey was hanging out with Judy when I called her. Judy called the rest of the crew, and before I knew it, all my girls were at my house. I told them the full story once everyone had settled in the living room.

"Damn. Raheem sent him a video of you two fucking?" Vivian asked, her eyes wide.

Her bluntness made me cringe. I nodded, feeling ashamed.

Chloe was slouched on the couch, with her arms crossed. She suddenly saw the bruises on my arm. "What happened to your arm?" she asked.

"Chris grabbed me," I said, looking at the darkening bruises.

"It looks like that motherfucker did more than just grab you!" Chloe said angrily.

I shook my head. "We were both caught up in the bullshit from the video. Chris would never hurt me. He was just—"

"That's how it all starts. First, they shake you, and then they beat you. There's no excuse for that shit. I don't care if you sucked Raheem's dick in front of him. He should keep his fucking paws to himself," Chloe asserted, fuming.

I knew there was no talking to her when she got hot like that, so I left her alone.

"Chloe is right. No matter what you did, he had no right to touch you," Vivian interjected.

I loved Vivian, but I felt like she was excited by all the drama and was saying things to rile Chloe up.

"What are you going to do?" Lindsey asked. She was sitting next to me on the couch.

"I'll do whatever I have to do to work things out with Chris," I answered. "I want my kids to see us happy. I want Chris not to hate me. I want everybody at my job to stop fucking talking about me. I want everything to go back to the way it was."

Lindsey took my hand and held it.

"I'm not trying to add fuel to the fire, K, but what if, after all this, your relationship is at the point of no return? What if it's beyond repair? You have to ask yourself if getting a divorce is inevitable at this point," Judy said.

Divorce. That frightful word had reared its ugly head again. The more I heard it, the more of a reality it became.

My eyes were swollen from crying. I hoped the next time Chris looked in them, he'd see I had never meant for any of this to happen.

Just then we heard movement at the front door. A key was inserted in the lock, and then the door opened. Chris walked into the house. I'd never been happy and sad to see someone at the same time. I prepared myself for another emotional experience.

Chris

I put my key in the lock and opened the door. Chloe, Vivian, Judy, and Lindsey were all in my living room, consoling Karen. Everyone turned and looked at me. Their piercing eyes felt like needles on me. Chloe sprang off the couch, charged at me, and shoved me.

"Don't you ever put your hands on my sister again!"

Karen rushed over to us. "Chloe, please stop!" she yelled.

Chloe stood nose to nose with me. She stood so close to me, I could smell her spearmint gum. Her eyes locked on mine. Vivian came over and stood next to Chloe, with a nasty expression on her face and her arms folded. Then Lindsey and Judy went and stood next to Karen to block Chloe and Vivian from getting any closer to me.

"I don't care how big you are. If you ever touch my sister again, I'll fuck you up. I can call some of my guy friends to fuck you up too, since you think it's cool to grab women," Chloe snarled.

"Chloe, you're not helping this situation right now," Lindsey said, trying to calm her down.

Chloe threw up her hands and said, "Fuck helping the situation."

Then she plopped back down on the couch and picked up her pack of Newports. She had a smug look on her face as she pulled out a cigarette. She turned to Vivian, who had followed her back to the couch and had sat down, and handed her one. Chloe flicked her lighter, took a long drag, and blew a smoke ring in my direction. She was pushing my buttons. I couldn't take her blatant disrespect. I walked over to her and snatched the cigarette from her lips and crumpled it in my hand. It burned like hell, but I didn't care. Chloe and Vivian stood up from the couch, and then Lindsey, Karen, and Judy walked over and pushed the three of us apart.

I looked over at Karen. "I don't have time for this shit right now. Where are the girls? I'm taking them with me to stay at Pops for the week, while we work on getting things started with our divorce."

"You're not taking the kids anywhere. Why are you even here? Leave. She was better off when you were gone," Chloe said.

"Mind your business. This doesn't concern you. Maybe if you worried about your shit and kept yourself out of mine, you could get a better job and find a man to put up with your rude ass." I turned to Karen. "Where are the kids?" I asked.

"They're in their room. Chris, don't do this. I know I fucked up—"

"Karen, don't beg him. He's the one that fucked up. If he had listened to you and given you what you wanted, you wouldn't have had to get it from other sources," Vivian said.

Unbelievable. They were blaming me for Karen cheating. I was way past being frustrated. I was tired of this double-standard bullshit. If the roles were reversed, and I had cheated on Karen for the same reasons, they would want to massacre me. It was okay for her to have cheated, because I supposedly hadn't given her what she *needed*. This was their justification for her infidelity. I ignored them and walked toward the stairs to get the girls.

"Are you deaf? You're not taking the kids anywhere," Chloe growled as she got in front of me and blocked my way to the steps.

I was done being polite. "Chloe, step aside, or get put aside," I snarled. "I'm taking my kids, and no one in this room is stopping me, do you understand?"

Chloe threw a punch at me. I sidestepped her and used her momentum to push her out of the way. She fell to the floor; I ran up the stairs. But then Chloe jumped up and chased after me. The rest of them followed. I stepped inside the girls' bedroom and locked the door before Chloe managed to reach me.

"Daddy!" the girls yelled excitedly.

"Hey!" I hugged and kissed them. Then I heard the handle on the bedroom door twisting. Then there was banging.

Boom! Boom! Boom!

"Open up the door, bitch!" Chloe yelled.

I ignored her. I dug into the girls' closet, pulled out two gym bags, and started packing the bags for the girls.

"Daddy, who is Aunt Chloe yelling at?" Jocelyn asked.

"Yeah. Why is she so mad?" Jaclyn asked.

"Aunt Chloe is mad at Daddy because I'm taking you guys to stay with me at Poppa's house for a while."

Boom! Boom! Boom!

"Why is she mad about that?" Jaclyn asked, frowning.

I didn't have time to get into it. I packed their bags with enough clothes to last about two weeks. I put the two bags over my shoulders, picked up the girls, and unlocked the door. Chloe opened it, ready to fight. I pushed past her and walked out of the room.

"Put them down, so I can fuck you up!" Chloe yelled as she punched me on my back.

When Vivian tried to pry the girls out of my arms, they started to cry.

"Stop!" Karen yelled. "Just stop, all of you," she cried, clutching the staircase banister. She collapsed to her knees. Lindsey and Judy consoled her, and Chloe and Vivian stopped hitting me.

"Chris, I know you need time away from me. I want to work things out. Take the kids, but only if you promise me we'll talk and try to fix things. I don't want a divorce. I don't want to break up our family. I just want things to go back to the way they were."

I wanted to ask her why she hadn't worried about breaking up our family when she was fucking Raheem and Tyrell, but I just nodded.

"Sis, you don't have to apologize to him. Fuck—"

"Stop it, Chloe!" Karen said. "I know you're trying to help me, but this isn't helping. I don't want this. Let him go. Let me handle this. I appreciate you being here for me, but we need to handle this between the two of us."

"We'll be with Pops. I'll talk to you later in the week," I said.

I walked downstairs with the girls and their bags and headed outside. I put them down once we got to my truck. I secured the girls in their car seats, then put their bags in the back of the truck. I was about to climb behind the wheel and leave when Judy called out to me.

"Chris, can we talk to you for a minute?" She was standing at the door with Lindsey, who couldn't even look at me. I sighed, closed the door to my truck, and walked over to them. I didn't want my kids to hear anything from this conversation.

"What is it? I have nothing more to say."

"Chris, Karen loves you. She fucked up, but she never meant for any of it to hurt you," Lindsey said, finally able to meet my eyes.

"You're doing what a good friend does, looking out for her. You were also her alibi when she was fucking around on me. Instead of covering for her, why didn't you try to convince her to stop? I'm not blaming you. I'm not mad at you. But how would you feel if you were in my place?"

Lindsey was about to answer when Judy asked, "While we're switching roles here, have you ever asked yourself how you would feel if you were Karen?"

I looked at Judy like she was out of her mind. "I wouldn't want to know what it feels like to lie to the person I'm supposed to love, and to cheat on them with not one, but *two* people. That's not something I would want to experience or put someone through."

"You're being a typical guy," Judy said.

Her statement pissed me off. I waved them away and turned back to my truck. Lindsey grabbed my arm.

"Chris, wait. Please hear me out," she said. "Judy isn't trying to insult you or upset you, but Karen wanted what pretty much all women want, to feel loved and appreciated. You might be different. It might not matter to you, but you have to put yourself in her place. These were things that were important to her. I'll be honest. We all knew she was stepping out on you, but she never once considered leaving you for them. She didn't think they were better than you. It was all emotional for her. She does love you, Chris, but the key to Karen's heart isn't through sex or material things. She needs to feel that you appreciate and love her."

My first thought was to say I had done everything I possibly could to show her those things, but seeing the honesty in Lindsey's eyes made me stop and reconsider. Had I really put my all into giving Karen what she needed? I wondered. Could I have done more to prevent this from happening? I didn't like second-guessing myself.

"We know it's hard, Chris, but before you think about getting divorced, think about what we said," Judy chimed in. "Karen might lose you and her job. Raheem and Tyrell both fucked her over. We all make mistakes. Try to forgive her, so you can both move on."

I wanted to say that Karen had brought this shit on herself. Hearing Raheem's and Tyrell's names irritated the shit out of me, but rather than make this worse than it was, I nodded and said, "I'll consider it."

"Thanks, Chris," Lindsey said.

Judy nodded.

I returned the nod and walked back to my truck and got in. I drove away, leaving them standing there. Too bad that I couldn't leave my problems behind with them.

Karen

I was sitting in a corner booth at the Friendly's in Massapequa, eating a large Oreo ice cream sundae. After Chris had taken the kids, I had felt it was best to get out of the house and get some fresh air. My girls had agreed and had wanted to come out with me. I had let them know they could come along as long as our activities didn't involve anything with alcohol. Alcohol had already made things worse. I wanted something comforting, so I had chosen to come here. I toyed with my sundae and watched a family sitting across from me play with their children and enjoy each other's company. For the most part, none of my girls had mentioned Chris since we got to Friendly's, but leave it up to Chloe to address the elephant in the room.

"K, not for nothing, but if it were me, I would've never let Chris take my kids," Chloe said.

I assumed that she didn't mean anything malicious by her comment and that she was talking this way only because she was concerned, but her words pushed me deeper into a depression.

"But it's not you. It's me. And I felt it was best to let him have the kids, so drop it," I snapped.

"Damn. I'm sorry," Chloe said.

I shook my head. "No, I'm sorry for being snippy, but with everything that's been going on, Chris hasn't spent time with *our* kids. They miss him, and I know he misses them. They shouldn't have to suffer because of what's going on between us."

"I know, but if he misses them so much, he should've stayed his ass home," Chloe muttered.

"No, there's too much negative energy in the house right now," Lindsey said. "He needs to be away with the kids to get his head right. I think keeping the kids around him is the best way for him to consider working things out."

"Are you ever going to talk to Raheem again?" Vivian asked me.

"No. I'm done with him. He played me. I wish I had never got involved with him," I replied.

Judy rubbed my back. "Everything is going to be okay," she soothed. I wished it were true.

My phone vibrated just then. I retrieved it from my pocket and saw I had a text from Tyrell. I put my phone under the table and discreetly read the text.

So, corporate has been really interrogating me. Have they questioned you yet? I'm kind of worried.

After reading his text, I went from being sad to being nervous. On top of all the shit I'd gone through today, I now had to worry about what this asshole had told the higher-ups at the company I worked for. I responded to his text.

No, they haven't questioned me yet. I think their strategy is to gather as much dirt as they can to make me confess. What did you tell them?

He texted me back quickly.

They told me to be truthful, because my answers could lead to me being terminated.

His reply didn't answer my damn question. I needed to know his precise words to the investigators.

Stop dancing around my damn question. What exactly did you tell them?

A minute later I got my answer.

I told them nothing happened. I said you were trying to teach me how to do my job more effectively so I wouldn't be fired.

It wasn't the best excuse, but I could work with it.

What kind of questions did they ask you?

A minute passed before I got his answer.

They wanted to know how long you've been my supervisor. Have I ever felt taken advantage of? Have we ever engaged in sexual intimacy? Why have I spent so much time in your office? And some other bullshit questions.

I texted him back quickly.

What were your answers?

Another minute went by.

I told them that you've been my supervisor for about a year, that we've never been intimate, and that you've always been professional. I added that you didn't want to embarrass me in front of our coworkers, so you gave me additional training in your office to make me more productive.

His answers sounded decent, but his wife and the rumors were what worried me.

All right. You need to think about how you're going to convince your wife to keep her mouth shut.

He texted back right away.

I know.

I fired off an important message.

When this is over, stay away from me. This situation has the potential to fuck up both our lives.

He didn't respond to my last text.

"Who were you texting?" Chloe asked after I slipped my phone back in my pocket.

"Just more drama and bullshit," I answered, rubbing my temples.

"Care to elaborate?" Vivian asked, not letting me off the hook.

"It was Tyrell. My job started the investigation on me, and they asked him questions. So far, so good. I told him that when this is over, he has to stay out of my life."

I hoped he would listen.

We talked more about my drama, and my girls helped me to get mentally prepared for a week without my family.

I was at work, sitting at my desk, swamped with reports. Since the investigation into my actions had begun, I'd rarely left my office. It was too uncomfortable. Every time I passed other employees in the hallways, I saw their curious glances and heard their whispers. I felt their eyes on me. Their laughter, rude comments, and gestures tormented and taunted me. I felt like everywhere I went, shame, guilt, and insecurities followed me.

I finally mustered up the courage to leave my office and walk to the bathroom. I avoided eye contact with the mail carrier, who was awkwardly smiling at me while he pushed the mail cart. I closed my eyes and took a deep breath to center myself. I needed to keep my shit together. I couldn't break down in the hallway, in front of my subordinates and coworkers. To adjust my body language, I fixed my face, making myself appear more confident, and straightened my posture. I couldn't let anyone in this company see any signs of the turmoil I was going through. That was how it needed to be, that was how it should be, and that was how it was going to be. I handled my business in the bathroom, then swiftly walked back to my office.

I tried to stay focus on work, but I kept thinking about Chris.

What I had thought would be only a week of Chris having the kids had turned into a month, and it had felt like an eternity and an ongoing hell. I'd felt that if I played nice and let Chris have the girls a little while longer, he'd be more receptive to working things out. However, my stress from this situation, and the horror show that my job had turned into, had driven me to start smoking again The first week that Chris had the girls, I'd been emotional, scared, depressed, and nothing I said or did had made things better between Chris and me. Our communication had been forced and stilted, and it still was. I stopped by to see my little girls every day, but the fear that this could be our future scared the shit out of me.

And every day, after being tortured by the whispers and gossip at work, I went home to a quiet and empty house. I frequently looked at our family pictures or our wedding album and reflected painfully on the actions that had led to this sorry state of affairs.

My depressing thoughts were disrupted when Roger knocked on my office door. I told him to come in.

"Hello, Karen. I hope I'm not disturbing you," he said as he closed the door behind him.

"Of course not, Roger. You are never a bother. How are you?"

"I'm well. I wanted to let you know that within the next two weeks, the higher-ups will be calling you in to close out their investigation. They haven't set a date yet, but I was told things should be wrapping up shortly."

"Thank you, Roger."

"No problem." He paused for a moment as he stood there. "Karen?"

"Yes?"

"When the time comes and they're questioning you, please don't lie to them."

I nodded.

"Great. I will let you know if I hear anything else."

"Thanks again, Roger."

When he left, I put my head in my hands. I just wanted this fucking nightmare to be over.

Chris

I pulled up to my father's driveway and saw Karen sitting in her car across the street from the house. When she saw me, she stepped out of her car and crossed the street, rubbing her hands up and down her arms, looking remorseful. I hated that I still loved her.

"Hey, Chris," she called as she approached my truck.

I nodded as I opened the truck door.

"Chris . . . can we talk?" she said.

I sighed. "Sure."

When I opened the front door of the house, the girls saw us and ran to us excitedly. They hugged us and told us all about their day at school. Pops was in the living room, working on putting together a new entertainment center he'd bought at IKEA.

I stepped into the living room. "Pops, I'm ordering dinner. You want anything in particular?" I said.

"I'm not picky. You know what I like. I trust your judgment," he told me.

"Roger that, Pops."

I returned to the foyer and decided to be civil to Karen. "Would you like to have dinner with us?"

She smiled and nodded excitedly.

We ordered Chinese food and sat together like a family again. I had missed this feeling so much, but Karen had ruined everything when she decided to fuck those two assholes.

When we were finished eating, Pops agreed to watch the kids while Karen and I talked in my bedroom.

"What do you want to talk about, Karen?" I asked once we were alone in my bedroom and the door was shut.

"I miss you, Chris. I'm sorry I hurt you. I know I fucked up, but I'll do anything to fix this."

"We're too damaged. I don't think we can be fixed."

"Please . . . please. Let's at least try."

"I don't know if I can. I don't think I'll ever trust you again, and if I can't trust you, we won't have a real relationship. We'd just be going through the motions."

"In time, maybe I can earn your trust back."

I thought then about the video of Raheem fucking her, and the speck of hope I had for our marriage disappeared. "After I saw another man fuck you and cum in your mouth, I don't know if you could ever earn my trust back. And there wasn't only one guy you were creeping with behind my back. There were two. That's too much to forgive."

Karen's face flushed, and she frowned. "Fuck this! The reason all this shit happened in the first place was that I wasn't getting what I needed from you."

"So, what would change, huh? I'm the same person now that I was then, Karen."

"Fuck you, Chris!"

"No thanks. I'm sure you'll find some other brother to do that."

I knew I had struck a nerve and had hurt her, but I didn't care. Karen gave me a long look, then slapped me hard across the face. My hands trembled; I opened and closed them. It took everything in my soul not to slap her back. We stood there and stared at each other. Karen sucked her teeth and then stormed out of the room. I heard her say good-bye to the girls, and then I heard the front door slam. I looked out the window to see Karen speeding off in her car. Then I heard a loud thud in the living room.

Jocelyn came racing to my bedroom. "Daddy, Daddy, something's wrong with Poppa!" she yelled.

I ran into the living room, in a panic. My father was on his knees, sweating heavily and clutching his chest. I had never seen fear in my father's eyes, but I swore I saw it in that moment.

"Pops, are you okay?" I asked him.

I tried to help him up, but he frowned, slapped my hand away, and stood up by himself.

"Get off me. I ain't no damn cripple. I'm a man," he snapped.

"Pops, maybe you should see a doctor. You don't look so good."

"I'm fine. I'm tired, and I lost my balance. That's all."

As he said that, he winced in pain and collapsed to his knees again. Once again, and for the second time this evening, I saw panic in his eyes.

"S-son, I need to rest a little bit," he said as he stood up. He was wobbly on his feet and was panting.

"Pops, you're scaring me right now. We should go to the emergency room."

"We don't need . . . to go to the emergency room, because there's no emergency. I'll be fine," he insisted.

I frowned. "Pops, this isn't the time to be stubborn. Let me take you to the hospital. This looks serious."

"Son, just take me to my room. I think I overexerted myself today and need to rest. I'll be good as new in the morning."

I helped him up the stairs to his bedroom. His bed was neatly made. I expected nothing less from my father. As I stood there, refusing to leave him alone, he slowly changed his clothes and got into bed.

"Son?"

"Yes, Pops?"

"I heard you arguing with Karen. Make sure you never fight in front of the girls."

I looked at him curiously. "I won't, Pops."

"Arguing with a woman is like putting out a fire. Sometimes putting water on it makes things worse. Sometimes nothing you do will extinguish it. You have to let the fire burn out and run its course." Pops paused to catch his breath and then continued. "Arguing with Karen when both of you are mad isn't going to change anything. Fighting with her in front of the kids will only make matters worse. The only solution to your problem is time. You both need to calm down and speak to each other away from the children, and when you both can think logically. Don't let your emotions get in the way of logic, son."

I nodded. "I understand, Pops."

"I know I've always been hard on you, but I'm proud of you, son. You've grown up to become a good man."

"Thanks."

I'd never seen Pops look so sick. While I'd love to take him to the emergency room, I know he'd gouge his eyes out before he'd let me. My father rarely went to the doctor. He hated to look weak in front of anyone. I respected his wishes.

"I love you, Pops."

"I love you too, son."

I had never heard my father say those words back to me.

"Rest up, Pops," I said as I inched toward his door.

"I'll be all right. I'll see you in the morning, son."

"See you in the morning."

I left the room and closed his bedroom door. When I went back downstairs, I explained to the girls that Pops was sick, but that he'd be good as new in the morning. I played with them for a while and then put them to bed. I prayed for my old man before I went to sleep that night.

***

I woke up the next morning to my children's laughter. It was ten on a Saturday morning. As soon as I got out of bed, I went to check on Pops. I walked to his bedroom door; it was still closed. He was always up by five o'clock in the morning, six at the latest. I didn't think much of it, because I knew he was sick. So I headed to the living room, where I found my kids sitting on the couch, giggling at cartoons. I sat down and joined them.

At around noon, I went to check on my father again. His bedroom door was still closed. Sick or not, I'd never known him to sleep until noon. I knocked on the door. No answer. The door creaked as I opened it. Pops was still in bed.

"Pops, you must really be sick. I've never seen you sleep this late."

He didn't answer. I walked over to the bed.

"Pops?"

Still, he was silent. I shook him.

"Dad!" I shouted.

He didn't answer. His eyes were closed, and he had a peaceful look on his face.

"Pops, please! I can't lose you! I need you more than ever now. Please God, don't take him from me. Please don't do this to me now. Haven't I gone through enough?"

Karen

I stubbed my fucking toe on the bathroom door as I rushed out of the shower to grab my ringing cell phone. I was in a hurry to get dressed for Pops's funeral.

"Hello?" I said, wincing and massaging my toe.

"Hello, Karen. It's Roger."

"Hey. How are you?"

"I'm well. You've called in sick most of the week, and you left work early yesterday, before Human Resources, your union delegate, or I had a chance to talk to you. Human Resources, your union delegate, and I have left you numerous messages throughout the week, and we all called you last night, but you haven't returned our calls."

"I'm sorry. I had a lot going on . . ."

"I'm calling because I have to deny your request to take more time off. Human Resources and I have been calling you and emailing you to tell you that the higher-ups want to close out this investigation today. They want you to report in at seven."

I couldn't believe that of all days for this shit to happen, it had to be today. I pleaded with Roger.

"Roger, please, is there any way we can reschedule this for tomorrow or later on during the day today?"

"I know you requested time off today, but no. When corporate wants you to show up to close out an investigation, there are no excuses. Everything is on their terms. I wouldn't even bring it up to them, out of fear that they could use it as leverage to let you go."

"Roger, I know I haven't mentioned it to you or to anyone at the company, but Chris's father died last week. His father's funeral is today. I can't come in to work. I haven't responded to calls or emails, because I, along with my family, have been mourning. I didn't say anything to anyone at the company about it, because I wanted to keep my personal life private."

Roger sighed. "I truly wish you had told me this earlier. First, my condolences to you and your family. I'm very sorry to hear about your father-in-law passing. I will relay the message to the higher-ups, but I will be honest. Seeing that you didn't say anything, it might come across as you delaying the process out of convenience. I don't see the meeting being very long. Do you think you could handle things here and make it back in time for the funeral?"

My heart was telling me not to take the risk. I truly wanted to be there for Chris and my kids and show my respects to Pops, but I knew that going to this meeting and fighting for my job was the logical choice.

"I'll be there," I said.

"Great! Good luck with everything today. Remember what I told you. Be truthful with your answers."

"I will. Thank you for everything, Roger."

"You're welcome. Take care of yourself today."

I ended the call and immediately felt nauseated. Lately, all this stress had been making me queasy. I took a deep breath and prepared myself for what I'd say to Chris. I knew he would be angry and would possibly hate me forever, but I had to do this if I wanted to have a chance of keeping my job. If we were to survive as a couple, we couldn't survive on a single salary. If shit happened and we got divorced, there would be no way I could survive if I was unemployed.

I called Chris and explained the situation with my job, and I told him I'd probably be late to the funeral. Hearing the disappointment and anger in his voice killed me inside. I felt like everything I did ended up hurting him. I cried when Chris ended the call. I was tired of feeling like a villain.

Chris

I looked up at the overcast sky and sighed. The down-pour on this dreary day emphasized the fact that my father was gone. My daughters were inconsolable. They were crying as they held my hands. I won't lie. I was devastated and would've loved to go somewhere and bawl too, but like Pops had always taught me, I had to be strong for my children.

The service was filled with my father's old military friends and construction buddies. The reverend, a friend of my father's who had served with him on active duty, gave a nice service. When he was finished, he motioned for me to approach the podium to say some words on my father's behalf. I kissed the girls, and Nadine held their hands while I stood in front of everyone and spoke about how great my father was. I took a moment to compose myself, and then I told them about the last conversation I had had with Pops. I said that even though we didn't always see eye to eye, I wouldn't change anything about him. He'd always been there for me, and he'd made me the man I was today, and for that, I'd always be grateful.

A few moments later I stood next to Nadine and my children as my father's casket was lowered into the grave next to my mother's. My little girls sobbed and held on tightly to me. I tried to be strong, but seeing Pops being lowered into the ground, hearing my children crying, and not having Karen with us were killing me inside. My hands trembled. Nadine touched my shoulder and hugged me. Will and Lou patted me on the back. I took a deep breath, stood up straight, and remained strong for my children.

When it was over, my father's friends lined up to shake my hand and give their condolences. Hearing them tell me funny stories about my father, and say how much I reminded them of him, made my grief worse. I held my pain inside and thanked everyone for coming. Nadine stayed with the girls while I did what I needed to do. I appreciated her being there after Karen called and said she couldn't make it.

Things with Karen had been better this past week. Pops's death had me emotional, and I had felt all week as if it was helping to bring us closer together. I had started to believe that in time, maybe we could work things out, but her absence today had ruined any reconciliation we could've had.

The beginning of the end had started at 6:00 a.m., when she called me.

"Chris . . . ," she'd said tentatively after I picked up the phone.

"Are you on your way here? You're late. The limo will be here at seven to take all of us to the funeral service."

"I . . . I'm probably going to be late to the funeral today, Chris. I'm sorry."

I'd taken a deep breath. "Why?"

"The higher-ups at work want to settle everything with my 'situation' this morning. Since I was already on thin ice, I requested to take the day off, but I never told them there was a death in the family. My supervisor just called to tell me my request was denied, and I'm to report to the conference room to close out the investigation."

"Did you tell them you have to reschedule? Did you mention that your husband's father died?"

"Chris, I couldn't reschedule—"

"Are you telling me you're not coming to my father's funeral? As much as he did for us, you owe him that much."

"You make it sound like I want to miss it. I know how important this is to you, to us. I loved Pops too, Chris. You know that, but this isn't personal. This is business. If I don't go to this hearing, I could lose my job—"

"If you hadn't been fucking around, you wouldn't be in this situation in the first place. This *is* personal. It's personal between me and you. You have to choose, Karen. Are you coming to the funeral, or are you going to work? Is it going to be business or your family?"

"Don't do this, Chris. I'm sorry. I'm not choosing business *over* my family, but I have to go to this meeting *for* my family. We can't survive on a single salary alone."

I shook my head in disgust. "There's always an excuse with you, Karen. If you miss this fucking funeral today, don't bother talking to me again."

"Chris . . . wait. Please listen to me."

"No, *you* listen. If you miss my father's funeral, I don't want shit to do with you anymore. We're done. Do you understand?"

"Chris, you're upset right now, and you're not thinking clearly—"

"I can't be any clearer. Your actions today will show me what I mean to you."

"That's not fair. You know I love you. You're blowing this way out of proportion."

"Either come to the funeral or stay the fuck away from me. It's as simple as that!" I yelled.

I ended the call before she could say anything else. I was tired of hearing her bullshit. I turned around and saw my kids watching me from the doorway. I remembered what Pops had said about fighting with Karen in front of them, and I felt like shit.

"Were you talking to Mommy, Daddy?" Jocelyn asked.

I didn't know how to answer that. "Yeah . . . I'm a little upset because Mommy has to work and won't be able to come to Poppa's funeral."

"You and Mommy are always fighting," Jaclyn said.

At that moment, I knew my father's advice was right. Getting divorced from Karen would be hard enough on the kids. To avoid completely fucking them up mentally and emotionally, I had to avoid fighting with Karen in front of them.

Nadine, Will, and Lou were the first group of people I saw at the funeral when the girls and I got there about an hour and a half after hanging up with Karen. I briefly told Nadine what had happened with Karen, while Will and Lou chatted with the girls.

"I'm sorry . . . ," Nadine said.

"Why are you sorry? You didn't do anything."

"I know, but you're hurting, and I wish I could do more for you."

"You being here means a lot to me," I told her.

My friends were here, but the woman who was my wife wasn't. It was time to make some adjustments in my life.

Karen

My anxiety was killing me. I had waited an hour and a half outside the conference room before I was called in to see the investigators. I had thought that this would be a quick meeting and that I wouldn't be too late for the funeral, but that didn't happen.

I walked into the conference room, where three male representatives from corporate; Helen, the representative from HR; a female delegate from my union; and several others were waiting. They all wore serious expressions and gave me questioning and accusatory looks. I felt like I was doomed before they asked the first question. One of Helen's assistants from Human Resources read me the rules for the company and explained that this investigation would be recorded. Next, he clicked on a small black recorder, and the representatives from corporate began rattling off questions. I answered them, sticking to the story Tyrell had told them.

"Mrs. Davis, can you explain why you felt the need to give Mr. Stevens additional training on the side?" the lead corporate representative asked.

"Tyrell's job performance was poor. He was very close to being let go because he wasn't grasping the job quickly enough. After speaking with him, I felt he had the potential to do his job more efficiently with the right supervision."

"Have you ever engaged in sexual intercourse with Mr. Stevens?" asked another of the three corporate representatives, an older man with salt-and-pepper hair.

A wave of heat hit me. My mouth went dry. I swallowed hard. "No, I've never engaged in any type of sexual intimacy with Mr. Stevens."

Their questions became more aggressive and accusatory. They read anonymous testimonies from other employees and brought up nasty rumors that had spread around the office.

"This anonymous testimony states, 'I watched Mrs. Davis and Tyrell go in her office late at night and come out smiling, laughing, and adjusting their clothes after being in there for close to twenty minutes," said the lead representative from corporate.

I shifted in my seat, and he continued.

"This testimony states, 'There have been lots of people who have had bad evaluations, and Mrs. Davis never attempted to give any of them additional training. It's almost comical that she thinks no one knows that they are having sex."

I took a deep breath. Everyone in the room was analyzing my every move, so I tried to keep my facial expressions neutral. I didn't want to come off as guilty.

"You say that you've never engaged in sexual intercourse with your subordinate, but why are there so many employees saying the two of you have been intimate in your office? Tell us the truth," demanded the third corporate representative, a middle-aged man in a pinstriped suit.

I couldn't stop the tears from running down my face.

"If you're being honest, why are you crying?" asked the lead corporate representative.

"I'm crying because I'm being falsely accused with these hurtful allegations. I didn't do any of the things that are written in those testimonies. I never slept with Tyrell."

My answer made them back off a bit. They stopped grilling me for a moment and looked at each other.

"Are you aware of the rumor that Mr. Stevens's wife, Pamela, has also had intercourse on corporate grounds?" asked the representative in the pin-striped suit.

I didn't play into the question. I kept my answer simple. "I've heard the rumor, but I don't believe it, because I've never seen anything that proves it, and there are always rumors going around the office. Most times they're false."

The representatives from corporate nodded.

"We are going to recess for one hour. We should have a decision when we return," the lead representative announced.

I left the conference room, shaking. The delegate from my union followed my into the hallway and approached me.

"I think you handled the questioning well," she said reassuringly.

I gave her a curt smile.

She patted me on the back. "I wouldn't worry about anything. It sounded like they have nothing, and they were trying to pressure you into confessing."

"I hope you're right."

After she stepped away to take a call, I paced the hall and constantly looked at my watch. Eventually, I sat down on the bench outside the conference room and texted Chris, but he didn't respond. I tapped my fingers against my legs, anxiously awaiting my fate with the company.

When the recess was over, I returned to the conference room, sat down, and tried to see if I could read anything from the near expressionless faces of the three corporate representatives. When everyone was present and seated, the lead representative, who sat between the other two, spoke. He was a white man with an intimidating face, thick square-rimmed glasses, and a yellow and blue polka-dot bow tie.

"While we were conducting our investigation, we determined, based on the video footage from our cameras around the premises, that the allegations about Pamela Stevens sleeping with another employee are true."

I was nervous again. I wondered whether at any point I'd slipped up and they had footage of Tyrell and me.

The lead representative went on. "When we confronted her with the footage, Mrs. Stevens became irate and was threatened with termination. Her allegations about you and her husband were conflicting, and when we interrogated her further, she dropped all her accusations against you and Mr. Stevens. She was subsequently suspended. We still needed to do a thorough investigation, which is why we have interviewed you and others in your department."

My heart was pounding. I couldn't take the tension of not knowing what was going to happen next.

"Upon further investigation, we haven't found anything that disproves your testimony," the lead representative noted. "Mr. Stevens's job performance improved substantially after your additional training. Considering, too, the fact that Mrs. Stevens had a motive for being dishonest with her accusation, we find you not guilty of improper conduct, but a verbal warning will be noted on your record for having Mr. Stevens in your office for unauthorized reasons."

I didn't give a shit about the verbal warning. I was elated to have my fucking job.

The lead representative cleared his throat, then declared, "Mr. Stevens will be transferred to another department. This investigation is closed. You may go back to performing your usual duties."

I stood up, shook everyone's hand, gathered my purse and coat, and left the conference room. I ran into the nearest bathroom and cried tears of joy. I was lucky to emerge unscathed by the investigation. I gathered myself and headed to Roger's office.

"Congratulations, Karen. I heard everything went well," Roger said when I stepped inside his office and came to a stop in front of his desk.

"Yes . . . I'm very happy."

"That's good to hear. I know you need to go to your father-in-law's funeral. Do you want to take the remainder of the day off?"

I nodded, and my eyes filled with tears. Roger noticed, but he didn't pry.

"Enjoy the rest of the day. Go and spend time with your family. I'm sorry for your loss."

I thanked him and headed to the door. As I reached for the door handle, Roger said, "Karen?"

I turned to face him. "Yes?"

"Whatever you had going on with Tyrell, I hope this was a wake-up call."

My eyes widened. I nodded, then left his office and closed the door slowly behind me.

I shook off my queasiness, adjusted my heels, and hurried to the function Chris had planned for after the funeral. I figured that if I showed my face, Chris would see that I cared. When I entered the building, I stopped in my tracks in the doorway. Jealousy swirled in the pit of my stomach. A woman was standing next to Chris and was consoling my children. The way she stood so comfortably by him, and the way my children looked so at ease in her embrace, brought me to tears.

"What are you doing here?"

I jumped when I heard Lou's question. I quickly straightened up, wiped my face, and turned to face him. Will was standing beside him.

"Yeah, Chris said you were too busy to make the funeral," Will said.

"I came right after work. Who is that woman with my children?"

"That's Nadine. She works with Chris. Unlike you, she wasn't too busy with work to be here today," Lou replied coldly.

"Fuck you, Lou. You don't know what I had to go through today. I'm hurting just as much as Chris is."

"Are you serious? You're really trying to compare your shitty day to Chris's? Chris lost everything. And when he needed you the most, you weren't there," Will said.

"If I didn't take care of what I needed to today . . . You know what? I don't need to explain myself to you. I did what was best for my family. I'm here for Chris now," I snapped.

"You stopped caring for Chris and your *family* when you opened your fucking legs for those other men. You hurt him enough. Leave and be gone, bitch," Lou growled.

I balled up my fist. I was ready to start swinging. I wanted to curse and beat their asses. I wanted to scream. I looked at Chris, who was still standing comfortably next to that woman Nadine with our children. I sighed, opened my fist, turned around, and walked out the door. I knew if I went in there, I'd make a scene. I was too angry, and out of respect to Pops, I knew this wasn't the time or the place for that. I climbed back in my car, started the engine, and drove off. Maybe it was better if I wasn't around.

Chris

I tucked my daughters gently into bed. They were exhausted from the funeral. I softly closed the door to their bedroom and walked into the living room. Nadine was standing next to the fireplace, looking at photos of me and my father on the mantel. She heard me come in the room and turned around.

"How are they doing?" she asked.

"They're good. They passed out as soon as I put them in their beds."

"How are you doing?"

"I'm fine. I have a few things to handle for my father, but I should be back to work in a week or two."

"Chris, I'm worried about you."

"I'll be fine . . . I'm fine."

"I know you're trying to be tough and to hold everything inside, but it's easy to see that you're hurting."

I shifted uncomfortably.

The look in her eyes was sincere as she continued. "I know you're strong, but you don't have to act tough in front of me. Talk to me. Tell me what you're feeling. Holding it in is toxic. If you need to vent or yell or cry, it's okay. I'm here for you, Chris."

I was overcome with emotion. I thought about Karen and how quickly my life and marriage had started to unravel. My father was the only person in my life who had ever given me meaningful advice, and now he was gone. A wave of loneliness washed over me. My lips quivered. I felt tears welling up in my eyes. Nadine wrapped her arms around me, and I cried long and hard. In my mind, I heard my father's voice. *Stop acting like a pansy. Be a man. I didn't raise a daughter. I raised a man.* But for once, I ignored it.

When I had no more tears left, we lay down on the couch. Nadine wrapped her arms around me and gently kissed my forehead. I fell asleep in her arms and slept more comfortably than I had in a long time. Nadine helped me to release the stress that was killing me inside. She helped to remind me that my tears weren't a sign of weakness. Nadine was there when I needed someone to be there for me. In one day, she did more for me than Karen had done in years.

"Hey, Daddy. Look at me!" Jocelyn yelled.

She zoomed past her sister on her skates. Jaclyn was trying her best to keep up, but she was losing the battle. We were at Hot Skates, a roller-skating rink in Lynbrook. Nadine had thought it would be good for me to get out of the house and do something fun with the kids.

"Are you going to just watch them or join in?" Nadine asked, handing me a cup of coffee as I sat at a table and watched the girls.

I shook my head and toyed with the stirrer in my cup.

"Snap out of it, Chris. You have to start having fun and enjoying life. That's the only way you're going to feel better."

I knew she was right, but I wanted to sulk and wallow in my sorrow. Nadine wasn't having it.

"Hurry up and drink your coffee," she ordered. "I'm taking you out on the rink with me. What size skates do you wear?"

"Nadine . . . I'm not going out there."

"Yes you are, Chris. I'm not going to leave you here to mope around while your kids are enjoying themselves. You need some fun in your life. Now, what size are you?"

I sighed and reluctantly said, "Size twelve."

"Now, was that so bad?" Nadine asked, smiling at me.

She rented us skates, and we spent half the time busting our asses all over the skating rink and the other half racing and laughing with the kids. Nadine was right. I needed this. Skating with my kids was a great distraction from the disaster called my life. It felt good to laugh again. It felt good not to think about my problems.

"Good night, girls," I said, tucking my daughters into bed hours after we returned home from the rink.

"Good night, Daddy," they chorused, giggling.

I closed their bedroom door and went into the kitchen to join Nadine, who was standing at the window and looking out.

"I had so much fun with you and your kids today," Nadine said and smiled.

"They enjoyed you too," I said as I went to stand next to her.

"What about you? Did you have fun?" she asked, winking at me.

I smirked. "You know I had a good time."

"I don't know anything unless you tell me."

"I had a great time. I'm glad you dragged me out of the house. Seriously, *thank you*. You were right. I needed to get my mind off things and have some fun with my kids."

"It's no problem. I'm happy I could help you, Chris. You're a good man . . . I like you."

"I appreciate you," I told her.

"What are you doing this weekend?"

"I honestly don't know. Karen is taking the girls. With everything that's going on with her and my dad passing, I feel like my life is so out of order. I'm probably going to move my Mustang here and spend my weekend working on it."

Nadine nodded. "I have a thought. Hang out with me this weekend."

"What do you want to do?" I asked her.

"I'll plan everything, just say yes."

"Okay."

"Okay, what?"

"Okay, *yes*," I laughed.

"Cool."

Nadine took my hand and gave it a squeeze. She raised her other hand and caressed my face. I was happy that she was here to cheer me up, but I was also irritated that Karen wasn't doing that. And I was scared, because I didn't know what the future had in store for me. Then I summoned some courage. I wrapped my hands around Nadine's waist and pulled her into my arms. I drew her face close to mine and kissed her. Nadine wrapped her arms around my neck and deepened the kiss.

After she slowly pulled away, she smiled and said, "Good night, Chris. I can't wait to spend the weekend with you."

"I look forward to it too."

I walked her to the front door, and she gave me a nice firm hug. I watched her climb behind the wheel and pull off in her car, and then I closed the door. I hoped I hadn't scared her off or made her feel uncomfortable by kissing her.

PART FOUR

To Love and to Cherish

Chris

"Who's the bitch in your car?" Karen asked bluntly.

It was seven in the morning. Karen stood in the front doorway, wearing her silk pajamas and tapping her fingers on her crossed arms. As soon as I had rung the doorbell to drop the kids off, she'd flung open the front door, her nostrils flared and her eyes narrowed. I figured she had looked through the bay window before I rang the doorbell and had noticed Nadine sitting in my truck.

Chloe was sitting on the couch in the living room, playing with the girls, when she heard Karen's question. She walked over to the front door and stood next to her sister.

"She's not a bitch. She's my friend from work. She's been helping me cope since Pops died," I said.

"I bet she has," Chloe said, then made a blow-job gesture as she sauntered back to the couch.

"Why is that cunt here?" Karen shouted. "I don't care how friendly you are with her. I don't want that bitch around my kids."

I shook my head and sucked my teeth. "First of all, they're not *your* kids. They're *our* kids. And nothing is going on. She's been good about keeping their minds off Pops's death."

"You've had this . . . fucking strange woman I've never met around my kids on a regular basis? How long has this been going on?"

"Really? You're asking me how long shit has been going on? She was the one who convinced me to come back home to you and try to work things out, before I saw that fucked-up video from Raheem. She was at Pops's funeral. She was there to help me and the kids mourn. Where were you?"

Karen tried to talk, but no words came out.

Before she could answer, I said, "You know what? I don't want to know. The divorce papers are being drawn up. I'm out."

"Wait, what do you mean, divorce papers?"

"I'm done."

"So, what? You're leaving me for her?"

"I'm leaving you because of you. She has nothing to do with this. *I've* always been faithful to you. *You* did this to us."

"You know what? Fuck you! Good riddance, Chris," Karen said as she slammed the door in my face.

As I walked back to my truck, the front door flew open. Karen and Chloe ran toward me. The kids stood in the doorway. Karen caught up with me when I was reaching to open the driver's door on my truck.

"No, fuck this! Bitch, were you fucking him this whole time? Did he have me thinking I was the only one doing dirt, and he was fucking around too?" Karen screamed through the truck window.

Karen ran around to the other side of the truck and tried to open Nadine's door, but it was locked. When she couldn't get it open, she pounded on the window. By then Chloe had caught up with me. I dodged punches as Chloe swung at my face. I grabbed Chloe by the wrists and threw her on the grass. Then I ran around the truck and grabbed Karen from behind. She squirmed, kicked, screamed, and cursed at Nadine.

"Get off her!" Chloe screamed as she punched me.

Some of our neighbors had their doors and windows open by now. They mumbled and pointed at the scene we were making. I spun Karen around and shook her.

"Our fucking neighbors and kids are watching you act crazy right now. Is this what you want them to see?" I yelled.

I let her go, and Karen calmed down. She stopped Chloe from hitting me. Chloe's chest heaved while she glared at me. I just got in my truck and sped off. I turned to Nadine when we were halfway up the street. She looked shaken up.

"I'm sorry you had to see that," I said.

"I'm okay."

I sighed, then pulled the truck over to the curb, came to a stop, and faced her. "If you want to hang out some other time, I completely understand."

Nadine smiled. "No way. Let's make the best out of this weekend!"

Karen

Chris had some fucking nerve bringing that bitch to my house.

"You see, this is why I have no respect for him, K. He's trying to be slick, and he brings some other chick in your face out of spite," Chloe said.

That feeling of queasiness hit me again. I rushed to the bathroom and threw up in the toilet.

"Damn. You okay, sis?" Chloe asked as she stood in the bathroom doorway.

"No. The stress from all this shit has me fucked up. I've been sick to my stomach and throwing up a lot lately."

"Throwing up? K, are you sure you're not prego?"

The realization that this could be a possibility hit me. The last time I slept with Raheem, he didn't use a condom. Chris didn't use one, either, and I wasn't on birth control.

I covered my face and screamed, "Shit!"

"You want me to go to CVS and get some tests?"

"Yeah. And call Lindsey."

"You want me to call Vivian and Judy too?"

"No, just Lindsey. If I am pregnant, I don't want them to know about it. They already know too much of my business."

My hands trembled. I sat on the edge of the tub, shaking my head in disbelief. I had taken five different fucking tests, and they all had shown the same result. I was pregnant. I stood, washed my hands in the sink, and splashed water on my face. Chloe and Lindsey were playing with the girls, but all eyes were on me when I walked out of the bathroom.

"What's the verdict, sis?" Chloe asked.

My eyes filled with tears, and my throat tightened. I slowly nodded and burst into tears. Seeing me crying, the girls ran and hugged me.

"Are you sad, Mommy?" Jocelyn asked.

"A little bit," I replied.

"Is it because you miss Daddy?" Jaclyn asked.

I didn't know how to answer that.

"Girls, Auntie Lindsey and Auntie Chloe have to talk to Mommy. Do you guys want to watch a movie?" Lindsey said.

They nodded in excitement. Lindsey set up the Disney movie *Brave* for the kids, while Chloe and I sat on the living-room couch. Chloe rubbed my back.

"What are you going to do? You know I got your back, no matter what," Chloe said.

"Thanks." I held her hand. "I don't know what to do."

"Fuck it. Keep it! If you get divorced, you can get even more money from Chris."

Lindsey heard Chloe's response. She sat down on the other side of me on the couch. "K, you know I'm not trying to disrespect you, but is Chris the father?" Lindsey asked.

"I don't know," I said, ashamed.

"Sis, what you mean, you don't know?"

"I honestly don't know. It could be Chris's or Raheem's."

"Shit!" Chloe said.

"K, this is your decision alone to make, but I think you should reconsider having this child. If the baby is Raheem's, do you think you'll be happy raising the child with him? Do you think he'll step up and be a good father? If Chris is the father, do you think he'll love this child after everything that went down before it was conceived? I don't know, K. I honestly don't think this is the right time," Lindsey said.

"I know I can't have this baby," I said, shaking my head. "This is a fucking disaster right now. I can't believe this is happening."

"When do you want to take care of this, sis?"

I hated having this conversation about aborting my child. Chloe had had a couple of abortions, but me personally, I had never imagined I would have one. I had never believed in doing that, and I was sure my parents were rolling over in their graves, seeing my actions lately. I hated myself because I knew I was going to go through with it. This had to be done, though. Right now, having a child wouldn't help me at all.

"I'm going to make the appointment for next Friday. I need to take care of this ASAP." I grabbed their hands. "Please, don't tell Judy or Vivian about this. If you see Chris, promise me you won't ever mention it to him. I never want him to know I was pregnant."

"You know I'd never say anything," Lindsey assured me.

Chloe stayed quiet.

I stared at my sister. "Chloe?"

"I'm really going to try, K. When I see his smug-ass face, sometimes I can't help myself."

"Chloe, promise me."

"Okay, okay. I promise I won't say anything."

I needed to take care of this pregnancy pronto. I had never thought I'd ever have an abortion, but there was no way I could have this child. Too many negative experiences surrounded this conception for the child to have the loving, nurturing environment it deserved.

Chris

"Hurry up, slowpoke," Nadine said. We held hands as we maneuvered through the huge Manhattan crowd. We were on Fifty-Fourth Street and were rushing to get to our room at the Marriott on Broadway.

"I can't keep up with you. We've been nonstop all day."

"I know. That's a good thing!" she retorted.

"I hate crowds—"

"Ah, you said *hate*. You know the rules. Five things!" Nadine had a rule that every time one of us used the word *hate*, we had to list five things we loved. It was her way of making sure we stayed positive.

"Ugh, I know. I love my kids, my pops, my Mustang, my house, and Kar . . ."

Shit. I had almost said Karen.

"It's okay. You still love her. There's nothing wrong with that."

Nadine had everything planned perfectly for this weekend. Yesterday and today, we'd been all over the city, doing things that tourists did but that most New Yorkers took for granted and never did. First, we'd visited the Statue of Liberty, on Liberty Island in New York Harbor. Then we'd gone from borough to borough. On Staten Island we'd visited *Postcards*, the sculpture honoring the Staten Island residents who lost their lives on 9/11. In the Bronx we'd gone on a tour of Yankee Stadium. In Queens we'd gone to the Museum of the Moving Image. In Brooklyn we'd strolled hand in hand on the Brooklyn

Bridge and explored Coney Island. We'd finished off our sightseeing in Manhattan by visiting the Empire State Building and seeing the musical *Jersey Boys*.

I felt so alive and comfortable with Nadine. She had helped me realize there could be a good life after Karen. We weren't constantly fighting, as Karen and I had on our date nights, but I wondered if this was because our relationship was new. I feared that the sugar with Nadine would soon turn to shit, like it had with Karen. While that was in the back of my mind, I couldn't deny I was having one of the best weekends of my life.

On our first night, when we'd entered our hotel room, I was surprised to find only one bed. I'd expected two.

"I'm going to shower," I said, feeling awkward about the sleeping arrangements.

"Okay. I'll hop in right after you finish. We have another exciting day tomorrow," she said, winking at me.

I was nervous. We had had a great day, but I felt I had made things awkward when I kissed her last time. I didn't want to ruin our trip.

We showered separately. While she dressed in the bathroom, I stood at the window in my tank top and pajama bottoms and stared blankly at the tourists still walking around Times Square below. Nadine walked out of the bathroom and wrapped her arms around me from behind. I turned and faced her. She had on a pink nightie that showcased her curves. She touched my cheek, then drew my face close to hers, and we kissed. My hands explored her body. Then I pulled her nightie over her head. She had nothing on underneath. She excitedly pulled my clothes off, and we stood naked in front of each other. Then I guided her over to the bed, pulled her down onto it, and kissed her.

"Wait," she said.

"What's wrong?" I asked.

"I really like you, Chris, but I don't want to be a rebound. I don't want to sleep with you, invest feelings, and you end up going back to your wife."

I nodded. I knew she was right. "I understand."

"Can I be honest with you?"

"Of course," I said.

"I've always had a crush on you . . . And I feel kind of guilty spending so much time with you when you're still married."

I held her hand in mine. "My marriage is over. Karen is getting served with our divorce papers on Friday."

"I never wanted to break up your family or disrespect your wife." She looked down at her feet. "I know what that feels like, and I don't want to be *that* woman."

"You're not, and you didn't. It's okay."

"I feel really stupid right now. Maybe this wasn't a good idea."

"No. You've been nothing but good to me. You've helped me more than you'll ever know. I couldn't be happier."

She smiled, sat up, and reached for her purse on the nightstand. She dug inside it, then handed me a condom.

"You sure?" I asked.

"I trust you. I'm not a casual-sex kind of woman. I'm sharing myself with you only because in time I feel we can be more than friends and have a future together. Do you feel the same way?"

"Yes, and I'm not bullshitting. I really mean that."

"Then I want to share this experience with you," she said.

The reality of what was about to happen hit me when I took off my wedding ring. When I'd acted out after finding out Karen was cheating, every time I slept with other women, I'd always left my ring on. A part of me had felt Karen and I would get back together. But now the act of taking off this ring to be intimate with Nadine helped to close the door on that part of my life.

Nadine playfully pushed me down on my back on the king-size bed. She held my manhood in her hand. She wrapped her fist around the base of my dick and worked her mouth up and down the length. She kept a strong suction around the head, which made my toes curl. I moaned, panted, and rocked my hips. I felt like I could cum any second. I gently stopped her and eased her away from my cock. The head glistened with saliva.

"I want you inside me," Nadine whispered.

I sat up and put on the condom she'd handed me.

Nadine patted the bed next to her. "Lie down," she whispered.

After I lay down next to her, she climbed on top of me and slid all the way down on my length. She moaned as she leaned back and placed her hands on the sides of her thick thighs. I twirled the tip of her clit with my thumb as she rode me. The headboard slammed against the wall. Nadine held it in place as she kept her rhythm going. I thrust my hips up while she gyrated. I pinched her nipples, and she swiveled faster and gazed into my eyes. I watched her face glow as her orgasm started to build.

"Oh God!" she screamed.

She quivered on top of me, wearing a smile on her face. Then Nadine slid off me and positioned herself to be taken from behind. I held her waist and worked my right hand up to her breasts. She turned her head, watched me, pushed her ass back at me, gripped the sheets tightly, and moaned through gritted teeth. She wasn't like Karen. Nadine liked it hard and rough. I squeezed her cheeks and smacked her ass. I slapped her hips and pulled on her long jet-black hair.

"Yes, Chris," she moaned.

She was lost in ecstasy. Hearing her say my name sent me over the edge. I felt connected with her. I felt like she was with me and only me. I quickened my pace. I gripped her shoulders. My orgasm snuck up on me. I came hard and fast, and then my strokes slowly wavered. We collapsed next to each other, panting. Nadine giggled.

"What are you thinking?" I asked.

"I needed that. I haven't had sex this good in a long time."

She laid her head on my chest. I ran my fingers up and down her skin as we held each other under the covers.

"I'm feeling you, Chris."

"I'm feeling you too."

We sexed each other up the rest of the night, exploring each other's bodies. I felt at peace. That was last night.

Tonight, after we got back to the Marriott and showered, Nadine stood in front of me, naked.

"You ready for an encore presentation of last night?" she asked, licking her lips.

"If it means falling for you all over again, I'm ready!"

Karen

"I got you, K," Lindsey said as she pulled up in front of my house.

I'd been vomiting and feeling nauseated ever since I left the clinic. That morning I had sobbed the whole way there when the reality hit me that I was actually going through with the abortion. Emotionally, I was sapped. Lindsey turned off the engine, got out, and hurried to the passenger side to help me out of the car. I grimaced as I got out. My abdomen was cramping, and I was achy and weak. She walked me to the door, fumbled through my bag, in search of my house keys, and finally found them. While I waited for Lindsey to open the door, a middle-aged white woman with bright red hair came out of nowhere and approached us.

"Excuse me, ma'am. Are you Karen Davis?" she asked as she looked me in the eye.

The pain in my stomach was killing me. "Yes," I said through gritted teeth.

She handed me a manila envelope. As soon as it was in my hand, the woman said, "You've been served, ma'am."

"What the fuck is this? Ah . . ."

I doubled over when I felt a sharp pain in my abdomen. Lindsey grabbed my arm and held the envelope for me. The woman swiftly walked to her car and drove off. Lindsey opened the front door and helped me inside the house. Chloe was watching TV, while the kids were playing with their toys.

"Mommy!" they yelled excitedly, then ran into the foyer and hugged me.

"Easy, girls. Your mommy isn't feeling well. That's why she went to the doctor," Lindsey said.

"Sorry, Mommy," they said in unison as they stepped out of the hug. Then they each gave me a kiss on the cheek.

Chloe walked up to me. "You all right?" she asked.

"I'm okay. Did a woman ring the doorbell while I was gone?"

She shook her head. "No. Nobody has called or stopped by while I've been here."

"Some white lady was waiting for Karen outside and served her with papers," Lindsey said.

Chloe and Lindsey walked me to the living-room couch. Lindsey pulled the ottoman out so I could put my feet up.

"I need to see what these papers are," I said. Lindsey handed me back the envelope.

The kids went back to playing with their toys on the floor, while I opened the envelope. I pulled out a three-page document. At the top of the first page, in big bold letters, were the words *Summons with notice*.

"That motherfucker!" Chloe yelled when I showed it to her.

"Ooh, Aunt Chloe said a bad word," Jocelyn noted and giggled.

"I'm sorry, girls, but your daddy is a piece of . . . work," Chloe said.

Lindsey took the document from me. "This is horrible timing right now," she said after she'd read the summons.

Of all days to be served divorce papers, this had to be the worst one. A feeling of heaviness came over me. This news only drove me further into a depression. As I was trying to deal with this latest blow, my phone chimed, letting me know that I had received a new text message. It was from Tyrell.

I miss you. Let's get back what we had.

I threw my phone across the room. I needed this fucking black cloud of bad luck to pass me already.

Chris

I had never thought I'd be doing this. I'd gone into my marriage with a promise that my kids would have both parents in their lives. I had wanted my marriage to be the blueprint for our children's future relationships, but here I was, driving a U-Haul truck with Will and Lou to pick up the rest of my things at a house that no longer felt like my home. This week I had made sure to stop by the house and pack my boxes while Karen was at work. She had texted me several days ago, saying that since I no longer lived there, I shouldn't be using my key to go in the house. I'd responded that since I was still paying most of the mortgage, I'd come and go as I pleased. That had led to her call me, and we'd had another huge argument.

Will interrupted my train of thought. "Yo, Chris. Chloe is gonna be there, right?"

Lou answered for me. "Yeah. Why you keep asking?" Lou shook his head.

"This fool wants to know because him and Chloe are feeling each other and won't admit it," I said.

"Nah, that ain't true," Will said defensively.

"Oh yeah? Every time you see each other, you squabble and fight. Then y'all end up fucking later on that night," I said.

Will nodded slowly and licked his lips. "Not *every* time, but she's a wild one."

Lou and I laughed.

Minutes later we pulled up to the house. I decided to ring the doorbell instead of using my keys. Chloe came to the door, opened it without acknowledging us, and then sat back down on the living-room couch, next to Karen. Lindsey sat on the other side of Karen. I knew they'd be there to support her, so I was glad I had Will and Lou around to have my back.

As usual, Chloe was the first to strike. She shook her head and snapped, "You know, that was a real dick move sending that process server here. Why couldn't you man up and give Karen the divorce papers yourself, you pussy?"

"Chloe," Lindsey said.

"Nah, fuck him. He gets no respect from me. He stays having some ugly bitch around K's kids and tries to rub it in her face by bringing her around when he drops them off. Now he springs this shit on her? He doesn't even know everything she's been through, so fuck him!"

"Chloe," Lindsey repeated. Karen and Lindsey looked at her like she'd said too much.

"I don't have time for your shit," I told Chloe and then turned to Karen. "Are the girls in their room? I want to say hi before we start loading my things on the truck."

"Where else would they be, Chris?" Karen asked snidely.

"There's no need for an attitude. I'm asking you a simple question."

"Ladies, ladies, y'all don't have to be so mean. Especially you Chloe," Will said, giving her a hungry look.

"Oh, shut up, with your corny ass. You shouldn't even be here," Chloe said.

Will chuckled and licked his lips. "Now, Chloe, you don't have to act wild in front of your friends. If you need a man in your life to tame you, I'm right here."

"Just because we fucked a couple of times when I was drunk and horny doesn't make you the shit."

"You weren't talking that shit when I was inside you."

"Oh please. You're only five inches," Chloe returned.

Karen's crew chuckled on the couch. Will played it off.

"I'm five inches, but I'm as thick as a soup can. Call me Mr. Progresso, baby."

Chloe couldn't help but shake her head, laugh, and blush.

"You're a clown," Lou said, patting Will on the back.

I appreciated Will's bickering with Chloe. It helped to ease the tension while I went to see the girls. I opened their bedroom door. They were playing with their toy kitchen.

"Hey, girls!"

"Daddy!" they yelled as they ran and hugged me.

I knelt down and gave them hugs and kisses.

"Mommy said you're not going to live here anymore," Jaclyn said with a frown.

"Yeah, she said you were going to live at Poppa's house now," Jocelyn added.

I sighed. "Yeah, that's going to be my house now."

"Why aren't you going to live with Mommy anymore?" Jaclyn asked.

"Yeah, Chris, why *aren't* you?" Karen asked from the doorway. I hadn't even noticed she was standing there.

"Daddy isn't getting along with Mommy, that's why," I told them.

"Real nice, Chris," Karen said.

I rubbed my face and stood up. "All right now, girls. Daddy has to pack his stuff. Mommy will bring you to my new house on Sunday."

Jocelyn was in tears. "No. I don't want you to go. You and Mommy are always fighting, and when it's over, you leave us," she said.

"How come you're not getting along with Mommy anymore? Is it me or Jocelyn's fault?" Jaclyn asked.

The girls cried hysterically.

I hugged my daughters, wiped the tears from their faces, and kissed their foreheads. The questions they had asked showed me the toll that this drama with Karen was taking on our children. They were just as hurt and affected by this as Karen and I were. Seeing my daughters crying broke my heart. I tried to find the right words to say to calm them down.

"It's not either of your faults that me and Mommy are fighting. Your mother and I don't agree on a lot of things, and it's making us argue a lot. We want you guys to be happy and not see us fighting all the time, so we think it's best that we live in different houses."

"But we don't want you to live in different houses. We want you guys to live in the same house, like we did before," Jocelyn said.

"We can't do that anymore. It wouldn't make me or Mommy happy, but it doesn't affect how we feel about you guys." I kissed them both again. "I love you two more than anything. Don't you ever forget that."

"Love you too, Daddy," they said in unison, giving me a big hug.

"All right. Daddy has to go—"

"No, don't leave us," Jaclyn said.

Both of the girls held on to my legs.

"Don't leave, Daddy," Jocelyn said.

I held back my own tears. I thought about what my pops had said a while back about being strong for me when my mom died. I couldn't cry in front of them. I need to be strong and assure them that everything would be fine. I sighed, took a deep breath, and gently pried their hands from my legs. "Everything will be fine. I'm going to see you guys on Sunday, I promise."

They calmed down somewhat, but they were still crying.

I walked out of the room before I lost it myself.

Karen followed me as I went from room to room.

"You're a fucking asshole, you know that?" Karen yelled.

"You're always so busy pointing out my negative shit, but you never take responsibility for the shit you do. *You* did this to us. *You* broke our vows. I loved you. You only *cared* about me. Our relationship was never even, and now I'm ending it while I still have my sanity intact," I said.

"If you go through with this divorce, I swear I'll crush you."

"There's the vindictive, manipulative Karen I know. It's good to see her again. You just proved my point. After all you've done to me, you're still playing the victim. Do what you feel you need to do, Karen."

"I hate you." The look of remorse on Karen's face told me that those words had slipped out, and that she regretted it.

"See? Anger makes the truth come out. I believe you," I told her.

"I didn't mean that."

"I'm sorry I wasn't the man you needed in our marriage. This divorce will correct the problem."

I brought the rest of my boxes into the living room. I needed Lou and Will to help me with some furniture.

"Where's Will?" I asked Lou.

"Do I really need to tell you? He's 'talking' with Chloe in her car," Will answered with a chuckle.

I walked outside to get him. When I looked in Chloe's car, they were tonguing each other down, and he was fingering her. They jumped when I knocked on the window. Chloe rolled down the passenger window.

"Don't touch my fucking car!" Chloe yelled.

I ignored her and looked at Will. "Come on, man. I didn't bring you out here to fuck around. I brought you here to help."

Will rolled down his window. "Give me ten minutes. I got some things I need to tell Chloe."

I sighed and walked back into the house.

"Will is going to finish up his talk with Chloe. He's coming in ten minutes," I told Lou.

"You sure about that, brother?" Lou asked.

"Yeah. Why?"

"Because they just pulled off."

I sucked my teeth and shook my head. "Whatever. Help me lift some of this stuff into the truck."

My argument with Karen today showed me I was doing the right thing by going through with the divorce. There was no point being with someone who not only didn't respect me but also hated me.

Chris

Pops's phone had been ringing almost nonstop. He had scheduled lots of home improvement jobs, and his clients were calling to confirm that he would be doing the work. For a retired man, his side business had been booming. I saved the messages and planned on dedicating an entire day to calling all his clients and canceling the jobs.

"Why don't you take on the work? You did these jobs with him your whole life. It's a great way to hold on to a piece of him by continuing his work and keeping his home improvement business," Nadine said as we sat at the kitchen table at my house.

I thought about it. There were some risks, but her suggestion wasn't too crazy. There were pros and cons, but it could be done.

"It's a big risk. I'd need a lot of help doing everything," I replied.

"You could use all the men your father used. Plus . . . I'd help you."

I kissed her.

Nadine has been by my side every day since our trip around the city. She was helpful with my kids, she uplifted me, and simply put, she made me happy.

Nadine's best friends, LaTesha and Jasmine, met us at my house later that day. Nadine had planned an event that was supposed to be a surprise for me, and we were all going together in one car.

"So, you're the 'perfect guy' that's been stealing all Nadine's time," LaTesha said as Nadine made the introductions.

"I'm not perfect, but I do cherish every minute I spend with her . . ." Then I paused and looked at Nadine. "You were talking about *me*, right?"

She punched my arm.

I laughed. "I just had to make sure," I said.

"Um, she has good taste. You got a brother?" Jasmine asked.

"Nah, no brother, but my friend Lou is single."

I knew she was Lou's type. She was mixed, half Asian and half black, and Lou loved the exotic types. She had almond-shaped eyes and soft Asian facial features, but her body was all sister. She had shapely hips and a round ass.

"You might have to set that up, then," Jasmine said and smiled.

"Screw this heifer. She gets enough men. I'm the one in need," LaTesha laughed.

LaTesha was gorgeous. She had a butterscotch complexion and chestnut eyes. Her breasts were huge. It was hard not to stare at them.

"My friend Will is single too," I revealed. "I'll invite them over one night, and we can let fate do its thing."

"I knew I would like him, Nae," Jasmine told Nadine.

"So where are we headed?" I asked.

"Baby, it's a surprise," Nadine said. "Everybody ready to go?"

We left the house and piled into Nadine's car. Twenty minutes later we arrived at a dance studio in Brooklyn.

"Brooklyn Pole Dance?" I said, reading the sign on the building.

"Yup. I'm taking you to my pole-dancing class," Nadine said.

I shook my head. "I'm going to look like a total perv in there."

"Don't worry, baby. I asked all the other girls, and the teacher said it was cool. You'll be our audience."

I laughed. "You're such a freak!" I said, chuckling.

"And you know this, man!" Nadine said.

The class was amazing. I tried my hardest not to booty watch, but I lost the battle. At the end of the class, Nadine's teacher, Mrs. Green, had Nadine dance for me.

"All right, ladies. Nadine is going to show Mr. Davis here what she's learned," Mrs. Green announced. "Do you think he's ready?"

"No!" the class shouted.

I laughed.

Mrs. Green pushed a chair close to the pole. "Have a seat, Mr. Davis," she said.

LaTesha played Usher's "I Don't Mind" on the sound system. Nadine stood near the pole and swayed her hips seductively to the beat. She wiggled her ass and flicked her tongue at me. I looked over at LaTesha and Jasmine; they were cracking up. Nadine slowly approached the brass pole, wrapped her leg around it, and twirled. I had to admit, she was really good at pole dancing. She did so many tricks, I wondered if she stripped on the side. At one point, Nadine went down into a squat, with the pole between her thighs, and then dropped down into a split. By the end of her dance, I had to cross my legs to hide my hard-on.

The class gave her enthusiastic applause.

Nadine kissed me and said, "So I see you liked it."

"How do you know that?"

"If you uncross your legs, I'll have to fight off every girl in this room." She leaned forward and kissed me again as we laughed.

I loved that she was spontaneous and outgoing. She'd seen me at my worst, so it was easy for me to be myself around her. We hung out with her friends a lot after that, but we also had our date nights. She even went to car shows with me, and I went to pottery and jewelry-making classes with her. Nadine was down for whatever and enjoyed being with me no matter what activity we did. Besides my kids, she was the best thing in my life.

She wasn't like Karen; I didn't feel like I had to work hard to make her happy.

"Yo, Chris. Your girl here is a cheater," Lou yelled.

"Oh stop. You need to step your game up. Now, come on and take this ass whupping!" Nadine joked.

We were at my place. Nadine had challenged Lou to a game of *NBA 2K* on my PlayStation and had destroyed him.

"Damn! How'd you get beat like that?" Will asked.

"Shut up!" Lou pouted.

We laughed at him.

"Aw, don't be mad," Nadine said, hugging him.

Lou smiled.

"Your girl is going to fit in just fine hanging out with us," Will said, slapping his hand on my shoulder.

Karen had the kids, so I had invited Nadine over to my place to hang out with my boys and me. I had known by the look on their faces when they saw her at Pops's funeral that they thought she was sexy. I was even happier when they got to know her. She laughed with them, talked sports, and we all had fun together. Karen's friends had never been too fond of me, and my friends had never been fond of her. So it felt good to finally have a woman in my life that my friends approved of.

"Chris, Nadine is all that. You did good with that, kid," Will said after Nadine had gone home. We were huddled around my kitchen table.

Lou nodded in agreement. "Oh, absolutely," he said.

I shifted in my chair. "I'm feeling her a lot. We have a good time whenever we're out. I'm happy that for once you guys like who I'm dating, but I don't know what the future holds for us. All women start off great. I worry she'll turn into another Karen once she's comfortable."

"I'm going to tell you a story," Will said.

"Oh God, here we go," I sighed.

Will ignored me and launched into his story. "I used to have this Honda Civic, right? I spent crazy money trying to turn it into a beast on the road."

I was confused about where he was going with this story.

He went on. "The car was cool after all the upgrades, but it was still a Honda. Nothing could change that. After having it for a while, I understood what I wanted from a car, and bought my BMW. My Beamer performs the way I want and has everything I want, without me having to change things about it. Eventually, I sold my Civic, and I've been happy sticking with my Beamer ever since."

"Brother, you lost me," I laughed.

"What I'm saying is Karen is your Honda Civic, and Nadine is your BMW. Your first were with Karen, and you tried to help her get her shit together, but she is who she is. She can't change that. Nadine has everything you want."

I nodded. "You're right . . . but did you just compare women to cars?"

"You got what I meant, so that's all that matters."

We laughed at his silliness, but he did have a point.

"Can you toss me that wrench over there?" I asked Nadine.

"Sure," she said, pulling the wrench out of my toolbox.

We were in the garage, working on my Mustang. Nadine leaned over to watch me work under the hood. She didn't know much about cars—I didn't even think she liked them—but she was eager to help me.

"You're bored out of your mind, aren't you?" I asked.

"Nah. I'm learning a lot. I love the look in your eyes when you talk about cars. Plus, I enjoy spending time with you."

"I like having you here with me. It feels nice. I'm used to working on it alone."

"Well, I figured if I keep helping you work on your car, one day you'll have the same passionate look in your eyes when you talk about me," she commented.

I smiled. I dropped one of the screws for my exhaust manifold. "Shit. I hate when—"

Nadine wagged her finger at me. "Five things you love."

"Okay, okay. I love my kids, this house, my car, my pops . . . and you."

"What did you say?"

I kept my eyes focused on searching for the dropped screw and mumbled, "I love you."

"Do you mean that?"

I looked up at her. "Yeah . . . I do." But then I started to have second thoughts. Maybe I was moving too fast.

"I love you too, Chris."

She leaned her forehead against mine. I lifted her chin and kissed her softly.

"I really do," I said.

"I know it might sound fucked up, but I'm glad fate brought us together. We both went through horrible situations, but we met each other for a reason," she mused.

I smiled. She was right. In the short time we'd been together, I'd been happier than I'd ever been with Karen.

"All right. That should do it," I said, tightening the last screw on the exhaust manifold.

"You want me to try to start it up?"

"Yeah."

Nadine got behind the wheel, turned the key in the ignition, and started the Mustang right up. It sounded perfect. This moment was perfect. I'd been working on this car for a long time. My blood, sweat, and tears had gone into this project. When I was a kid, I had loved Mustangs and had promised myself that one day I'd own one. I'd wanted to restore it slowly because, as with my marriage, I'd felt that if I worked with it and was patient, the love and hard work I put into it would truly make me happy. I found it symbolic that I was finally able to finish the work on the Mustang with the woman I was truly in love with.

Karen

"Okay, Karen, if you'll just sign here and then here, that should complete everything," said Chris's lawyer, Mr. Morrison.

We were in Mr. Morrison's office. Chris and I sat across from each other, with our lawyers at our sides. A knot was in my stomach. I had never thought he'd go through with the divorce, but here we were. I had agreed not to take alimony from him if he paid off the house and signed it completely over to me. He had agreed and had used money from his father's insurance to pay off the house.

The thought had crossed my mind to demand half of his father's insurance money and half of his 401(k) out of vindictiveness. He had wanted this divorce, not me. I had wanted to work things out, but he had brought out the bitch in me. As it turned out, I had refrained from going after the insurance money and his 401(k) due to the fact that he might have turned around and ask for half my pension, and my pension was significantly bigger than both the insurance money and his 401(k) combined. So he would have ended up with the fatter check. I had thought for sure he'd try to fuck me over and go after my pension even if I didn't target his 401(k) and insurance money, but he didn't want anything from me. All he wanted was to end our marriage.

So we had agreed not to touch each other's retirement funds. The one thing we had fought over was *our* kids. We'd argued over them for the longest time. Chris had begged me for custody. He'd told me if I let him be the custodial parent, I could see the children anytime I wanted. He'd added that he wouldn't ask for any child support. While a part of me admired him for wanting to be a great father to our kids, another part of me felt he had put up more of a fight trying to keep them than he had trying to fight for our marriage. Deep down, I was ashamed of being jealous that he loved our kids more than he loved me. Out of spite, I had fought with him relentlessly. I had wanted to crush him with child support, but with my work hours, it had ended up being better to have Chris as the custodial parent.

So I fulfilled Mr. Morrison's request now and signed the document.

"Since we're all in agreement, we're done here," Mr. Morrison said when I had finished signing. With a smile, he pushed his chair away from his desk.

"I'm glad we were able to wrap things up quickly," my lawyer, Mrs. Harrell, said, shaking his hand.

I felt like shit, while Chris looked relieved. I curled my bottom lip and reached out to shake Chris's hand.

"Happy?" I asked.

He shook my hand but didn't respond. There was no love in his eyes when he looked at me. His gaze was cold and empty.

Once I was inside my car, I leaned my head against the steering wheel and wept. My marriage was officially dead and buried.

"Sis, you need to pull yourself out of this funk and go out with me tonight," Chloe said as we sat at my kitchen table.

"I'm not really up for going out," I said.

"Oh, c'mon. We're going to go out and be skinny, skanky, and slutty."

I laughed. No matter what anyone said about Chloe, she always had my back.

"Now you can add *single* to the list and find the guy you deserve," she said.

"Chloe, I don't want another guy. I had the guy I deserved, and I fucked it up."

"Fuck Chris. This divorce was the best thing that could've happened to you."

I took a cigarette out of my purse, lit it, and took a long drag. "I still don't understand why you hate him so much. Let that grudge go," I said.

Chloe watched me smoke and said, "Sometimes the things we want aren't good for us. Chris wasn't good for you. He's comfortable, and you love him, but he's not what makes you truly happy."

I rolled the cigarette between my fingers and then put it out in the ashtray. "Maybe you're right."

"Oh, there's no maybes. I know I'm right. Now get dressed. We're going out. We're going to have a great night, and later we're planning your divorce party!"

I shook my head, stood up from the table, and prepared myself for a night of partying.

It was 6:00 a.m. on a Sunday morning, and I was tiptoeing out of a random guy's hotel room. With my purse in one hand and my shoes and car keys in the other, I did the walk of shame through the hotel lobby to my car. Overall, the guy was decent, but he was yet another meaningless fuck for me. I would never see him again, nor did I want to.

For the past six months, every weekend had been like this for me. Chris would have the kids, and I'd party hard, unrestricted, and free. I didn't care if guys were trying to run game on me. I lived in the moment and blocked all my pain with alcohol and sex.

My head was still pounding from my hangover when I pulled into my garage. I figured I would use the rest of today to recuperate.

It felt weird not seeing Chris's Mustang parked in there anymore. He'd been moving more of his things from the house every time he dropped off the kids, further distancing himself from me. I leaned my head back against the headrest. I sighed and prepared myself to be depressed for the rest of the day.

I slowly made my way from the garage to the kitchen. I made some coffee, turned on the TV in the living room, and scrolled through all the shows on my DVR. My plan was to catch up on the ones I had missed during the week. As I sipped my coffee, Lindsey called. I thought about answering the phone, but I let the call go to voice mail. My head was throbbing, and I wanted to be alone. But five minutes later the doorbell rang. I got a text from Lindsey saying she was outside. I answered the door.

"Hey, bestie," I said.

"Hey," she answered.

She walked in, and we hugged.

"You want some coffee?" I asked.

"Nah. What are you doing today?"

"Nothing. Gonna relax and catch up on my shows. My head's still bumping from last night."

"I actually came to talk to you about last night," she informed me as she followed me into the living room.

I had known this was coming. Lindsey was my best friend, and even though she loved me like a sister, she wouldn't hesitate to check me when she felt it was needed.

"What's up?"

"I know you're going through a lot of shit, but this has to stop. This isn't you anymore. You're better than this," she blurted as we both took a seat on the couch.

I ran my hand over my hair and down my face. "This *is* me. With Chris, I lost who I was. I wasn't the fun party girl I used to be. My life had become routine and boring."

"So, you think getting drunk all the time and partying will improve it? Things have changed, K. You're an adult now. You have responsibilities and children. I agree, you do need to have fun, but part of life is growing up and leaving that childish shit behind."

I stared at my wedding ring. I was too damn emotional to respond.

"Every weekend, you're partying and sleeping with guy after guy. Is that really making you happy?" she said.

I managed to get my emotions under control enough to answer. "I'm not happy, but what am I supposed to do? When I'm home, I'm depressed as shit. Things at work are starting to get a little better, but the whispers are still there. People are still gossiping about me, and it hurts."

Lindsey put her hand on my shoulder.

"I'm divorced, Lindsey. At first, I felt that it was only some stupid paperwork, that in time everything would go back to normal, and that this would only be temporary, like a bad dream. But when I look in Chris's eyes, I know it's real. I know it's over." My throat tightened. Tears welled in my eyes, and my lips quivered. "That love he had for me is gone. He's given it to Nadine. He's happy with her. I'm nothing more than the mother of his children, and I'm scared I'll never find someone to make me happy."

"Karen, you have to let go. You'll find the right guy for you. It might not happen right away or when you want it, but you will. I want you to promise me something, though."

I huffed. "What?"

"When the right one comes around, you'll work things out with him whenever there's a problem."

"Of course I will . . . What do you mean?"

"With Chris, a part of the reason things didn't work out is that you compared him to too many other men. You compared him to Raheem. You compared him to Tyrell. You even compared him to Jeff."

I nodded. She was right.

"Of course, you want to help your man become better, but don't try to turn him into something he's not. Learn from this experience so history doesn't repeat itself," she advised me.

We hugged. We spent the rest of the day talking. It was time I started to apply Lindsey's advice.

Another six months passed, and during that time I swore off men completely. I didn't even entertain the idea of dating, because in my mind, finding a good man was like finding a unicorn. I was alone, but I wasn't lonely. I had my friends, my sister, and most importantly, I had myself. Chloe tried numerous times to convince me to party and fuck my pain away, but I didn't allow myself to be persuaded. I told her I was sticking with my decision to swear off men, and even though she strongly disagreed, she respected my decision.

These past few months had shown me I didn't require a man in my life to be happy. I needed to find happiness within myself first and understand that when the time was right, a man would enhance my already happy life. For years, I had felt I had to find a Prince Charming to rescue me so I could live happily ever after. This whole ordeal with Chris had helped me to break out of that fantasy and had forced me to grow up.

Things with Chris had improved somewhat. I had had to realize that no matter how much I wanted things to be the way they were or how much I tried to repair our past, things would never be the same with us. The only thing I could do now was make the best of the situation for the sake of our children. Now whenever Chris and I interacted, we weren't cold and argumentative. We were cordial. As far as Chris's girlfriend, Nadine, was concerned, I had stopped thinking about her as the woman who took my man. I'd even met her a few times, and she was always pleasant. She was nice to my kids, and while I could never be friends with her, the least I could do was be somewhat friendly toward her.

I was jolted back to the present when my tire pressure light came on after I hit two huge potholes on the road. My car started shaking and sputtering.

"Fuck, fuck, fuck!" I screamed. I was driving to work, and now I knew I was going to be late.

I steered my car onto the shoulder of the expressway, out of the way of traffic. I slapped the steering wheel in frustration.

"Fucking great!" I yelled.

I called Chloe. No answer. I called Lindsey. Her phone went straight to voice mail. I remembered she always turned her phone off when she was teaching. I called Vivian and Judy, but no answer. As a last resort, I called Chris.

"Yeah? What's up?" he answered.

"Are you still home, or are you already in the city?"

"I'm in the city. Why?"

"My tire blew out, and I'm stranded on the side of the road."

"Our . . . You should still have triple A on your car. Look in the glove compartment. You should find all the info in there. That should help. I gotta go."

"All right. Thanks."

He ended the call. I followed what he'd said to do, and discovered that our fucking AAA had expired. I stepped

out of the car to assess the damage. It was fucking freez-
ing. While I was surveying the tire, a black BMW 6 Series
pulled up next to me.

The driver rolled down his window. "Excuse me, miss.
Do you need some help?"

Any other day, I would've told the dude to keep stepping, but it was too damn cold to have an attitude.

"Yeah. These two massive potholes came out of nowhere,
and now I have a flat."

"Do you have a regular spare or at least a doughnut?"

I shrugged. "I don't know anything about that stuff."

"Do you mind if I check your trunk?"

"You can, but I don't think there's one in there."

He parked behind me, put on his flashing lights, then
climbed out of the BMW. I popped my trunk for him. He
fished around inside, raised the lid on the compartment
underneath, and found a doughnut spare tire and a jack.

"I can help you put this on if you want," he said as he
pulled out the doughnut and the jack.

"Please do."

He knelt down and got to work on my tire. It had been
a while since a guy had caught my eye, but this one did,
so I checked him out a bit. He was tall, about six feet five,
and he had a mocha-colored complexion. And he was in
decent shape and *fine*.

He wiped his brow when he had finished changing
the tire and stowing the flat one in my trunk. "There
you go. That should get you where you're going, at least
temporarily."

"Thank you so much." I reached in my purse. "Let me
give you a few dollars for your time."

"Nah, I'm good."

"No, no. Time is money," I insisted.

"Seriously, I'm good." He pulled out his wallet and
handed me a business card. "I own an auto shop not too

far from here. When you want to replace that tire, stop by.
I'll take care of you."

I was tired and stressed from this early morning
tire bullshit, so I thought about taking the day off and
handling this tire right away. I needed a mental health
day from work, anyway.

"Are you headed to your shop now?" I asked.

"Yup."

"Would you be able to help me replace the tire now?"

"Sure. Just follow me."

The only reason I was being bold and agreeing to
follow this random stranger—random *fine* stranger—was
that I'd driven past his business before, so I knew it
existed. I called my job, told my supervisor, Roger, I had
car trouble and needed the day off, then followed Mr.
Handy and Handsome to his shop. Fifteen minutes later,
I was inside the shop's waiting room.

"All right, Mrs. . . . ."

I had my gloves on, so Mr. Handy and Handsome
couldn't see my wedding ring, but I corrected him. "It's
Ms., and my name is Karen."

"Well, Ms. Karen, my name is Andre. Please have a seat,
and my men will take care of you."

He talked to his staff. I saw them nod, and then one of
them drove my car into the garage. I sat in the waiting
room for about two and half hours, reading the magazines that were around, drinking coffee, and playing
games on my phone. Finally, Andre reappeared with
paperwork in his hand.

"Karen, can you come into my office for a minute?"

"Coming." I followed him into his office and sat in the
chair in front of his desk.

"How much is everything?" I asked.

"Well, for starters your front brakes were shot, you
badly needed an oil change, and your windshield wipers

were beyond worn. We took care of all those for you, but we also needed to replace both of your front tires. I gave you a break with everything, so I'm only charging you two hundred seventy-five dollars. The tires alone cost that much."

"Thank you for that, but this isn't what I fucking need right now. I didn't know tires were that damn costly."

He stared at me. "I guess this expense isn't good for your budget, huh?"

I sucked my teeth. "No, it's not."

He shifted in his chair. He looked uncomfortable. "Please don't take this the wrong way. I'm not trying to be rude or come on too strong, but how about you go out to lunch with me today, and we'll call it even?"

I gave him the side eye. "Excuse me? It sounds like you're trying to pick me up."

"I am . . . sort of. Look, you seem nice. I work all the time, and I don't get to meet a lot of nice, attractive women. I'm just asking you to bless me with your presence for lunch. That's all. If you have a good time, maybe we can exchange numbers and have dinner sometime. If not, at least you'll have a free lunch, and you'll have your car fixed for free today. It's a win-win."

He was right. Either way it was good for me. If he was an ass, I'd never talk to him again, and I'd still have my car fixed and a free lunch. If he behaved himself and proved interesting, maybe I'd let him take me on a real date. *Maybe.* I had a feeling he thought I'd be an easy piece of ass. If he believed that, he had another thing coming. I hadn't touched a man in months and had no plans to break that streak now.

"I'll play nice and have lunch with you, but I'll follow you to the restaurant in my car," I told him.

"How do I know you won't drive off and ditch me?"

I shrugged. "You don't."

He laughed. "Fair enough."

Although the thought did cross my mind to ditch him, I followed him along Route 110 to Blackstone Steakhouse. He opened the door for me, which was a plus, and pulled my chair out when we sat at our table. I loved that he was gentlemanly, but I figured he was just running game. Raheem had put up the same façade when he was courting me.

"Order whatever you want," he said as we gazed at our menus.

I gave him a small grin. "I plan on it. You invited me out to lunch. I didn't expect to have a limit on the price of what I could order."

He laughed. I didn't even crack a smile.

"You look nice today," he said after he closed his menu.

I sighed. "Thank you for the compliment. I'm flattered, but I'm not up for games. Compliment me when you mean it. If you want to get to know me, be real and honest with me."

"I meant what I said. Trust me, I'm not into playing mind games, either. If you allow me to get to know you, you'll see that I'm a genuine brotha."

"We'll see about that."

"So, do you work around this area?" he asked.

"Yeah, I work for National Grid. Are you married?"

He looked at my hand and noticed my wedding ring. I still hadn't taken it off after all this time. "Divorced. You?" he said.

"The same. Was your divorce a hot mess or peaceful?"

"Uh, a hot mess."

"Why?"

He fidgeted. My direct questions made him nervous, and I liked that. His discomfort could help keep him honest or at least help me to decipher if he was bullshitting. It wouldn't be much, but his answers would expose little pieces of himself to me and would let me know what type of man I was dealing with.

"You want the politically correct answer or the truth?"

"Humor me. Give me both."

"The politically correct answer would be, we grew apart. The truth is, I cheated on her because our marriage lacked passion. I could lie, but I want to be real and honest with you."

I nodded. "Keep going."

"You want to know more about my old marriage?"

"Yup. If I know why it failed, it'll help me to see if you're worth dating or if history will repeat itself. We both established that we don't want to waste each other's time."

"Fair enough . . . She never gave a shit about anything. She was always nonchalant. She had no dreams, hobbies, or passions. I couldn't live like that. I didn't want to break her heart completely and leave her, so I cheated."

Now I was the one shifting uncomfortably. "Did she ever find out?"

He looked pained by that question. "No. To this day, she still has no idea. The woman I cheated with was married. I thought she shared the same feelings I had and was going to leave her husband, but she had a change of heart and decided to stay with him. The damage was already done for me, though. I had already ended things with my ex."

"Does this ex of yours have a name?"

"Does it matter?"

I nodded. "It matters to me."

"Her name is Qiana."

"Cute name."

He shrugged.

"You have any kids?" I asked.

"She didn't want any. She had her tubes tied before we married, and never told me. I found out one day, when we argued over the possibility of starting a family. All right. You've been asking a lot of questions. It's my turn."

I didn't have to answer shit. He was the one pursuing me, but I humored him. I sighed and said, "Ask away."

"Do you have any kids?"

"Yup. I have twin girls."

"Cool. Do they live with you?"

"No, they stay with my ex-husband, but I see them almost every day."

"Does this ex-husband have a name?"

"Chris. Now back to you. Why didn't you try to get Qiana back after things fell apart with your side piece?"

He cringed when I said, "Side piece."

"If I'd gone back to her, I'd have only ended up cheating on her with someone else. It wouldn't have been right, and I didn't want to continue being a liar and a cheater."

His pain echoed my pain. I told him about Chris and the horrendous saga that had led to our divorce. I felt oddly comfortable talking to him. I felt like he understood me because we had similar situations. He explained that his divorce had made him into a better man. He was more ambitious, wanting to expand his business to more locations, and true to himself. He had promised himself that if he were ever to marry again, he'd marry the "right" woman for him. It was still too early for me to determine what kind of man he was, but so far, he had my attention.

In the weeks that followed, Andre and I went on more dates. He was good company and someone I could vibe with. He was easy to talk to, he made me laugh, and he understood I was in no rush to enter a relationship.

Overall, he was a good guy. He was someone with whom I could have dinner, catch a movie, and go to functions when I needed a male companion. He was a deep brother. Mentally, he stimulated me, and that was a huge turn-on. What I liked about him was also what I feared about him. The things he would do and say had the power to create a false sense of hope, and I didn't want to get hurt. I wished I could stop the feelings that were blossoming, but I couldn't help it. They were there.

On our sixth date, we kissed. It was at the company Christmas party. I usually brought Chris to the party, but that was over. I didn't want to go alone, so I took Andre.

"It's good to see you, Karen," Roger said when we bumped into each other.

"Thanks. It's good to see you too. This is my . . . uh . . . friend Andre."

Roger and Andre shook hands.

As soon as Andre and I left Roger's side and turned around to mingle some more, Tyrell was smack-dab in my face.

"Hi, Karen. Can we talk?" he said.

I sighed. "What do you want to talk about, Tyrell?"

"All I'm asking for is five minutes . . . Please."

I mouthed to Andre, "Give me a minute."

Andre nodded.

Tyrell and I stepped off to the side so that we could have a modicum of privacy.

"Karen, I've been calling, texting, and emailing you. You haven't answered any of my messages."

"Because what we had is over, Tyrell. I lost a marriage over my mistake with you."

Andre was sitting at our table now, giving me space, but his eyes stayed on Tyrell and my every move. I nodded to let him know everything was okay.

"You got thirty seconds. Say your piece," I told Tyrell.

"Let's get back what we had. I know I was fucked up with the way I acted, but you know how I feel about you."

"And how is that?"

He leaned in close to my ear. "I love you, Karen."

"Oh, stop. The only thing you loved was fucking me. Those times are dead and gone. Have a good night. And say hello to your wife, Pamela, for me."

I was turning to head back over to Andre when Tyrell grabbed my arm and spun me back to face him.

"I'm not done talking to you yet. Who's the dude you're with?" he said.

I yanked my arm away. "He's none of your concern, and don't you ever put your hands on me again."

"I'm sorry, all right? I just feel like you're not seeing I'm being real with you."

Having read my body language with Tyrell, Andre stood up from the table, walked over, and gave him a stiff shove.

"Your time is up, brother. She's with me," Andre said.

"Mind your business. I'm talking to Karen."

Andre shoved him again. "This is the last time I'm going to tell you. Back off. She's with me."

They stared each other down. Roger and some other coworkers looked in our direction. I stepped between Andre and Tyrell before things got out of hand and I ended up embarrassed in front of important people in my company.

"Tyrell, have a good night," I said.

"So that's it? After all the things we did and all the time we spent together, that's it?" Tyrell muttered.

"That's it," I said.

He shook his head, huffed, and stormed out of the party.

Andre took my hand.

"Thanks for rescuing me," I said, smiling at him.

"Was that the Tyrell you told me you had the past with?"

"Yup, that was him."

Andre kissed my hand.

"I'm glad you're here with me," I said.

"I'm glad you invited me."

I hugged him. "Seriously, thank you. That was hard for me."

He leaned in, and we kissed. His soft lips felt heavenly on mine.

"I'm here for you, K. I want you to see that."

On our tenth date, I went to Andre's condo. We had finished having dinner, and he invited me to see where he lived.

"Well, this is the place I call home," he said as we stood in the entryway.

"You mind if I walk around?"

"You want a tour?"

"Nah. I can manage on my own."

I strolled from room to room, admiring his home but also looking to see if there were any signs that he was living with a woman. He had a modest place. It wasn't cluttered or messy, but it could use a woman's touch.

A few minutes later Andre and I sat down on the couch. His hand grazed my breast as he drew me close to him. We shared a nice soft kiss. My wandering hands traveled down his chest to his crotch. I rubbed, massaged, and measured the outline in his pants, which was swelling and throbbing. His hands traveled under my skirt. He pulled down my thong and massaged the head of my clit. Our gaze was so intense; our breathing, so thick and heavy. I thought about the last sexual experience I had had, the one where I had creeped out of a random man's hotel room early in the morning. I had disrespected myself for too long and had shared my treasure with men who weren't worth my time. I stopped massaging his dick and moved his hand from my clit.

He looked confused. "What's wrong?" he asked.

"Not yet."

"Did I do something wrong?"

"No. I need more time to get to know you before I share myself completely."

Disappointment was in his eyes. He sighed and adjusted himself in his jeans.

I thought that maybe it was a mistake to be here. I started to get up to leave, but he gently held my hand and said, "Stay. We don't have to do anything you don't want to. When you're ready, I'm ready."

I smiled at him.

After that night, I felt comfortable hanging around his house. We would often end up falling asleep while holding each other on his couch. Sometimes our passion would lead us to a lot of touching and kissing, but he never pressured me. There was no fucking involved, though. I didn't want to waste a number on another loser. I needed to be sure he was worthy of experiencing the privilege of being intimate with me.

We talked on the phone every day. He would stop by my job on my lunch hour to take me out, and if I was swamped with work and couldn't have lunch with him, he'd bring lunch to my office.

By date twenty-five, I felt I was ready. We went to the boardwalk at Jones Beach, held hands, and walked and talked.

"I want you," I said.

He looked me in the eyes and said, "I want you too."

"I mean, I'm ready to share myself with you completely."

"Are you sure? I'm a patient man. For you, I'm willing to wait. I want our first time to be special."

"I couldn't be surer."

"What made you realize that you wanted to be intimate with me?" he asked.

"I appreciate the little things you've been doing for me. You've been respectful, a gentleman, and I trust you. I haven't trusted a man in a long time."

Andre wrapped his arm around my waist, pulled me to him, then slid his tongue in my mouth and kissed me. This wasn't our first kiss, but this time it felt different, more genuine. Each second I kissed him, I felt my heart thawing and welcoming his embrace.

Our clothes were scattered all over Andre's bedroom floor. We'd been all over each other, kissing and groping as soon as we reached his front door. We stood next to his bed now in our underwear, holding each other, our breathing choppy and erratic. He pulled off his boxers, then slid my panties down my legs and dropped them to the floor. I tugged and twisted my engagement ring and wedding band. Once I got them off, I placed them on his nightstand. I felt naked without them, but it was time to move on and let go. My body desperately needed this. It had been so long since I had felt the need to have a man fill me, stretch me, and fuck me.

Andre kissed my neck while he held my breasts.

"Mmm," I moaned.

He leaned down and sucked my nipples, alternating from one to the other. Then Andre took my hand and laid me on the bed. He knelt down, caressed my legs, and sucked on my toes. I was in complete bliss. My treasure was wet and aching for relief.

I looked at him and said, "I'm ready."

He nodded, stood up, and opened one of his dresser drawers. After retrieving a condom, he tore open the packet. His dick looked scrumptious as he rolled on his condom.

Andre climbed on the bed and lowered himself gently on top of me. I was trying to hold back my emotions. I was also attempting to convince myself that I wanted this to be no more than another meaningless fuck with a fine man, but that was a lie. I wanted this to be real. I wanted this to have meaning and to lead to more.

I gazed into his eyes. "Don't . . . hurt me, okay?"

He cradled my face, gently stroked my cheeks with his thumbs. "I have no intention of ever doing you wrong."

He kissed me, and at that moment, all my negative thoughts, worries, and emotions vanished. The way he handled me made me believe his desire was deeper than sex.

He placed soft kisses on my collarbone, then on my nipples. I felt the plump head of his cock graze the entrance to my treasure. I writhed and moaned in anticipation. I caught my breath when he entered me. He started out slow and steady. I shivered at the sensation of his fullness traveling between my lips, into my slit, and deep inside me. He spread my thighs even more. I got even wetter as I watched his thick dick work its magic as it slid in and out of me. The wait was worth it!

I held on for dear life, at his mercy, as his pace quickened and his depth increased. I reached up and caressed his face. He sucked on my fingers and continued his deep strokes. Each stroke broke down the walls I had built around my heart. Eventually, I pulled my fingers from his mouth and gripped his shoulders. Consumed by pleasure, I held Andre close and kissed the side of his face as I trembled at the strength of my orgasm. Andre kept pumping into me. Then his breathing quickened, and he moaned into my mouth. His eyes were shut tight, and he bit his bottom lip. He groaned and shuddered as I felt him release. His dick pulsated inside me when he came.

Afterward, I lay on top of Andre as we both panted. I was still shaking from my orgasm as he placed soft kisses on my neck. Our sex was so intense and so good. It was exactly what I *needed*. At some point, I rolled off of him, and we spooned. I felt butterflies when he kissed the back of my neck and rubbed my shoulders. Then we fell into a deep sleep.

I woke up in the morning in Andre's arms. He was still sleeping comfortably. In my head, I began to consider whether he was better or worse in bed than Chris. I closed my eyes and stopped myself, blocking out that thought. They both pleased me in different ways, and in order to truly let go, I had to stop comparing every man to Chris. I had had a beautiful, satisfying evening. I savored the moment and snuggled closer to Andre. In my head, I'd already accepted that nothing would come out of fucking him, but I decided to enjoy this moment. I figured that either he would either hit it and quit it or he would want to be a steady booty call. The choice to keep him as a booty call was mine alone, but If he wanted that option, I would cut his ass off in a second. I was sure this would be a one-time affair.

I couldn't believe I was telling myself this, but Andre Miles had stolen my heart! This wasn't supposed to happen, and I sure as hell wasn't looking for it, but fate had brought him into my life and had ignited feelings in me I thought were long dead and buried. I had thought that as soon as he got some ass, he would be gone, but he had stayed around. I had figured I'd keep him around as a lover, as someone who wasn't technically *my man*, but he wanted to be exclusive and official. I had thought that as time went by, he would get too comfortable, and all the things I loved about him would fade, but he'd been consistent.

My sister and my friends loved him. He had gone out dancing with all of us several times and had enjoyed relaxing and having a good time with us after a long workweek.

Tonight we were at Avenue, a nightclub on Tenth Avenue in Manhattan. Chloe was dancing with Lindsey, while Vivian and Judy danced with guys they had met at the club. Beyoncé's "7/11" boomed from the club's speakers. As I ground my ass against Andre and twerked like a stripper, he held on to my hips and rubbed his cock against my ass.

"Ooh, get it, sis," Chloe yelled.

I turned around, wrapped my arms around Andre's neck, and swayed to the beat. Andre looked at me like I was the only woman in the club. After a couple more songs, I decided to sit some out. I left the dance floor and sat down next to Chloe and Lindsey, while Andre danced with Vivian and Judy.

"Sis, your man is too fine," Chloe said, fanning herself.

"Thanks. I enjoy him," I said, looking at Andre with admiration.

"It's nice to see you so happy again, K," Lindsey said.

"I'm not trying to bash Chris anymore, but you're a much better fit with Andre. He gives you more of what you want. I never really hated Chris. I just wanted to see you happy," Chloe commented.

"Are you saying that now because you're secretly dating Will?" I asked.

"Way to ruin a nice moment, sis."

We laughed.

When the song that was playing ended, Andre walked over to Chloe, grabbed her hand, and took her to the dance floor, where they rejoined Vivian and Judy. The four of them danced to "Tuesday," by ILoveMakonnen, and made funny faces at me.

"Look at you. You're glowing, K," Lindsey said as she gazed out at the dance floor.

I giggled. "I know. He makes me very happy."

Andre was everything I needed.

He was *attentive*.

For example, one day when I was at work, finishing a huge report, my phone rang.

"Hey, baby," Andre said when I picked up.

"Hi, honey. I was just thinking about you."

Doing his best Stevie Wonder impression, he sang, "I just called to say I love you!"

"Aw, I love you too."

Andre made sure to text me and to call me every day to see how I was doing. And even when I talked his ear off, he listened to me. It made me feel warm inside when he remembered small details from previous conversations.

He was *giving*.

He sent flowers to me at my job. He made romantic plans for us at least once a week. And sexually, he always made sure I was satisfied.

Andre was *understanding*.

For instance, the other day I was presented with quite a dilemma, and despite the fact that it was a bit awkward for him, Andre offered to help. When I turned down his offer, he completely understood where I was coming from.

"Fuck!" I shouted as I stood in the kitchen, preparing a cup of tea.

"What up, babe?" Andre said as he stared at me from his spot at the table.

"Chris just texted me. The kids have a birthday party they're invited to on Saturday, and he can't take them, because he made plans with Nadine. I planned on going into the office to do OT, but I guess that's not happening now."

"If you want, I'll take them to the party so you can work," he offered without blinking.

I smiled. "Thanks, but you would be a total stranger to them."

"Whose fault is that? I'd love to meet your kids. I'm down for helping you with them anytime."

"Soon. I'm not ready to introduce you to them yet. I need a little more time in our relationship before I'll be comfortable with that, okay?"

"I get it. Does Chris know about me?"

"Not yet. I don't discuss my love life with him. It's a little weird, since our divorce . . ." I sighed and held his hand. "I'm not ashamed of you. I just need your patience with these things, please."

"I'll fall back and let you and Chris handle things for now, but I'm in this for the long run. I want to be fully involved in your life."

In all honesty, if things ended quickly with Andre, I didn't want Chris to think I was always in failing relationships. I shouldn't care what Chris thought about me at this point, but I did. I was lucky to have someone like Andre, who knew when to give me my space and when to give me extra love and affection to make me feel better.

Andre complimented me often and made me feel special. I saw the sincerity in his eyes when he told me that I was beautiful and that he loved me. He included me in his plans and saw a future with me. Most importantly, Andre did all the little things I liked without me asking him to. He was crazy about me. Furthermore, he appreciated me, and I made sure he knew I appreciated him too. He put in the effort, so I matched his work. I thanked him, complimented him, and told him how much he meant to me often, something I had neglected to do when I was married to Chris.

When we had our little spats, this time around I held nothing inside. I told him what bothered me, but I also took the time to determine the things that I had fucked up on. When I messed up, I owned it and apologized. For example, one evening I gave Andre a really hard time about going to hang out with his buddies without me. Then I realized how selfish I was being. I owned it when I saw him later that night at his place.

"I'm sorry. I know I was selfish. You work a lot, and the little bit of time you do have, you mostly spend it with me. I shouldn't have given you shit about hanging out with your friends," I said.

Andre nodded. "It's not like I don't invite you out to hang out with us. Tonight was guys' night, and we rarely have those."

He was right. Most of the time, he invited me to hang out with his friends Kyle, Brandon, and Keith. They were good guys, all married and successful. Andre had been friends with them since elementary school. Now and then, we would all go out as couples.

"I'm sorry. Do you forgive me?" I said.

"You know I can't stay mad at you," Andre said, then kissed me.

Andre wasn't perfect; he had his flaws. Everyone did. But he was definitely the type of man I needed.

Chris

The club was packed. The music thumped, and everyone moved and grooved to the rhythm.

"Baby, can you get me something to drink?" Nadine asked me.

"Yeah. What would you like, my dear?"

"You know what I like," she said, licking her lips.

"Don't start nothing you can't finish in here," I joked.

"Who said I would finish it in here?" she said, bouncing her eyebrows.

"I'll hold you to that when we get home."

"You better!" Nadine playfully slapped my ass when I turned to get her drink.

I pushed through the crowd and headed for the bar. In front of me a woman with a shapely figure was swaying her ass to the music. When she turned around, she damn near bumped into me. Of all the places I could've bumped into Karen, it had to be at this club. I didn't want to be rude, so I spoke to her.

"Hey, Karen. How are you?"

"I'm well. I'm surprised to see you in here. You hate clubs," she replied.

"Yeah, well, Nadine likes to dance, so—" I began, but she interrupted me.

"I liked to dance when we were together too—"

I interrupted her and changed the subject. "Who has the kids?"

"Lindsey and Chloe are staying overnight at the house. They're treating the girls to the movies and ice cream."

"Cool. Are you here with Vivian and Judy?"

She fidgeted, and she had a little smirk on her face. "They're over there." She pointed them out on the dance floor. "But I'm actually here with my man . . ."

I swallowed hard. "Oh . . . I didn't know you had someone new in your life."

"I know."

There was a long, uncomfortable pause.

She pointed. "There he is."

I saw a tall brother heading toward us. He walked up and looked me up and down. The dude was tall, but he had nothing on me. If he thought he was intimidating me, he was highly mistaken. He leaned in, kissed Karen, and wrapped his arm around her. It was obvious he thought I was trying to hit on her.

"Look at you, sexy. I leave to go to the bathroom for five minutes, and brothers are flocking to you," he told Karen.

"Honey, this is actually my ex-husband, Chris. Chris, this is Andre."

I braced myself for tension, but the guy's expression was pleasant.

"Oh, how are you, Chris?" He shook my hand. "I'm Andre. Karen speaks very highly of you. She said you're a good brother that takes care of his children. I respect that."

His statement shocked me. I could tell Karen was just as surprised, but she smiled and hugged him.

"Well, thank you. I appreciate it," I said. "I got to order my lady her drink, but it was nice meeting you, Andre. Take care of Kar . . . I mean, you two have a good night."

Karen smiled at me, and I gave them both a friendly nod.

I went to the bar and ordered a martini straight up with a twist for Nadine. I walked back to her and handed her the drink.

"Is that who I think it is?" she asked.

"Yup."

"Is everything cool? Do you want to go? We don't have to stay here if you're not comfortable."

"Are you having a good time?" I asked her.

"Yes, but—"

"Are you happy?"

"Yes."

"Then everything is cool. Karen's toned down her bitchiness, and her new man is respectful. We're good."

Nadine smiled and gave me a light kiss.

"What's that for?" I asked.

"I'm sure you don't want to be here, especially now that Karen is here, but you want to stay because you know it makes me happy."

I nodded.

"That's what I love about you," she told me.

Chris Brown's "New Flame" came on. The DJ called for all the couples to make their way to the dance floor. Nadine grabbed my hand and pulled me to the dance floor. I held her close and stared at her, in awe of how good she looked with her head on my chest. We swayed to the music, and she looked like she was in heaven. At some point I glanced over at Karen and her new guy. I watched as he pulled her close. She held his hands, smiled, and stared lovingly in his eyes. The way she looked at him, I knew she loved him.

As I watched them, a flame of jealousy sparked inside me. Nadine had my heart. I loved her, and she'd been my rock, but when I looked over at Karen, I saw my past. Seeing this man succeed in making Karen happy made me feel like a failure. It sucked. But I shook those thoughts off and thought about the woman who was in my arms, the woman who deserved my heart.

I leaned close and whispered in Nadine's ear. "You look beautiful, baby."

"Aw, thank you."

"I love you, Nadine."

She looked up at me. "I love you too, Chris."

I couldn't deny that I felt some type of way seeing Karen with another man, but we were over, and she deserved someone who could make her happy. That responsibility wasn't mine anymore. I had what I needed in Nadine.

Karen

"I know you have the kids coming, so I'll go now. I'll text you when I get home," Andre said as he stood in the middle of my bedroom.

I yawned and stretched as I stepped out of bed. "No, you don't have to leave. Stay."

"You sure?"

"Yup. It's time."

Andre had met my friends and my sister. He had finally met Chris, though not exactly the way I would've planned it, but it had still worked out. The only thing I needed to do now was introduce him to my children.

An hour later Chris brought the girls over to the house.

"Hey, Mommy!" Jocelyn said when she ran through the front door.

"Morning!" Jaclyn said.

"Hey, girls," I called as I walked toward them, with Andre right behind me.

They stopped in their tracks when they saw Andre.

"Girls, this is Mommy's friend, Andre."

They said hello to him, shook his hand, then ran to the couch and turned on the TV.

We laughed.

"Good morning, Chris," I said, kissing him on the cheek.

"Good morning." Then Chris looked past me and said, "Hey, Andre."

Andre stood next to me and shook Chris's hand. "What's up, brother? How are you?" he said.

"I'm good."

Andre looked past Chris and out the window and said, "Is that your Mustang out there in the driveway?"

Chris nodded. "Yeah. You want to check it out?"

"Hell yeah!"

"You got it working?" I asked, surprised.

Chris nodded again. "Yup."

Chris took Andre for a quick drive around the block. A part of me was worried that they'd discuss me or end up fighting, but all I could do was trust that things would be fine. In their absence, I talked to the girls about Andre. I explained that he made me very happy, and that he'd be hanging out with us for a while.

Chris and Andre came back inside the house and wouldn't shut up about cars. While it annoyed me to hear them babbling about different engines and horsepower, I was glad they got along.

As the days passed, Andre spent more and more time with the girls and me. He helped them with their homework; took them to amusement parks, like Adventureland and Great Adventure; and read them bedtime stories on the nights I was exhausted from work. The kids were fond of him, but Chris was the most important man in their lives, as he should be.

Chris

I'd been with Nadine for over a year, and I couldn't be happier. She had sold her house. She'd said the memory of her ex-husband cheating on her still lived in those walls. She'd explained that living with me in my . . . *our* house would be a fresh start.

She'd been with me through my toughest times: Karen's cheating, my father's death, and my divorce. I cared for her. I trusted her. I loved her. Nadine made me better. But there were times when I would fuck up and go back to my old habits. Today was one of those days.

"Baby, I'm going to shower. Come and join me," Nadine said as we stood in our bedroom.

I was exhausted from working all day and playing with the kids afterward. "Nah. I'm just going to watch some of this Nets game. I'll be here when you come out."

Nadine undressed, stood in front of me, rubbed her breasts on my face, and said, "I'm not taking no for an answer."

I thought about the times when Karen had asked me to shower with her and I had turned her down. I didn't want history to repeat itself.

"Well, in that case, you have my undivided attention," I said.

I tore my clothes off. Nadine giggled as I lifted her up and carried her into the shower. We bathed each other, and I gave her the affection she craved.

What I loved about Nadine was that instead of fighting with me or letting things build up, she took the initiative. If she wanted me to hold her hand, she grabbed my hand. Her straightforwardness was what *I needed*. It helped me realize when I was acting like a jackass, and since she didn't complain all the time, I *want* to do those types of things for her. For instance, I hated clubs, but she loved dancing. Out of love for her, I sucked it up, danced, and had a good time when we went to them.

With Karen, I had never been vocal about my feelings. And Karen had felt that I didn't see her as more than the mother of my children. She hadn't felt appreciated. She'd felt that I didn't listen to her, and the times that I had, she'd thought I believed her feelings were bullshit or not important.

With Nadine, I was much more expressive. I told her I loved her every time I felt it. Since I was in love with her, I said it often, and it was always genuine. I would also send Nadine random "I miss you" texts and tell her how important she was to me. I complimented her on her hair and her outfits. I hit PAUSE on my movie or the show I was watching on the DVR to see how her day was. And whenever we fought, I was more tactful with how I spoke to her.

When I'd looked back on my failed marriage with Karen, I'd realized that it was the little things that made a big difference in a relationship, and this time around, I promised myself I would pay attention to those little things. I wanted this relationship to work.

After a lot of thought, I decided I wanted to be with Nadine in a forever type of way. I talked to my boys about it when they were over at my house one day after work.

"Man, you're crazy. You got something good going here. She's not pressuring you for marriage. You've been married before. She's been married before. You didn't learn your lesson the first time? Just enjoy each other," Lou said.

"The concept of marriage doesn't have much meaning to you, but it means something to me. I believe in it and what it stands for. I want that with Nadine." What I did say was that I had learned from my marriage and my divorce, and this time around, I wouldn't make the same mistakes.

"Good for you, Chris. Don't listen to this fool. He hasn't found the right woman yet," Will said.

"And you have? What do you know about finding the right one?" Lou asked.

"Chloe and I fight a lot, but she's the only woman that keeps me on my toes. Later on down the road, I could see myself settling down with her," Will asserted.

Lou shook his head. "Oh my God. Y'all are ruining the plans we've had since college. We're supposed to be successful bachelors."

"We were boys when we made those plans. We're men now. It's time to let go of that life," I argued.

Karen had the kids. I had planned another weekend in the city with Nadine, and off we went. Since there wasn't much to do on Staten Island, we revisited the Statue of Liberty. In the Bronx, we went to the Bronx Zoo. In Queens, we went on a tour around Citi Field, the Mets' home turf. In Brooklyn, we went rock climbing at Brooklyn Boulders. On Sunday, after we saw *The Lion King* on Broadway, I dropped down on one knee in the middle of Times Square and proposed to Nadine.

"Nadine, I planned this weekend because the first time we did this trip, it transformed our friendship into a relationship. This time around, I wanted this trip to transform our relationship into something more . . ."

Nadine covered her mouth with her hand. Tourists and passersby from all over stopped to watch us. I reached in my pocket and pulled out her ring, a certified four-carat cushion-cut diamond ring I had made specifically for her.

"Nadine, will you marry me?"

Tears streamed down her face as she nodded. Then she stood me up and kissed me. Random strangers cheered for us. I had found true happiness with Nadine. I didn't fear going into a marriage with her, because she'd always help me get through any drama and pain. I'd evolved into a stronger, better man. I loved Nadine, and I was ready to face any and all challenges that awaited us.

Karen

"Mommy!" the girls yelled excitedly as they ran toward me and hugged me.

"Hey, girls!" I said, accepting their warm embrace.

The girls ran to their bedroom. Chris was fidgeting in the front doorway.

"Hey, Chris," I called.

"Hey."

"How are things going with you?" I asked him.

"Really good, really good. You mind if I come in to talk to you for a minute?"

"Sure. Come in."

Chris stepped inside and walked a couple of steps past me as I pushed the front door closed. Chris seemed anxious, like something weighed heavily on his mind.

Andre was sitting on the couch when Chris waved and said, "What's up?" They exchanged pleasantries, and Andre went back to watching the news. I loved how they were so civil with each other.

Chris turned to face me.

"Everything all right?" I asked.

"Everything is cool. I know this might be weird to ask of you, but I wanted to invite you to my wedding." Chris pulled an invitation from his pocket and handed it to me.

"Wow! Congratulations. I'm happy for you. Let me check my schedule, and I'll get back to you. I'll definitely try to make it, though."

"If you can't, I understand."

"I'll let you know."

Chris nodded, then said good-bye to Andre and me and headed out the door. I sat next to Andre on the couch and handed him the invitation.

"So, you gonna go?" Andre asked after reading the invitation.

I wouldn't lie. When Chris had handed that invitation to me, I had felt a twinge of jealousy. My first reaction had been to turn him down, but there was no need to be jealous. We both had people in our lives whom we loved and who made us happy. Our time together was history.

"Yeah. Why not? I'll support him. Besides, I know he's going to have an open bar, so at least we can get our drink on."

"Now you're talking."

Months passed, and the day finally arrived. I was attending Chris's wedding reception, toasting to his marriage. Will and Lou gave great speeches, and to my surprise, they didn't mention anything negative about his first marriage, or about me, for that matter. Since Will and Chloe were official, she was at the wedding too. She hugged Chris and congratulated him. She and Chris didn't bicker at all anymore. When our marriage ended, their beef with each other died with it. Chris had invited Jeff and Lindsey to the wedding also, which I thought was nice, because I knew that was Chris's way of making sure I was comfortable and wasn't sitting awkwardly with strangers. He had Lindsey, Jeff, Andre, and me all share a table together.

Chris looked so happy and in love with Nadine. I felt a little sad, because I remembered when he had looked at me that way. However, I put my sadness aside when I walked up to him and Nadine.

"Congratulations to you both! I wish you guys nothing but blessings and success," I told them.

"Aw, thank you, Karen." Nadine beamed.

"You look amazing, by the way. Your dress is all that!" I exclaimed.

"Thank you so much! I'm going to make my way around the room. I don't want to be rude to my other guests, but I'm really happy that you're here to support us," Nadine said.

We smiled and gave each other a hug.

While Nadine made the rounds, Chris and I stood next to each other.

"You look very handsome," I told him.

"Thanks. You look beautiful too."

"I'm happy for you, Chris. You deserve someone nice. I know I never told you this, but I'm sorry—"

Chris pulled me in, hugged me briefly, and kissed my forehead. "It's okay. I forgave you a long time ago. I appreciate you coming. Things with us are over, but a part of me will always love you."

"And a part of me will always love you too."

There was an awkward patch of silence.

"Do you ever wonder what things would be like if we had worked things out?" I asked him.

"Every day, but everything happens for a reason. We both found people that love us the way we want and need to be loved."

I nodded, not quite agreeing, but I understood what he meant. I was getting choked up by then. The girls were playing with Andre, but then they ran up to Chris and me just then. I dabbed my eyes with my sleeves.

"Hey, girls! Are you guys happy for Daddy?" I asked.

They giggled and yelled, "Yes!"

Things with the kids were bittersweet. They were comfortable around Nadine and Andre, but they were also a little older now and understood that their father and I were no longer together. I loved that they got along with our new loves, but the situation itself always left a bitter taste in my mouth.

Will and Lou walked over and patted Chris on the back.

"What's up, Karen?" Lou asked.

"You look nice," Will added.

"I'm good, Lou. Thanks, Will."

"Excuse us, Karen. We need to take Chris over to Nadine. Some folks want to take pictures with them," Lou said.

"It's cool," I said.

I gave Chris a kiss on the cheek.

A little while later, as a surprise to Nadine, Chris sang—well, he tried to sing—"Just the Way You Are," by Bruno Mars. It was cute watching him sing and seeing her blush from embarrassment. When the DJ announced it was time for the first dance, the two of them embraced, looked lovingly into each other's eyes, and danced slowly to "I Love You," by Faith Evans. Nadine wrapped her arms around Chris's neck. They looked euphoric in each other's arms.

This may sound weird, but being at the wedding gave me closure. While there were lots of things I would've changed with how our marriage ended, I was happy we had both found our true soul mates. I'd always love Chris. He was the father of my children and a good man. I harbored no animosity toward him. I had let those negative feelings go a long time ago.

After the first dance, Chris and Nadine stood together at a small table and cut the cake. As they were feeding each other pieces of cake, Andre leaned in close to me and whispered, "You ready to go? Lindsey agreed to watch the kids for you and Chris, so I wanted to use this night to sex you up something proper."

I giggled. "I'm ready."

We congratulated Chris and Nadine again and made our exit. Andre opened my car door for me. As I got in, he dropped the car keys on the ground.

"Damn. I think they fell under the car," he muttered.

He got on his knees and started searched for the keys.

"Got them?" I asked when a minute had gone by.

"I got them, but while I'm down here, I want to ask you a question."

Andre reached in his pocket and pulled out something. He opened it. Nestled neatly in the folds of the small velvety jewelry box in his hand was a gorgeous diamond ring.

"It might be in bad taste to propose to you at this event, but I don't give a shit. I want to spend the rest of my life with you. I love you. Will you marry me, K—"

Before he could say the rest of my name, I kissed him, nodded, and said, "Yes," as tears ran down my face.

He slipped the ring onto my finger.

"I love you so much," I said, kissing him again.

There was no man I'd rather be with. Some women never found men that loved them. In my lifetime, I had been lucky to find two men that loved me unconditionally. Over time, I had learned what I truly needed versus what I wanted. I didn't know if this made sense, but I was sorry for what I had done to Chris, but I didn't regret it. In a way, our drama had changed us both for the better.

Seeing Chris at the club with Nadine had proved to me that he had learned from his mistakes with me and now wanted to do an activity his girl liked, even if it wasn't a favorite of his. And I had learned so much from our experience too. For instance, I had learned that I needed to stop comparing the man I had to everyone else, and that it was important for me to appreciate my man for who he was and for what he did for me. And I had learned that I needed to communicate better and be more under-standing and less selfish.

It had been a long time coming, but I'd finally found love and happiness.